THE ARK

Life of the Dead Book 3

TONY URBAN

PACKANACK
publishing

Dedicated to George A. Romero, the father of zombies. Without George and his groundbreaking films, I never could have created these books. Stay scared & R.I.P.

INTRODUCTION

Author's Note

"The Ark" is the third book in the Life of the Dead series and begins several months after book 2, "Road of the Damned", ended. There's a bit of nonlinear timeline hopping which I hope I've pulled off without being confusing.

I hope you enjoy the book and reading what becomes of our large cast of characters.

The life of the dead is placed in the memory of the living.
  - Cicero

And every living substance was destroyed which was upon the face of the ground, both man, and cattle, and the creeping things, and the fowl of the heaven; and they were destroyed from the earth: and Noah only remained alive, and they that were with him in the ark.

Genesis 7:21-23

PART ONE

CHAPTER ONE

The worst thing about this end of the world zombie shit is that women don't wear yoga pants anymore.

That thought rolled around Caleb Daniels mostly empty head as he approached the gym. Neon yellow paint above a row of glass windows declared it 'Fanatical Fitness'. Yoga pants were pretty much the only reason he'd ever gone to the gym. He hadn't even cared much about the size or shape of the wearer. Truth be told, he preferred if the girls were on the big side. Like his dad always said, 'That's more cushion for the pushin.'

It had been over almost half a year since those assholes at the Ark abducted him. Him and Juanita, the woman he'd been traveling with at the time. And on days like this, he wished he'd have taken a different route south and avoided them altogether. The only good thing about the Ark was that it was safe. There weren't zombies everywhere, waiting to eat your balls or rip your face off every time you rounded a corner, and he appreciated that. But Caleb Daniels wasn't an idiot, or so he thought. And he knew that, as far as pecking orders went, he was barely above that hick farmer with the stupid name.

Caleb didn't hate Wim, even if his name was weird and the man was too damned quiet. He liked him for the most part. His annoyance stemmed from the fact that the two of them, plus whatever lackey Doc deemed dispensable, kept getting sent out into the danger zone. No one cared that Caleb and Wim risked their lives every time the Ark was running low on canned fruit or pig slop or fuel for the generators. The important people, Doc and his ass sucking followers, they never abandoned the safety of the walls. Nope, they stayed inside where it was safe and they could pretend the world was still hunky dory.

Every time one of these missions (suicide missions, he often thought them) arose, Caleb told himself that this time he wasn't coming back. That he would hot wire a car (an act he'd never so much as attempted, but it looked easy on TV) and hit the road for Texas. That place was so damned big he could build himself a ranch on about a thousand acres and never have to deal with this zombie shit again. That was the plan, but every time they went on a supply run, Caleb did as told and brought back whatever they wanted. No car. No hot wires. No Texas. No ranch. Only obeying.

He hated that about himself. Hated getting bossed around all the time and never doing a thing to stop it. Even in the apocalypse, he seemed destined to be a follower. In life before zombies, his passive, do as he was told attitude had landed him a peach of a job pushing carts at Walmart for a buck over minimum wage. For that barely livable salary he had the pleasure of getting reamed out by the manager every time he moved too slow or blocked the aisles too long or didn't flash big, fake smiles at the customers all day long. Like they gave two shits about the guy pushing buggies anyway.

The first time Caleb saw zombies he was at work. He'd rounded up thirty or so carts and was steering them toward the entrance bay when the bastard came hauling ass across the parking lot. He slammed right into Caleb's centipede of shopping carts without so much as an "excuse me." He was a middle-aged man, only half a decade or so older than Caleb himself, and he wore a Marlboro jacket. There was blood smeared on his coat. Blood which was hard to see against all the red. Caleb remembered that specific detail because he always wished he could afford Marlboros. But he couldn't, not on cart pusher wages, and he had to settle for generics that tasted like week old ass.

The Marlboro man bounced off the carts and tumbled onto his skinny rump. Caleb was halfway to rushing to his side to see how bad he'd hurt himself when the man hopped back up and made a beeline for a woman on a motorized scooter. The old gal, who reminded Caleb a bit of his own grandma, floored the accelerator and the scooter lurched forward at three miles an hour. That wasn't nearly fast enough and the smoker tackled her like a linebacker taking out the star QB. The next thing Caleb knew, the woman was screaming and a pool of blood ebbed out around them and turned the dull, sun-faded gray pavement black. Caleb grabbed his walkie, ready to radio in, but realized he hadn't a clue what to say. There sure wasn't a code for this. That was when he realized the Marlboro man was eating the scooter rider. He'd taken three big bites out of her double chin but seemed to lose interest when a trio of teenage girls stumbled onto the scene.

When the zombie took off after them, the woman who'd been his midday snack climbed to her feet. At first, she stumbled around like she'd just come awake after a long nap, but then she shook her whole body like she was doing some exotic Indian rain dance. Then, she didn't need the scooter anymore and in a half dozen lumbering steps she disappeared into the store.

Caleb stood there, too shocked to move. Shrieks and squeals from inside Walmart spilled through the automatic doors along with a sea of shoppers, many bloodied and frantic as they dashed toward their vehicles. There were more zombies amongst them, running with and through the crowd. Occasionally there'd come some sort of guttural roar and a human would fall and the zombies would dive onto him or her, ripping and tearing and eating. It reminded Caleb more than a little of the nature shows he often watched where a bunch of lions or tigers would attack a herd of zebras. Only this wasn't Africa and these were people.

His walkie had crackled and he heard a voice he recognized all too well as that of Drayton Sawyer, the Assistant Manager, mumble something about 'calling the fucking police' and 'blood everywhere' but the noise was cut short and the box on Caleb's thigh remained silent from there on out. Around him, the people who had been attacked and munched on were rising to their feet. One woman had an eyeball dangling to and fro from the socket. He watched it sway back and forth so long he worried he might get hypnotized by the movement.

Hypnotized, he thought, realizing that he almost was. All around him chaos reigned and there he stood doing nothing but staring. Useless as a scarecrow.

With a shake to clear his head, Caleb abandoned his carts and sprinted up the lot toward employee parking. He tried three times to pull his keys from his pocket as he ran. Finally, on the fourth try and five yards from his Ford, he succeeded. He dove into the driver's seat and gunned the engine, drawing the attention of Lynn, a plain, but buxom girl he recognized from working in the 'Beauti-que' hair salon. She clutched a pair of scissors in her fist and Caleb thought he saw blood dripping from the blades.

He waved her toward him. "Get in!"

Lynn the hair stylist jogged in his direction, but she didn't see the toddler. It was five years old tops, but the blood ringed around its plump lips showed it was just as dangerous as the other zombies. The tot jumped onto her, catching hold of her ample thigh and chomping down on the exposed skin below her denim skirt. Lynn flailed and struggled, knocking the kid to the ground, but Caleb had already seen enough to know she was toast. He stomped on the gas pedal and put his career pushing carts in the rear-view mirror.

In the days afterward, when everyone else was dying, he clung to a small piece of hope. Not that things would get better, but that maybe he could be different now. Maybe he could be someone who mattered for once. That crashed down on his bald head when he met Juanita. She saved him from getting chomped by one of the zombies while he stood outside a gas station and tried to write his name on the concrete block wall with his own piss. He'd just finished the 'e' when he heard a rifle report, then felt the undead bastard crash into his back. Juanita was only 20-something, much younger than him, but she was already the boss.

When he wanted to head west, she insisted they go south instead. And he obeyed. "Yes, ma'am. That's a fine idea, ma'am." "How about you sit in the back seat while I drive you ma'am." It was along one of her stupid detours where they came up on a road block, got gassed, and ended up in the Ark.

There, life returned to the same old, same old, only without the benefit of cable TV to take his mind off his shitty life at the end of the day. If he wasn't being shipped out on supply runs, he was burning trash or emptying the composting toilets, which were really nothing more than fancied outhouses. Even during the apocalypse, Caleb's life sucked ass. And meanwhile Juanita had run off for greener pastures while he stayed behind, stuck and miserable.

An opaque layer of dust cloaked the windows to Fanatical Fitness. Caleb tried to peer through it, but had no luck. He knew he should continue, to locate a store with food or toilet paper or any of the other things on his list, but he couldn't get the idea of yoga pants out of his head. Maybe some little sweetheart had been working out in there when the shit hit the fan. And even if she was a zombie, it would still give his sore eyes a sight he'd been yearning to see. After all, it had been almost six months.

Caleb spat into his palm, then rubbed his hands together. Once thoroughly lubricated, he used them to wipe clear a ten inch by ten-inch section of glass. He pressed his face against it, pushing his nose sideways as he peered into the cavernous gym.

Was that movement? He thought so. But who or what? He strained, trying to see inside. Something moved to his left, he was sure of it that time. He hocked another wad of spit into his hand and just as he started to wipe clear more of the window, the glass shattered.

Large chunks sprayed outward, crashing onto the sidewalk and exploding. A shard the size of a slice of XL pizza fell into Caleb's face, peeling open his cheek, but he barely noticed because something was coming through the hole in the window. No, not something. Someone.

A man who Caleb thought looked as big as one of those wrestlers on *Monday Night Raw* pushed his way through the broken window. Glass clawed and tore at his gray flesh but the man was dead and no blood flowed from the wounds. Caleb spied a large tattoo on his bare chest. 'No pain, no gains' it declared, in harsh, script font. As soon as he was through, another zombie appeared at the window. That one had upper arms which were as big around as Caleb's head and thick, black veins popped up like he had yards of rope embedded underneath his flesh.

Caleb took a staggering step backward, trying to grab the pistol he had tucked in the small of his back. In the process, he pushed the gun all the way into his jeans and he felt it slide down against his ass cheeks. He gave a little shiver as the cold metal hit his hot flesh.

As he backed away from the bodybuilder zombies, his right foot dropped over the curb. The four inches drop to the road was enough to send him careening down where he slammed onto his back. His head bounced off the pavement and everything went black. Then he felt two hands grab his ankles.

His sight came back in flashes. The first zombie was at his feet. Pulling at them. Its fingers entwined in his boot laces.

Black.

The vein-riddled zombie was above him, leaning down, expelling the rotten stench of hot death from his mouth. Caleb saw vaguely white mucous seep from its slack, gaping jaws and fall free.

Black.

He felt the zombie's slobber splash onto his face where it dribbled down his cheek before ending up in his own mouth. The pungent taste of it made Caleb think of spoiled fish.

He gagged and his vision returned. The drooling zombie was inches from him now, coming in fast for a bite of filet a la Caleb. He flailed with his arms in an attempt to push the zombie away, but it caught hold of his hands. Even in death its grip was unbelievably strong and Caleb thought it might break his bones. Instead, it pulled.

The zombie at his feet grunted and jerked his body in the opposite direction and Caleb felt himself rise off the ground as he became stretched out between the two monsters. The creature with his hands yanked and he felt a shoulder dislocate, sending shockwaves down his left side. Before he could concentrate on that pain, his legs were forced in the opposite direction. Joints popped and cracked. Muscles and tendons ripped, then burst. He stared up at the overcast, milky sky above and tried not to hear his skeleton coming apart. He tried to think of anything but that. But the pain was too intense. He couldn't even conjure up a vision of yoga pants.

The pain in his arms and legs was replaced by an excruciating fire in his abdomen. It was unlike anything he'd ever felt before. He wouldn't have imagined such agony could be real if he wasn't experiencing it firsthand.

Caleb screamed, the high pitched, wounded wail of an animal in the throes of death. It was like every nerve ending in his torso had been doused in kerosene and set ablaze.

And then it stopped.

He was moving again.

The zombie which had hold of his arms dragged him along the street, bouncing him over potholes and debris, but Caleb was so relieved that the tug of war was finally over that he didn't mind the rough ride.

His head felt cloudy, like he'd gulped down a six pack too quick. And his eyes, they seemed so heavy. Must be from cracking my noggin.

He raised his head up and, in doing so, looked down his body toward his feet. But his feet were not there. Neither were his legs. Or his hips. Or his pelvis. Not even his damned dick. His body now ended in a ragged jumble of tattered flesh and intestines that were strewn out before him like streamers.

Then, he spotted the tattooed zombie sitting on the sidewalk. The creature still held the lower half of Caleb's bisected body, but now he raised it to his mouth and ate from it like he was holding a rack of ribs.

"Well, shit," Caleb said as he let his eyes fall shut. He'd seen more than enough.

* * *

THE FEED SACKS WEIGHED FIFTY POUNDS EACH AND WIM CARRIED THEM two at a time. The mill had been free of zombies but filled with a variety of animal feed, grains, seeds and fertilizer. It was a treasure trove and, being less than an hour from the ark, an asset for which he thanked God. Nevertheless, it annoyed Wim that he had to make regular trips here.

Doc and the others who had started the Ark should have planned ahead. They should have bought and amassed their own warehouse full of supplies. For a group of people who referred to themselves as 'preppers', Wim thought they were woefully unready for a disaster such as the one which occurred the previous May.

The two bags dropped into the back of the pickup with a thud and a cloud of dust that rose up and surrounded Wim's head like a fog. The bed was nearly full now and he knew he should stop. He needed to save room for whatever goods Caleb had scavenged, but the animals and crops were Wim's responsibility and, so far as he was concerned, they took priority.

He returned to the almost endless rows of pallets and grabbed two more bags. As he did, he glanced over to Clark Raber whose attention was focused on an adult magazine which he held sideways to get a better look at the centerfold. His belly sagged over his belt and Wim quickly looked away when Clark's free hand fell into is lap.

Clark Raber was there, in theory, to assist and supervise Caleb and Wim on their duties. But the fact that he allowed Caleb to wander about town proved to Wim that Clark was little more than his own personal babysitter. A poor excuse for one too. He told everyone he was a sergeant in the Army but Wim doubted that. The man didn't carry himself like a soldier. Nevertheless, Clark had been given a position of power at the Ark, one he enjoyed flaunting.

While Wim found the carelessness of the Ark's founders frustrating, he greatly enjoyed his time away from it. The quiet reminded him of life on his farm and there were many days when the idea of returning to Pennsylvania and leaving the Ark behind sounded not only plausible, but desirable. Even knowing he'd be returning to nothing - no mama, no pa, no animals to tend to - still seemed more appealing than the thought of a life lived behind the Ark's walls. Of being given a list of chores each week like he was some sort of over-grown toddler working for an allowance. Of pretending that any of this was normal and that the world outside of the twelve-foot-tall timber barriers that lined the Ark like prison walls hadn't gone to hell.

None of the founders of the Ark - Emory called them OG's which Wim didn't understand even after his old friend had tried to explain the term - talked about the zombies. They never acknowledged that the world had collapsed. They simply went on as if everything was normal and that bothered Wim more than anything else. So far as he could tell, just about everyone was dead and to not even talk about them, to question why it happened, it seemed wrong on a moral level and Wim didn't care to be around people who could go on as if nothing had happened.

The only reasons he stayed were Ramey and Emory and Mina. He felt responsible for them and couldn't bring himself to leave them behind. And he knew Ramey would never leave her father. That man, Doc, had been a sore spot in their relationship since his group arrived at the Ark. Wim didn't trust him and, even more, didn't like him and he suspected the feeling was mutual.

Doc said all the right things. He blathered on about how they were starting a new, better world, but Wim thought the man was as phony as a high school student in a class play. He said the words like they were lines in a script, and to Wim's ears, they rang hollow.

Emory shared his opinion. Caleb too, for the most part, but Caleb was always careful to keep his criticisms in check, like he was afraid someone was trying to get him to slip up so they could run and tattle. Wim couldn't really blame him as such tattling was a regular occur-rence at the Ark. If someone missed a chore or snuck an extra ration or spoke critically when the wrong ears were listening, it wasn't long before Phillip, Doc's right-hand man, would sidle up to the offending party and scold him or her.

Usually, a punishment followed. It could be as minor as no dessert after supper, or a day or two doing the Ark's less desirable jobs, such as emptying the composting toilets. But for more serious offenses, like possessing contraband, there was a three feet wide by five feet high steel shed that stood at the far end of the compound which everyone called 'the box'.

Doc said it was a place to clear your mind and think about what you'd done, but Wim knew what it really was. A jail cell where you were confined with no food or water until your release. Most only ended up in the box for a day, but once a man named Waylon who had arrived at the Ark a few days before Wim and his companions, got drunk on homemade whiskey and started shouting in the middle of the night that they were all hostages and that Doc was a dictator. Waylon spent three days in the box after that tirade. When he was let out, Wim thought he looked like he'd aged ten years and the man never spoke out of turn again. Rarely spoke at all, matter of fact. Wim had never ended up in the box, but its very existence was yet another reason why he wished he'd never found that X on Ramey's map.

When it came to discussing Doc with Ramey, Wim had hemmed and hawed and beaten around the proverbial bush on numerous occasions but never worked up the nerve to come right out and share his opinion on her father. And considering the way Ramey looked at Doc with eyes gleaming adulation and spoke of him in a tone that exuded love, that was probably for the best. If Doc was a magician, he certainly had his daughter under his spell.

Wim understood a child's love for its parents for he had found his own to be just about flawless and he knew that keeping his big mouth shut was for the best. Still, Wim felt like Doc was a splinter under the skin of their... he wasn't sure what they had. Friendship. Relationship. Romance. Whatever it was, that splinter was festering and it was only a matter of time before infection and pus pushed it to the surface and they'd be forced to address it. Wim suspected it would end badly and hoped to delay the inevitable for as long as possible.

Wim was half way back to the truck when he heard the scream. It was low and masculine and, as he'd never seen a living person in this town on their four prior trips, he had a good idea it must be Caleb. He dropped the feed sacks which created another mushroom cloud of dust as they collided with the floor, and started for the door but Clark had heard the scream too and it had finally pulled his attention away from the dirty magazine.

"Stay here and finish loading the truck," Clark said as he went toward the door, drawing his pistol.

"We should go together. It's more safe."

Clark paused, considering it, then shook his head. "No way. Maybe you two got something planned. I'm not taking any chances. You stay. If I need you, I'll fire off a round."

Wim thought he was making a mistake, but kept silent as Clark disappeared out of the building. He only had time to load four more bags before he heard the gunshot.

* * *

THE TOWN HAD A SMALL CROSSHATCH OF STREETS AND IT TOOK WIM less than two minutes to stumble upon the scene. He saw the zombies first. A near giant of a man that made Wim think of a gray version of Arnold Schwarzenegger, shambled down the street, a dribble of blood staining his chest like an infant whose Kool-Aid had missed its mouth. Wim raised the pistol and sent a perfectly aimed shot into the creature's forehead. It took an awkward step forward, then crumpled to its knees. Wim thought it might be staring at him and almost shot again but then the zombie toppled over in a backbend that would have reminded Caleb of a yoga pose.

A hissing growl to his right caught Wim's attention and he turned to see Clark Raber. Most of the skin from his nose down was gone revealing gristle and bone and bottom teeth that Wim thought looked scary and long. Clark's eyes had gone gray and Wim didn't hesitate before firing a shot that poked a hole just under Clark's right eye.

As he fell, Wim saw a second musclebound zombie further away, sitting on the sidewalk before a pile of bloody clothing. Blue jeans? Wim wondered and tried to remember what Caleb had been wearing that morning. Before he could recall, the zombie rose to his feet, tottering as it stabilized itself and prepared to move. Before it could come toward him, Wim shot again and the left side of the monster's face collapsed inward like a tiny bomb had gone off inside its skull. It fell forward, landing face first in the rain gutter.

Wim hurried across the street to where the motionless zombie had taken its final dive, but he wasn't concerned with the dead man. He knelt beside the mound of blue jeans which were soaked purple with blood. At first, he couldn't understand why the fabric was so voluminous but when he reached out to pull them closer, he realized the unusual density was because they still contained a pelvis and legs. Leftover bits of bowel spilled out when Wim lifted them and hit the pavement with a wet thwack. Wim dropped the jeans, causing more tissue to tumble free.

He was almost certain the jeans belonged to Caleb and whatever small percentage of doubt he clung to disappeared when he heard noise behind him. It was a heavy, scraping sound with an undercurrent of throaty gasps and labored breathing. Wim didn't want to turn around, but he did anyway.

Caleb, or what was left of him, dragged himself up the street, toward Wim. Blood leaked from his mouth and, further up his face, his dead eyes stared ahead in that desperate, insatiably hungry gaze that Wim had seen all too often since the plague.

Wim had known splitting up was a bad idea, but Caleb always insisted they'd finish their runs in half the time by doing so and, since Wim tried to avoid conflict on general principle, he always relented. Now it was Caleb that was split up. His bottom half laid useless at Wim's feet and he pulled his upper body along the roadway with his fingers which had become destroyed in the process. Wim could see shards of broken fingernails peeling back as the zombie clawed its way toward him. In some places, the flesh had totally torn free and white bone gleamed through the gore.

None of it slowed down the dead man and Wim pondered

whether zombies could feel pain. He suspected not. Not the physical kind anyway. But occasionally he'd see something in their eyes, some small bit of tortured humanity trapped inside, and that made him wonder. He tried to ignore that. Tried to tell himself it was his imagination and that might very well be true, but late at night when he'd closed his own eyes but sleep wouldn't come, the memory of that pain in their eyes was impossible to forget.

In six long strides Wim reached Caleb. The half man pushed himself up on its bloodied elbows and its head flopped back as it peered up at Wim. Caleb's mouth hung ajar and a quivering, raspy groan tumbled out. Hunger or hurt, Wim thought, then quickly tried to push the question away. He tilted the barrel of the pistol down and shot a round through Caleb's forehead. The zombie fell to the pavement and Wim couldn't avoid seeing the splintered burst of skull that had broken apart in the back of the man's head.

"Sorry about that," Wim said to the dead man.

He considered dragging Caleb's torso over to his severed legs and reuniting the pair, then thought the idea foolish. Neither half had any use for the other anymore. So, he left them lying twenty feet apart and returned to the mill where he finished loading the truck. Caleb wouldn't be able to retrieve whatever items were on his list and Wim wasn't rifling through his pockets to find it. The Ark would have to make due with feed and fertilizer and if that didn't satisfy them, oh well. Wim found himself not caring much at the moment.

When the truck bed was so full that the back end sagged down and threatened to brush against the rear tires, Wim figured he had enough for the day and climbed into the cab. He knew he had an hour or so drive back to the dock where Hal would be waiting for him. For *them*. He didn't look forward to explaining why three had become one and suspected he'd catch the blame someway or somehow.

* * *

EVEN THOUGH THE FALL AIR HAD TAKEN ON A DECIDEDLY WINTERISH feel, Wim drove with the windows down. The sun had dipped near the horizon and he realized it must only be a few weeks until the winter solstice. And Christmas too, for that matter, not that he felt much like celebrating. As he tried to do the math in his head and remember the exact day, he almost missed seeing the figure standing in the roadway ahead of him. When he did see it, he slowed the truck from forty down to twenty but didn't give much consideration to stopping. Just another zombie, after all.

As he got within five yards of it, he thought it looked almost skinny enough to be a skeleton and he slowed down a little more. He didn't want to risk running it over and having a bone splinter and puncture a tire, not with another thirty miles to travel. He leaned out the open window and aimed the gun at the thing's head but waited to fire.

When he got right up next to it, he saw its face was nearly black with dried blood. All that broke the ebony mask were the whites of its eyes and mounds of mustard yellow pus that oozed from around its mouth like lava. Wim had never seen infection on a zombie and he stopped the truck dead.

At first, the figure didn't react. It stood in the road like a statue. Body motionless. Eyes unblinking. Wim could smell the sickness coming off it but as noxious as the smell was, it wasn't the aroma of spoiled, rotten meat that typically accompanied the undead. He realized then that this thing was alive.

"Hey." It was all he could think to say. He considered following that up with something equally useless, perhaps, 'Are you all right' even though it clearly was not. Instead of saying anything, Wim pulled the emergency brake and stepped out of the truck.

He looked closer at the person. It was hard to see detail through the caked-on blood but from the slender build he thought it to be a teenage boy or maybe a girl who hadn't developed yet. Its hair was shoulder length, but dirty and matted, clinging to its head like a mangy cap. Wim eased his big hand onto its shoulder and felt hard bone poking at the skin.

It was at his touch that the person reacted. It turned its head slow, like a rusty wheel which hadn't been used in ages, and looked up at Wim who towered over it by nearly a foot.

"I can get you help," Wim said and when the person heard his voice, its eyes grew wide and Wim heard a gasp as it gulped in a mouthful of air. "You'll be all right." Damn, he thought as soon as he said that, what a dumb thing to say.

He realized just how dumb the words where when the person opened its mouth, but instead of its lips parting to form words, its entire face split in two from the corners of its mouth to its ears. More pus seeped from the wounds and fresh blood joined in, mixing into a pink fluid that Wim thought had the consistency of sour milk. Through the torn - not torn, cut, Wim thought, flesh Wim could see every tooth in the person's mouth, all the way back to the molars. He heard air escape from that too wide opening and realized it was trying to speak.

"Stop now. You don't have to say anything. I'll take you somewhere safe."

"He..."

It was a deeper voice. A young man's voice, Wim was certain. The boy said something else but the words came out in a jumble that Wim couldn't solve. The boy tried again. "He..."

Wim didn't want the young man to speak. Every time he tried, more infection and blood broke free of its face, but he could tell by the look in his eyes that he wasn't going to stop until Wim heard what it was trying to say.

"Is someone with you? Are you looking for someone?"

The young man shook his head slowly, like every movement took considerable effort or caused unbearable pain, or both.

"Help me."

Tears dribbled from his eyes and glistened against the black blood that marred his face. Wim saw his eyes flutter and knew what was about to happen. The young man swayed on his feet and Wim reached out and grabbed him around the waist, catching him just before he lost consciousness. Wim carried the man to the truck bed, thinking he might weigh less than two sacks of feed, then eased him into the vehicle. Wim rested the young man's head against a feed bag, then resumed his spot behind the wheel. He drove faster now, anxious to get this person help, but also to get away from this place.

As the truck barreled down the deserted road, he wondered who could have hurt this boy so bad and why. What type of monster was out there?

CHAPTER TWO

Harvey Dade, known as Hal to members of the Ark, let the cold water of the lake wash to and fro across his bare feet as he sat on the dock. He'd been reading from a tattered paperback book when he heard tires approaching. He knew the odds were great that it was Clark and the newbies - he still thought of them as newbies even though they'd been in the Ark for months - returning from their supply run, but you could never be too careful. He folded over the corner of the page that had been interrupted and set the book aside as he stood up, wiping his feet against the rough wood of the dock to dry them.

Dust rose in the distance and the cloud blew nearer and nearer until the pickup broke free from it and sped down the dirt and gravel ramp that ended in the water.

"What's he in such a damned hurry for?" Hal muttered as he slipped on his shoes. He stepped off the dock and onto mostly dry land, wincing as his right knee gave a little pop.

The truck skidded a yard as the brakes locked up, then stopped a few feet from the water's edge. The engine rumbled to a halt as Wim climbed free of the cab. Hal noticed the passenger seat was empty, then looked toward the truck bed.

"Where's Clark? And Caleb?" Hal said as he limped toward Wim.

Wim didn't look at the 55-year-old man whose hair was still so thick and curly that it looked like he'd just received a perm from a salon. The only difference between now and thirty years earlier was that Hal's locks were gray, not blond.

"Dead."

"Dead?" Hal asked.

"That's what I said."

Hal didn't like this at all. Clark was one of his friends. And Caleb wasn't anyone's favorite resident of the Ark but Doc didn't like change and liked mistakes even less. If what Wim said was true, and Hal had no reason to doubt him, these would be the first members of the Ark to die and Hal knew someone would catch the blame. And he didn't want it to be him.

"What happened?"

Wim had moved behind the truck and dropped the tailgate. "I'd imagine they got careless and, out there, careless people get killed."

When he reached the cab of the truck, Hal peered inside and saw it empty. "What about their bodies?"

"Clark's missing most of his head and Caleb's in two pieces back in Jolo. If you want to clean up the mess, help yourself to the truck."

Hal turned back to Wim, his face screwed up in annoyance. He didn't know why Doc and Phillip assigned him of all people to help unload whatever bounty the others had gathered. Him being close to an old man, after all. And now he got smart-mouthed on top of it? That's not right. Not right at all.

"Well that's pretty rude. Those were our frien—" Hal realized Wim wasn't pulling a bag of feed out of the truck bed. What he carried was a human being that looked about light as a feather in Wim's thick arms. "Wim?"

"This boy needs help."

Wim carried the young man past Hal who saw, upon closer inspection, that he was covered in dried blood. And he smelled like sickness.

"Looks dead to me, Wim. Did you bring back a zombie? What are you trying to pull?"

Wim glanced back at him, his fierce eyes conveying that he wasn't interested in a discussion. "He's not dead yet. Now get in the boat."

Hal's stomach went sour. This was bad news. This was why they should let him stay inside the Ark.

"Doc's not gonna like this, Wim. You know no one's allowed inside except—"

Wim gently sat the boy in the rear of the boat. Then he let his free right hand fall against the butt of his pistol. "I'll accept the responsibility. All you got to do is drive the boat."

Wim took a seat as if the matter was settled and Hal supposed it was.

Hal snuck a look back to the truck. "What about the feed?"

"Drive, Hal."

Wim extended one of his big, calloused palms and Hal let him help him into the boat. He didn't like this. Not one bit.

CHAPTER THREE

"I told you. Beautiful, ain't it?"

Before them, the blue waters of a spring glistened under the cloudless sky. It was the kind of day Ramey knew was coming to an end with winter fast approaching and, although there was a chill in the air, she was loving it. She turned toward Phillip and nodded.

"How did I not know this was here?"

"Almost no one does. I sort of keep it to myself. I like to come here and clear my mind."

Phillip McKeough was such a typical Irish cop that he would have seemed a stereotype if this were a movie and not real life. He was tall, but not as tall as Wim, with hard muscles that made themselves visible through his snug, long sleeved t-shirt. He wasn't handsome. He had beady eyes, a soft, receding chin, and oversized teeth that made Ramey think of the Cheshire cat. His skin was so white that it was almost translucent and that made his curly hair, which could only be described as 'carrot' even more dramatic. Freckles covered his flesh but they had started to fade now that the days were shorter and less sunny. Nonetheless, he had a certain charisma that made spending time with him enjoyable.

"Clear your mind and seduce naive, young girls," Ramey said. Her eyes blazed as Phillip's white face flared a mottled eggplant color.

"No. I. No. You don't—"

"I'm just busting your balls, Phillip. But if you get any redder I'm going to start to think I was right."

He turned away from her, back toward the cerulean body of water. The lake surrounding the Ark wasn't visible from here. It was only untamed devil-grass and occasional rocks that burst up from the ground like it was giving birth. That made the water even more impressive.

"Let's swim," Phillip said without looking at her.

"Are you insane? It's not even fifty degrees. I'll freeze my pretty little toes off."

He did turn to her then. The embarrassment had fled his face, replaced with a grin that made him look younger than his 26 years.

Younger then Wim, Ramey thought.

"No. It's a hot spring. Water's 110 degrees at least."

"Bullshit."

"I'm serious. Jump in and you'll see."

He was already stripping off his shirt and as it came up, Ramey could have sworn he flexed his abs to make the muscles pop even more. Such a showboat. Unlike Wim.

Phillip dropped his shirt into the grass and started on his jeans.

"Phillip! Stop! We don't have any suits."

That was stupid, she thought. She knew exactly what this man was doing and it didn't require bathing suits or swim trunks.

"I won't complain," he said as he deftly unzipped his jeans and pushed them down in one smooth, practiced motion. His walkie talkie clattered against a rock and gave a short gasp of static. "Come on. I wouldn't lie to you. This is like Mother Nature's hot tub. You'll love it."

And then Phillips fingers were in the waistband of his black boxer briefs. Ramey thought about turning her head but he was too fast and they too hit the grass. His long, flaccid penis was even more white than the rest of him and it was topped off by a shock of that same carrot-colored curly hair. The vision of it made Ramey think of a circus clown. 'Hey Ramey, watch me pull of rabbit out of my hat!' She almost laughed and bit her lip to stop herself.

Phillip didn't notice because he was spinning around and flashing his bare buttocks at Ramey (who noticed that they too were covered with freckles) as he took a swan dive into the spring. Water splashed back against her flesh and she could tell instantly that he was right, it was hot. And it felt good.

He disappeared for a moment before bursting theatrically back to the surface. His curls had gone limp under the weight of the water and clung to his forehead in random streaks. Small rivulets trickled down his chest, over his toned pecks, and Ramey again mentally compared him to Wim, noting that Phillip was much harder than the man who had saved her life several months earlier. Yet on the mental check list she'd been compiling, Phillip still lagged far behind.

She'd loved Wim after that, at least as much as she'd ever loved anyone and as much as a teenage girl could. But things changed when they got to the Ark. Wim changed and Ramey supposed she had too. Here she had her father. She made friends fast too, friends like Phillip who was, from as far as she could tell second in command even though no one in the Ark talked about a hierarchy. And while she made friends and got to know these new people within the safety of the Ark's walls, Wim worked. From sunrise to sunset and most days before and after too. Often, it seemed like he'd rather spend time conversing with the cows and pigs than her and if that was who he'd rather surround himself with, maybe she should move on and let him be. After all that had happened, Ramey was ready to live.

It didn't help matters that the tension between Wim and her father was as obvious as the noses on their faces even if neither of them admitted it. Her father aka Doc aka Douglas Younkin, had been her world growing up and losing him had damaged her in ways she still didn't quite understand. After all this time, he was back in her life and she wasn't about to fowl that up.

It was her father who encouraged her to get to know Phillip. The young man had been a beat cop in Albany, where her father had been the head biochemist at the Miner & Zito Research Facility before his sudden departure. Phillip moonlighted as a security guard at the lab and, as Doc explained it to her, "Was a man of rare character and like mind. The kind of man the world needs more of."

From afar Ramey thought Phillip to be comprised mostly of bluster and bravado but as weeks became months she saw that there were other, more appealing, aspects of his personality. It helped that he was one of the few younger people on the Ark. And she enjoyed the way his tongue became tied in knots when she teased him about one thing or another. While many on the Ark thought he was too strict, too quick to remind others of the rules, she understood that their safety here was almost entirely dependent on men like Phillip and her father. This was a paradise amid a fallen world and they needed to protect it. To protect themselves.

"Come on, Ramey! Don't make me get wet all alone!"

She opened her mouth to say no, but stopped herself. Why shouldn't she? She was one month past her nineteenth birthday and she wasn't married to Wim. On many days, they didn't speak a hundred words to one another. If he wanted her, wanted to be with her, he'd done little to prove it and after six months, maybe it was time she take a hint and move on.

Ramey lifted her hands to her waistband and unbuttoned her low-rise jeans. Phillip's eyes grew wide in either surprise or excitement, Ramey couldn't tell which and supposed it didn't make much difference. They were two sides of the same coin, after all. She pushed the denim downward rocking her hips as the rough fabric slid across her thighs.

"Phillip! Come in! We've got an emergency at the gate." The voice crackled through the speaker of the walkie talkie which had been discarded in the high grass. Ramey jumped at the sound of it and pulled up her jeans as she looked from the radio to Phillip and back again.

She heard water splash as he worked his way to the edge of the spring. Grunting as he lifted himself from the pond.

"Phillip! I need you!" A garble of static obscured a few words.

"brought someone with him. Someone— "More static. "Dead. Where are you? Doc's gonna freak the fuck out!"

Ramey didn't realize Phillip was at her side until he pushed past her, still naked as the day he was born, and grabbed the walkie talkie from its holster on his discarded pants.

"Vince, this is Phillip. I'm on my way but only got about half of that. What did you say?"

The voice resumed, "Wim brought someone inside. Threatened to shoot me if I didn't let him in. The guy or kid or whoever he brought, he looked sick as fuck and about ready to die."

Phillip glanced at Ramey who thought she saw blame -Your guy did this! - in the look he cast her way, or maybe it was her own guilt.

"What about Clark and Caleb?"

"They're dead."

"Shit!"

"Yeah. Shit is right man. Oh shit."

Phillip spoke as he redressed. "Don't let them past you, I'm coming."

"He's already on his way, man. He took my four-wheeler and tossed that sick fucker on the back and took off. He'll be in the village any minute."

Phillip didn't respond as he shoved the radio back into its holster. He looked at Ramey again. "We have to run. Can you keep up?"

"I'll try."

He ran, his long legs outpacing her in just a few strides. As she watched the distance grow she couldn't stop wondering, what has Wim done now?

CHAPTER FOUR

"D id you see that birdie?"

Mina had been so caught up in reading the bible, or trying to read it, that she'd almost forgotten Emory was there. She sat slouched back in a wicker chair which would have been comfortable if she had more meat on her bones so the hard seat wouldn't have pressed into her hips. She'd always been slim, but she'd left slim in the rear-view mirror months ago and now skeletal was the more appropriate adjective.

Emory had been the one who saw her wasting away, or at least the first one to mention it to her, and he suggested she read the bible to try to find some sense in everything she'd gone through. That they'd all gone through, she knew, but in the aftermath of Bundy, the only man she'd ever loved, blowing himself to bits in order to save her, she grasped hold of her grief like it was a life preserver and wallowed in the selfishness of it. It was, after all, the only thing she had left.

She found the bible mostly confusing and more than a little boring in places. Some parts she just couldn't get her head around, like why God cared whether people ate shrimp or wore cotton-poly blend. Emory assured her that it got better when Jesus came into the picture so she trudged on.

At the moment, she was a third of the way through the book of Job and the more she read the angrier she got. Why would God allow someone who loved him so to be tortured all because of a silly bet with the devil? It seemed like a very human thing to do and she'd always expected God to be better than the wretched people who treated each other so poorly on Earth. With her mood already sour, Emory's question cut through her like a blade. Why would he call her 'Birdie', that horrible name that her father used to make her feel ugly and worthless? How did he even know about it? She'd never told anyone about 'Birdie' except Bundy and she was certain he wouldn't have spilled her dirty secret.

Mina glared at Emory who wasn't looking at her but instead staring into a thicket of pine trees that rose above the sprawling building that served as that the Ark's meeting place and mess hall.

"What did you say?"

Emory looked over at her, then raised a crooked finger and pointed at the trees. "Did you see that birdie? I think it was a pileated woodpecker."

Mina felt her anger dissipate like air gushing out of a balloon. "Oh. No, I didn't."

"Grant used to feed the birds. He kept a moleskin notebook filled with the various species, what they ate, the time of day he saw them. He was very detail oriented."

Mina thought that sounded like a rich person's hobby, but didn't say that out loud. She liked Emory even though she knew he was the kind of person she'd never have associated with before the plague. No, if she'd have so much as seen Emory Prescott it would have been while she was pushing a cart of dirty linens up a hotel room hallway and he was going to or coming from his room. Although, she suspected Emory was much too rich to have stayed at the hotel she worked at. He'd never talked about money, but a poor person could tell a rich one, especially a really rich one, just by looking at them. It wasn't their clothes or car or wallet. It was the way they stood up and carried themselves, all straight and perfect because they hadn't been beaten down and stooped by life. Even if Emory was 80-some years old, he still stood like a rich man.

Before the birdie comment, Emory had been using a paint brush to apply rich, cedar-colored stain to the log siding which had started to go gray. He and Mina had been taking turns, but it seemed like he did most of the work. Mina thought it a bit of a sin to let him, but he didn't seem to mind and the people who ran the Ark, Doc mostly, insisted that everyone had a job to do, even the old fogies.

The way Doc told it, the Ark was something of a hippie commune where everyone worked together to advance the greater good. But Mina never saw any of the higher ups digging ditches or emptying outhouse latrines. She supposed they did work but it happened behind closed doors and in secret. She was okay with that, as long as it kept them safe.

Aside from the log cabin, which was bigger than the school Mina had attended growing up, the Ark had several other buildings which spiraled out in circles. Among them was the medical clinic where Doc spent his days working on a cure and Ellen Sideris, the Ark's real doctor, treated people for sprained ankles and stomach bugs.

Further out there was a small community of single-story, four-room houses where most of the Ark's seventy or so original residents resided. Closer to the entrance, which was blocked by a tall wood and metal gate, were a half dozen decrepit house trailers where the few people who had arrived after the plague lived. The idea that they were segregated wasn't lost on her. But again, as she stared out at the walls which lined the community, the razor wire looped atop to add further protection, she knew she was safe and that was enough. Right?

She thought it was. She told herself that it didn't matter that they weren't allowed to pick what jobs they wanted to do, but that the chores were doled out like the big boss telling everyone on the plantation what needed done that particular day. She told herself that it was alright for there to be a 'safety squad' which was little more than a police force with a nicer name, one that she'd seen hand out punishment in the way of a billy club to the kidneys or a punch in the guts to men and even some women who they thought were causing problems. And she even told herself there wasn't anything wrong with the box. That it was a necessity to keep everyone behaving and safe. But even she didn't totally believe that one, no matter how much she tried to convince herself otherwise.

"That has me curious. The birds," he said.

In her daydream, Mina had forgotten about the birds and didn't know what Emory was talking about. Not that that was unusual.

"How's that?"

"Well, I've assumed the virus that started the epidemic was air born. That's the only way it could spread so rapidly. And it was ruthless in its attack, not just infecting the humans, but killing the animals too. Wim said his entire farm was destroyed within a day."

"Now, I can go along with the theory that this island is far enough from the mainland, and in a location remote enough that the virus couldn't cross the waters to infect the livestock. And the decontamination procedures we endured when arriving might cleanse us of the virus, although I'm quite dubious about that myself. But what about the birds? They fly back and forth from here to the mainland. Why haven't they brought the virus with them?"

Mina squinted her eyes, thinking. This was all so complicated and she wasn't sure how it even mattered. There weren't any zombies here and so far as she was concerned, that was good enough.

"Maybe they have. We're not sick even though we were out there. I just figured everything here was immune like us."

Emory's mouth formed a wry smile that Mina couldn't label as amused or condescending but the paranoid part of her, and that was a large part, leaned toward the latter.

"We know some people are immune, of course. And some animals too. But doesn't it all seem too perfect that the people who created the Ark, the animals they brought here, are impervious to a disease that killed approximately 999,999 people out of every million?"

Mina didn't feel up for a debate she was certain to lose. She tapped the bible on her lap and then cast a glance skyward.

"This book talks about all sorts of miracles. I don't see how what you just said is any more farfetched than a man getting two of every animal on the planet onto a little boat and not having the elephants squish the mice or chipmunks."

Emory's grin broke into a full smile and he let loose a tired, but joyful laugh. "I suppose you're right, Mina. It's all about faith, is it not?"

"I don't right know. I've got a lot of pages left to read yet."

Emory opened his mouth as if to speak, but the steady whine of a quad stole both of their attention and they looked toward the sound. Mina knew Wim was out gathering supplies and she always felt a little tied up inside with nerves until he got back. She hoped it was him.

They didn't share another word until the quad, and its rider, came into view in the far distance. Behind her, she heard shouting voices, their inflections panicked and angry. She knew one of the voices belonged to Phillip and at the sound, Mina's knot of nerves only got worse. She didn't remember much of her schooling, but for some reason she never forgot the way a history book had described Europe leading up to the first World War. The term that book used was 'powder keg' and she thought that was also the perfect word to describe the Ark.

CHAPTER FIVE

The heartbeat pounding through the stethoscope was strong and steady and the sound of it made Doc smile.

Ba bum. Ba bum. Ba bum.

He counted 142 beats per second. Fast. Might be a girl.

He could sense the woman staring at him. To Doc, she was little more than a vessel. A human Petri dish. But he felt obligated to keep her in good spirits for the sake of the life inside her and he eased a gloved hand down onto her skin, which felt hard and warm through the latex. He gave her belly a consoling, if awkward, rub and pat.

"Good. Very good. Everything is going remarkably well."

She might have smiled. He couldn't be certain because her mouth was a swollen, purple mass of ragged gums where her teeth had once been before Doc had extracted them with a pair of needle nosed pliers. Several had shattered in the process and he'd had to dig the shards free of her jaw. The process took hours and he lamented the fact that he hadn't recruited a dentist. But it had to be done and, although it wasn't pleasant for either of them, they were much safer this way. She was strapped to a hospital bed, her hands and feet belted tight and additional straps crisscrossed her chest and thighs.

Can never be to safe. He grabbed her chart and began scribbling notes when the radio squawked to life.

"Doc! Come in Doc."

It was Vince's voice and in only those four words Doc knew something was wrong. He'd brought Vince into the group five years earlier, at a time when the Ark was nothing but an idea inside Doc's overactive brain and when ending the world hadn't even crossed his mind. Vince, of course, didn't know that Doc was responsible for the virus that had gone a long way toward wiping out humanity. Only those he trusted the most knew that. And that number was quite small.

Doc peeled the gloves off his hands, which had gone moist and clammy under the latex. That made the air feel even colder. Because the laboratory was buried more than 20 feet underground, it was easy to keep the temperature at a steady 50 degrees. Doc preferred the cold for a multitude of reasons, the primary being that it kept the odors at bay. Plain white tile lined the floors and walls, adding to the sterile feeling. A few dry erase boards stood on easels, all filled with notes and dates and projections made in Doc's neat, tight writing. At the far end of the room were seven gurneys, each cloaked in white sheets which covered human-sized lumps. Doc found the sheets kept those lumps placated and quiet, which was appreciated as sound echoed down there.

"Do-"

Doc pressed the 'talk' button on the radio, cutting Vince off. "Vincent. I'm here."

"Oh, thank holy God. This is a shit storm, Doc. Clark and Caleb are dead. And Wim brought back some kid who looks like he's infected and if he ain't then he's practically dead anyway. He threw the kid on my four-wheeler and is heading for the village. I—"

Doc stopped listening. He didn't know if this qualified as a genuine shit storm but it had the potential to go very bad very quick if he didn't make the right decision. The residents of the Ark, people like Vince who didn't know the fine details about why they were alive and most everyone else was dead, were terrified of the infected. They droned on incessantly about their worries of getting sick and dying and becoming zombies. Their fear made them easier to handle. Easier to control. Doc needed to keep that fear alive and if Wim had indeed brought a sick or dying person into their midst, they had to stay afraid.

"Vincent, don't let anyone near Wim or the boy. Keep everyone at least 50 yards away from them until I get there."

"Okay."

Doc turned and looked back to the pregnant woman tied to the hospital bed. He seemed to recall that her name had been Juanita, but that didn't matter now. Her long, ebony hair was unwashed and matted under her head which rocked back and forth, the few millimeters movement the straps permitted. Her eyes, which stared back at him were pained, pleading. She groaned, a raspy, agonized noise. Waiting the next few months was going to be torture. He wondered if she grasped the importance of the life growing in her womb. About her essential role in the rebirth of mankind. He doubted she had the capacity to understand, but that was just as well. It wasn't the test-tube that mattered. It was the contents.

"And Vincent?"

"Yes, Doc?"

"Tell the others, if Wim gets himself or the boy near anyone, they have my orders to shoot them."

Doc shut off the radio before Vincent could respond. That should do the trick, he thought. Shoot to kill always managed to work the masses into a panic. And Doc enjoyed a good panic.

CHAPTER SIX

"Don't come any closer, Wim!"

Wim stared ahead where Phillip had an assault rifle aimed in his direction and his finger on the trigger. He wondered if he would really shoot. Sometimes he thought the cop was all ego, but he also knew ego often led to poor decisions. And with a good thirty or forty people watching the situation unfold, he had more than an inkling that Phillip's finger already had a one-pound squeeze on a three-pound trigger. Near him, four other men with guns, the ones who acted as the Ark's safety squad aka security force, also had their weapons drawn and aimed.

"Phillip, I'm not going anywhere. But this boy's dying and it's not from the bug that killed everyone else. He's injured and he needs help. Sooner too, because I don't reckon he'll be around long else wise"

Wim held the boy in his arms and he was so frail his muscles hadn't even begun to tire. He did notice the boy was taller than he first thought and suspected he might not be a boy at all. He was probably a teenager, although he couldn't hazard a guess whether he was early, mid, or late. Not with a face blackened with blood and swollen so full of pus that his skin looked tight as a water balloon getting ready to bust. Please don't bust. I don't want to see that.

A few yards behind Phillip, Wim caught Ramey watching. He couldn't tell if the look on her face was concern or fear or anger or a combination of the three. He'd noticed that Ramey arrived at this scene with Phillip. And he also noticed that Phillip's hair was wet and that Ramey's jeans were unbuttoned. He tried not to think about that and told himself there were more pressing matters but his mind kept wandering back to it nonetheless. What was up with those two, he wondered. Whatever it was, he was pretty certain he didn't like it.

Beyond them, he saw Emory and Mina's faces peering out from amongst the crowd. He was a little shocked to see Mina there as she usually kept to herself when she wasn't working. He wondered if everyone on the Ark had already got word of his exploits and from the way the crowd kept growing, he suspected that to be the case.

He didn't recognize the voice of the first person who hollered but their words came through clear enough. "You're going to get us all killed, you asshole! What were you thinking?"

With that, it was like a cork had been popped and a flow of angry shouts burst loose. Wim heard more accusations along with words like, 'traitor', 'murderer', 'idiot' and 'dumbass redneck'. He took a little offense at the latter. He always thought himself to be a hillbilly and a hick but he wasn't a redneck. A spattering of curses seasoned their accusations and Wim realized Phillip and his one-pound pull might not be the biggest of his worries after all. These people were one thrown rock or bottle away from becoming a mob.

How did we get to this point, Wim thought? Earlier that very year there had been hundreds of millions of people in the country and now most of them had either died or been eaten. It seemed to Wim that life should be more important now but as he stared out at that sea of accusing and angry faces, it seemed as if the only lives they cared about were their own.

He supposed that he was the fool in the situation. Nothing about life on the Ark had shown him that any of these people gave a second thought to the people who might be alive outside of this island. No one ever asked him if he'd found anyone alive during the supply runs. No one asked them what life was like out there. They were content to live inside their bubble and pretend as if the world wasn't burning everywhere else.

As their shouts and screams became a chorus too loud to decipher, Wim took one more look at Ramey. She wasn't crying out or joining in the verbal onslaught, but when their eyes met he saw something that hurt him more than if he'd have seen anger or fear, because, in her gaze, he saw disappointment.

Wim had little time to process that before Doc's voice blasted over the crowd.

"Quiet please, everyone."

As if someone had pressed the mute button on a remote control, the voices fell silent. All heads turned toward the sound of the voice and Wim watched as the crowd slowly parted. Through the now clear path, he saw Doc, at least he assumed that's who approached him, wading in like Moses walking through the parted sea. He couldn't be certain because the person coming toward him was clad in a HAZMAT suit with only a small rectangle of clear plastic to reveal the wearer.

Doc raised a megaphone to his face and his voice boomed out again. "Please, everyone go back to your business. This situation will be contained and any issues addressed. Everyone will be briefed at the meeting hall at noon tomorrow."

About a third of the crowd dispersed immediately. The rest lagged behind and they reminded Wim of the lookie loos who slowed down when passing a traffic accident or fire, not because they wanted to help, but to get a good look at someone else's misfortune. Soon enough, they too left.

All that remained were Doc, the men with guns, and Ramey. When Doc reached her, he covered her forearm with his gloved hand.

"Go on now, sweetheart. We'll take care of this."

She looked to Wim, then back to her father. "Don't hurt him."

Wim couldn't see Doc's face but when he saw the tension flow from Ramey's body he imagined the man had smiled. "Of course not. He made a mistake. A terribly dangerous one, but I suspect his heart was in the right place."

Now it was Doc's turn to look at Wim. "Isn't that right, William?"

Wim nodded. "Everything's going to be all right, Ramey."

She brightened and her reaction seemed to annoy Doc. "Sometimes our hearts get in the way of our brains, but that's just human nature." Doc gave Ramey's arm a squeeze, then nodded toward the direction of camp. "I believe you have some children waiting for story time, do you not?"

Ramey gave a grin full of tired relief. "I do."

"Then don't keep them waiting any longer."

Before she left, Ramey turned back to Wim and flicked her fingers in a barely there wave. He nodded in return.

"Guns down, gentlemen. William isn't going to do anything rash. Are you William?"

"It wasn't in my plans."

"Good. Good. Now tell me what happened out there today."

Wim did and Doc and the men with guns watched. He told them everything including the gory details and he noticed one of them, a man he thought was named Buck, looked like he was about to lose his lunch when Wim told of the two halves of Caleb. When he got to the part about the boy, Doc motioned for Phillip and the others to leave them. They did.

"You're aware that you took a terrible risk, are you not?" Doc said.

"I take a risk every time I go out there."

"Yes, but that's requirement. A necessary evil, you might say. If you and the men who gather supplies never left this island, we'd all starve."

"With proper planning, I'd say much of that could have been avoided."

Wim knew Doc was examining him even though the plastic face shield had gone cloudy under a haze of condensation.

"You're always willing to share your opinion, William. Regardless of the situation or to whom you are speaking. Some could say that's a character flaw."

"No sense sugar-coating things. I just say how I feel."

"Indeed, you do. And I'm pleased that I always know what to expect from you."

Wim shifted the boy in his arms and in doing so, a small sigh escaped through sick, cracked lips.

"Are you going to kill him?"

Doc smiled and Wim thought that an improper reaction to such a dire question.

"Am I going to kill him?" Doc took a step closer to Wim, to the boy. He was close enough to touch them but he did not. Instead he peered down on the boy's swollen, wounded face. "What a silly question, William. No, I'm not going to kill him. We'll take him to decontamination and, after that, to the medical clinic. Doctor Sideris will do her very best to make him well again, but if those efforts fail, I'm not going to kill him."

Doc turned his face from the boy to Wim. "I'm not the zombie killer, after all. You are."

CHAPTER SEVEN

"Beefaroni." Emory read from the label as he poured the contents of a can into a pot which sat atop a propane powered burner. "I believe this is a first for me. I wonder if it's as tasty as spaghetti o's."

"It's not."

Emory glanced over at Mina as she set aside her bible, then rubbed her hand against her right temple.

"You've eaten it before?"

"Any time it was on sale."

"But it's not good?"

"Not very."

"Then why did you eat it?"

"Because it was ten cans for five dollars every fourth week at Save-A-Bunch."

Emory had never shopped at Save-A-Bunch but recalled seeing them, usually in poor sections of the cities or in downtrodden rural areas, on his travels. He felt rather guilty for bringing it up and felt a change of subject was the wisest action.

"Still on Job?"

"No. I finished that one. I still think God came off like a bit of an asshole."

"Well, he is God. I suppose the complex must have started somewhere."

Mina's face clouded over and Emory again feared he'd made a faux pas. He liked the woman, but always felt like he was walking on the proverbial eggshells when in her presence. And since their current accommodations were a forty plus year old Airstream trailer, he had that feeling almost constantly.

He felt guilty that she should have to live in such conditions. The vinyl seats were cracked and torn. The floor creaked underfoot. The only blessing was that, autumn had brought with it cooler weather and the tin can in which they lived was no longer a sweat lodge. Yet, as the yin to that yang, he worried how they would stay warm through the coming winter.

Emory often thought that this shoddy dwelling well summarized their life in the Ark. Not even a week after they arrived, following hours of interviews about their experiences with the plague and subsequent travails, he, Mina, and Wim were led to a cramped compound on the outskirts of the island where a handful of run down mobile homes were stacked in with little room to spare. The other men and women who occupied those trailers had arrived in the weeks after the plague, but before Emory and his friends. No one had been admitted to the Ark since that day and, to Emory at least, it was clear that Doc only had interest in saving one person from the horror show that had become of the real world. And that was Ramey. Once she had arrived, the Ark was on lockdown and the ones who had gained admittance before or with her were second hand citizens in this new world, housed as far from the chosen ones as possible.

He often found himself wishing they could have avoided this place. Life was dangerous and terrifying and deadly outside the walls but somehow it was still better. Here they were trapped, caged up like dangerous animals and tossed scraps no one else wanted.

That brought him back to the Beefaroni and he again found himself feeling guilty over Mina's station in life prior to this. He'd always known he had lived an almost foolishly blessed life, but being around her and picking up the offhand remarks she made or the curious things she said made him realize just how privileged he had been. He'd often thought a rich black man was still less accepted in society than a middle-class white one, but he was certainly far more fortunate than a poor black woman.

As he looked at her, he saw her bones poking against her taut skin like wire hangers under cheap clothing. He almost said something. Maybe an apology of sorts. Was there such a thing as 'rich guilt'? He wasn't certain. It was probably for the best that the door opened before his mouth.

Wim stepped inside, his black hair dripping wet. He glanced up, saw Emory and Mina looking back, then cast his eyes toward the floor as he sat on a metal folding chair and began to untie his boots.

"It wasn't raining when I was last outside," Emory said and he tried to inject some humor into his voice. It half worked.

"Still ain't." Wim pulled off one boot and started at the other.

"Did they hose you down again?" Mina's voice was tight, nervous. She stood and crossed the short divide between them.

Wim nodded.

"Bastards." She grabbed a dish towel from the counter and handed it to him.

Wim used it to wring some of the moisture from his hair and dry his face. "Brought it on myself."

Emory didn't like that. Didn't like seeing Wim behave like a cowed dog. He'd changed so much in the last five months that Emory sometimes wondered if whatever force inside of him that had been holding everything together had finally broken.

"You did no such thing. You saved a life today. That's to be commended."

"Let's wait and see if he lives or not before you go patting me on the back. Might be all I did was delay the inevitable."

"You tried though. You tried Wim. And that's what matters."

Wim wrinkled his nose and, for a brief moment, Emory thought he was going to say he made a mistake. That he no longer wanted to be the hero. Instead he looked toward the stove.

"Something's burning."

Amidst his daydreams Emory had forgotten all about the beefaroni. He rushed to the stove to shut off the burner, as much as an 84-year-old man could rush, anyway.

Wisps of smoke drifted up from the pan and he saw the edges of the food were charred blacker than his own skin. "Oh, shit!"

Emory then heard a sound that almost made his old heart burst. Laughter. Wim's laughter. Emory couldn't remember the last time he'd heard it and when he turned around, pot in hand, he saw a broad smile across Wim's tired, face.

"What do you find so amusing? I've ruined our dinner."

"I do believe that's the first time I've heard you cuss"

It was Emory's turn to smile. "Well, Wim, what can I say? There are occasions when 'sugar' or 'shoot' just won't do."

"I reckon that's true." Wim peered into the pot. "What was it?"

"Beefaroni."

"Aw, heck, you can't ruin that. The burned parts might actually be an improvement."

"That's for damn sure," Mina said as she took a seat at their cramped kitchenette table. She grabbed a spoon and began dishing the charred food onto mismatched plates. "So, are you gonna tell us what happened out there today or do we have to wait for the town hall meeting? I'd rather hear your version."

Wim twirled a fork between his index and middle fingers. Emory looked down at his own meal and took a reluctant bite. Mina was right, this was far worse than spaghetti o's.

"I'll tell you. I'd say it might spoil your appetite but…"

Emory saw Wim's eyes flash and his heart gave another happy flutter. Wim might be bent but he wasn't broken. Not yet. Not ever, if Emory could do anything about it. And he knew what needed to be done. He needed to get all of them out of the Ark.

CHAPTER EIGHT

It was quiet on the Ark at night. There wasn't an official curfew, but most turned off their solar powered lights at dusk to save energy and, with sun setting before 5pm, many residents went to sleep early due to boredom. But Ramey had always been a night owl and found it hard to adjust, even after almost six months.

She lived in a five-room log cabin with her father, but he was usually in the lab, trying to find a cure to what everyone referred to as 'the zombie virus.' But when she used that phrase around him, he was quick to point out that the virus itself was not a zombie and that viruses were technically neither alive nor dead, that they were far more complex biochemical mechanisms than man. He prattled on but Ramey lost interest in short order. She always admired her father, but when he talked about his work and research his voice became that of the teacher in the Charlie Brown cartoons.

The trailer court, and despite what her father and the others in charge of the Ark claimed, that's exactly what it was, was located a quarter mile from the main dwellings. She rarely went there, partly because it reminded her of her old home and her drug addled mother, but maybe even more so because seeing it in person made it hard not to believe Wim and Emory's claims that they weren't really welcome here.

Her father insisted that the encampment was temporary. A place for the new arrivals to live until they fully acclimated to life on the Ark. It was also meant to allow the originals to get to know and trust them. But after all this time, Ramey doubted such trust would ever be found. Especially after a day like today.

The silence bordered on being eerie and the only thing that made the walk tolerable was knowing that she was safe. There weren't any wild animals lurking in the shadows. No creepers hiding behind buildings. And no zombies. That was the best part. No zombies wanting to eat her. That one simple fact made any doubts or questions she had about the Ark and the people who helped her father run it, fall far down the ladder of concern.

When the trailers came into view she was surprised to see a dim glow near Wim's Airstream. It came and went in a red flare and she initially thought it might be a lightning bug. The on and off flicker came again and then the smell of smoke hit her nostrils. Not tobacco smoke though. Marijuana.

Ramey considered spinning on her heels and heading back to the cabin, but before she could, a voice called out softly through the night.

"Ramey?"

She knew Emory's voice immediately, even though she rarely saw him these days. The raspy, but kind tenor was impossible to mistake and she continued until she found him sitting on a plastic crate outside the trailer.

"I see you've found an interesting way to burn the midnight oil."

Emory gave his soft chuckle. "Why, it's not even nine p.m." He extended the half-smoked joint in her direction. "Care to partake?"

The last time Ramey had smoked pot she ended up in the back of Bobby Mack's car, losing her virginity. She knew she was in no danger around Emory, but the memory still made her forearms prickle with goosebumps. Besides, an important conversation needed to be had and she wanted a clear head.

"No thank you."

"As you wish," Emory took another drag, then pressed the cigarette against the silver metal siding of the Airstream. It gave a short hissing sizzle as the dew snuffed out the fire. "How have you been, Ramey?"

"Good. I like it here."

"You do?"

This wasn't a discussion she cared to have. She knew Emory wanted out of the Ark and there was no changing his mind. But he wasn't changing hers either.

"It's safe here. And after the things I saw - we saw - out there, the people we lost, I like being safe again."

Emory considered that and gave a slight nod. She sensed he had more to say, and was relieved when he didn't pursue the matter.

"That's a perfectly reasonable viewpoint. I know Mina feels the same." He slowly rose to his feet and Ramey heard the joints in his knees pop like snapping twigs. "I assume you're here for Wim."

"I am."

"He'll be asleep most likely. As soon as his head touches the pillow he's dead to the world. But I'll fetch him for you,"

"I'd appreciate that. Thank you, Emory,"

As he started up the metal steps the Airstream Ramey couldn't resist one more question. "Can I ask you where you got the pot?"

Emory looked over his shoulder and she could see the moonlight reflecting off his vaguely yellow teeth, "I'm sorry, Ramey, but considering the company you keep, I believe I'll keep that to myself." He lifted his fingers to his lips and made a locking gesture before disappearing into the trailer.

The notion of an old man smoking pot and not wanting to reveal his dealer was so silly that Ramey wanted to smile, but she couldn't because she realized what it meant. Emory thought she had chosen a side. A side that wasn't his and he no longer trusted her. It made her throat tighten up, which prevented any comeback she might have attempted. That was probably for the best.

She heard no movement from within the darkened trailer and after a few seconds became two full minutes, she began to wonder if Emory had simply gone to bed and left her to stand there like a fool. But after another thirty seconds or so passed, the door reopened and Wim stepped into view. His hair was pushed askew and jutted up in the back making him look as if he had half a mohawk. The smile she'd wanted to show Emory earlier came easily now. It was always her first instinct when she saw Wim. No matter what, he'd always be her first love.

But Wim didn't smile back. Instead he covered his mouth as he tried and failed to stifle a yawn. Then he plodded down the steps but stopped a yard short of her. Why wouldn't he touch her, she wondered. She wanted that. Needed that. For him to take her hand, to hold her in his arms again. He promised her once that he'd never let her go, but he'd broken that promise after they arrived on the Ark and she still wasn't sure why. Did he too think she'd chosen a side? That she couldn't be trusted?

"Surprised to see you," he said.

"I wanted to talk about today."

"I already told your father everything that happened. Forward and backward several times over and my story stayed the same because it was the truth."

There it was. The divide between them wasn't three feet, it may as well have been a mile.

"I'm not here to interrogate you, Wim. I came to see how you were. If you're okay."

His posture sagged and Ramey hoped that was some of the tension leaving him. "Oh. I'm all right."

"Can we talk?"

He nodded. "But not here. Go for a walk with me."

They walked and walked, crossing the expanse between the scattering of trailers toward an open field where the farm animals Wim tended to slept in knee high fescue, but talk was sparse and superficial.

Wim motioned to a newborn calf. "That girl's only four days old. Had to pull it out of the mama. I wasn't sure either was going to make it through but they seem to be doing just fine now."

As if it knew it was being talked about, the calf lifted its head and looked at them.

"You go on back to sleep now."

The calf's head lolled to the side and rested against its mother and soon enough its eyes fell shut again.

"You're so good with them," Ramey said.

"It's no special talent. Done it all my life."

"It's because they know you're kind. That you'll take care of them." She reached over and grabbed his hand but he deftly slipped it free.

It always seemed to be like this now. Like the weeks they spent together before coming here had ceased to exist. That their bond had been a figment of her imagination. Maybe it was, she thought. Maybe Wim was simply protecting her because he was a good man. Maybe he never cared for her any more than Mina or Emory or Bundy or even these animals.

"I've been ordered to butcher three steer so there's meat through the winter. I told 'em it's too soon, that we need to build up the herd first. There's plenty of canned goods to go around. They don't need to be killing anything."

"I'll talk to my father."

"Orders came from him. Just like all the others."

"I can still try."

"Do what you want."

His words were curt, the tone cutting. This wasn't the man she thought she knew and she almost stormed away right then but she forced herself to stay calm. "Wim, why did you bring that boy back with you? You knew how everyone here would react."

He looked at her. Really looked at her, for the first time that night.

"You haven't been out there in months. Things haven't got none better. If anything, it's worse because everything, and I really mean everything, I've seen outside of these walls for months on end is dead. Either dead and rotting on the ground or dead and walking around and trying to eat me. I have no idea how many of those zombies I've killed now but its more than all the people I knew my whole life put together.

"I do it because it needs done. And because when I look into their eyes I don't see monsters, I see people who are dead but because of some awful cruel twist of fate, they aren't allowed to die. So, I give them that end they deserve. Not because they're evil, but because they're just as much victims in this as me and you.

"That boy today, he's the first living person I've seen outside these walls in five months. And you know, I'd started to think it really was over, that there wasn't anything left alive out there. That we were all that remained. But when I saw that kid, I realized I was wrong and I ain't never been so happy to be wrong before. That's why I brought him back. Because that boy means there's a chance. That there's still hope."

He looked down but before he did Ramey could see his eyes were wet. She again reached out and grabbed onto his hand and he again tried to pull away, but without as much force and she held on. "My God, Wim. I'm sorry. I'm sorry for everything you've seen and everything you've had to do."

"It's all right."

"No, it's not. You've been saddled with all this shit because you're stronger than the rest of us, but that doesn't make it alright."

Ramey looked up into his light blue eyes and watched as the tears spilled down the lower lids and drew glistening trails down his cheeks until the water got caught up in the black stubble of his beard. Suddenly being safe didn't matter. All that mattered was Wim.

"I hate that this place has pulled us apart. That you and my father don't get along. That you're stuck living in some piece of shit trailer and that that they make you go out there and see and do those horrible things."

She'd never seen him like this. So hurt and so wounded. She realized that maybe now he was the one who needed saved and she wasn't going to let him down. "And after winter, if you still want to leave, we'll leave."

His mouth dropped open in shock and Ramey couldn't help but think he looked as surprised as a little boy who just saw Santa Claus climbing down a chimney. "You'd do that?"

She nodded, squeezing his hand tight. His palms were sweating. She thought about her father. She didn't know if she could really go through with leaving him, but she hoped in time that would change because the man standing in front of her now was her future.

"I never said this out loud, but I love you, Wim. I don't know the exact moment it happened but I can tell you that I haven't stopped."

Wim stared at her so long Ramey thought he might kiss her, but instead he took her face between his calloused, working man palms.

"That night on the farm. When you sat down beside me in front of the bonfire and laid your head against my shoulders."

She waited for him to go on. He didn't. "What about it?"

"That's when it happened."

"When what happened, Wim?"

"That's when I fell in love with you."

Then Wim leaned in to her and they kissed, really kissed, for the first time. And even though they didn't do anything more than kiss, it was as perfect a moment as she'd ever experienced in her 19 years of life.

CHAPTER NINE

The seventy or so residents of the Ark congregated inside a wood sided building which was large enough to house twice that number. Most sat in folding chairs, feet shuffling, fingers tapping. They are a nervous bunch, Wim thought.

It was cool inside the cavernous room but sweat seeped through Wim's pores as he stood in the rear corner, trying to stay in the shadows. None of the natives had said a word to him since he arrived, but several angry looks had been hurled his way like daggers. He never did like being the center of attention and was even less fond of it now. The only person who seemed to look at him with compassion was Delphine Boudreaux. He caught her staring his way several times and once he even thought he saw a smile.

Wim didn't know much about Delphine, and it seemed neither did anyone else. The rumor was that she lived on the island before it became the Ark and that, while she wasn't part of Doc's original group, she was still privy to some of the inner workings. She had long braided hair which hung thick as a rope halfway down her back. It was white with dirty blonde streaks, but it seemed near impossible to tell her age for certain. Sometimes Wim thought she looked 50, others 70. He'd only had conversations with her in passing, but of all the people associated with the Ark, she was one with whom he felt he might share some common ground.

But right now, the only person he cared to see was Ramey and she sat in the front, stealing glances his way but not risking a reaffirming smile or nod. Not that Wim blamed her. He wouldn't have wanted to look like his own ally right now, not amongst this bunch.

When Doc arrived with Phillip and Ellen Sideris, the Ark's only actual physician, the crowd had risen to their collective feet, an act which both dismayed and disgusted Wim. He'd grown to understand how cult leaders like Jim Jones and David Koresh did it. He could only hope that Doc wasn't as evil as those men. But, if he had been a betting man, he thought those odds were quite poor.

After a few brief paragraphs reminding everyone why they were there, Doc got to the meat of it.

"We lost two of our own yesterday. Clark was an original member of the Ark. One of our hardest and most loyal workers. He was integral to establishing life here and keeping us safe. Life here will not be the same without him. And Caleb Daniels, although he arrived here after most of us, will also be missed. I'd like to take a moment of silence in their memory."

Wim watched as most of the people in the room shut their eyes and bowed their heads. He dipped his a bit, but kept his eyes open. He watched as Doc, Ellen Sideris, and Phillip huddled in a brief, hushed conversation up front. It ended before the supposed moment of silence and after two or three beats, Doc resumed speaking.

"And as you also know, William Wagner brought a very, very sick young man into the Ark."

Nearly every head in the room swiveled in Wim's direction. It made him feel a bit like a contestant who had just been chosen to compete on *The Price is Right* but no one was cheering him on and he was not inclined to rush the stage.

"Doctor Sideris," Doc tipped his head toward Sideris, a slight, but hard woman in her sixties with skin the color and consistency of shoe leather. "Is caring for the young man. At the present, he is unconscious and heavily sedated while we wait to see if the treatment is successful."

"What if he turns into a zombie?" Someone in the crowd shouted. A flurry of murmurs followed.

Doc waved his hands in a 'keep calm' gesture. "I understand your fear. Your worries. And I share them. If just one of the infected dead should gain access to the Ark it could - likely would - mean the end for us all. That's why we've taken precautions. This patient is not being housed in the clinic. He's confined to a portion of the research lab where he is, I assure you, no threat."

The chorus of murmurs slowed, then ceased. Wim couldn't understand how they could so easily be manipulated by the man at the microphone. How did so many sheep fall under the care of this wolf?

"Yet even though we are safe, this situation could have gone dramatically different. I understand that Mr. Wagner threatened one of our own with a firearm. Harvey?"

Harvey aka Hal, stood. "That's true, Doc. I told him that boy was dangerous and he showed me his gun and I knew I didn't have no choice in the matter."

Doc nodded and Hal sat. "And when they reached the gates, Mr. Wagner forced his way inside and stole the recreational vehicle belonging to Vincent Dufresne."

Vince nodded, but didn't speak. It didn't matter though, Wim thought, because this wasn't a trial, it was an inquisition.

"Mr. Wagner, do you have anything to say for yourself?"

Wim considered staying silent, but as he stared into the angry and confused faces that filled the room, which peered back at him accusingly, he felt it only fair to explain himself rather than let Doc's version of events muddy their thinking.

"I do and I'll keep it short. Two men with whom I've gone on countless supply runs died yesterday. Why, Caleb was ripped in half and despite that he still came back as a zombie. I had to put him down, along with Clark and the two zombies that killed and turned them in the first place. It wasn't the first time I've seen terrible things out there nor was it the first time I've had to use my gun to put an end to suffering. Because that's what it is. Suffering."

He'd hoped to find compassion in the crowd but saw none.

"And after that, while I made my way back here with the food and grain we'd all risked our lives to gather, I came upon the boy. Yes, he was sick. Yes, he might be dying. But yesterday, he was alive. And as far as I'm concerned, life still matters. Maybe it even matters more now than ever before because there's so little of it left. But I made a choice to try to save a life and no matter what anyone here tries to say, nothing will convince me that it was the wrong choice."

Whispers and hushed conversations spread through the crowd like a fire. Wim thought he might have won them over, or at least made them think. Maybe Doc sensed it too because he was quick to speak up.

"No one is doubting that your heart was in the right place, Mr. Wagner. But as you well know, these are dangerous days we are living through. And if we want to live, we must protect our home here at the Ark. That is why we have these walls. Why we have our rules."

The voices stopped and all eyes were trained on Doc. Wim knew he'd lost.

"We are a community of rules. And we cannot allow anyone to flaunt them with impunity." Doc glared at Wim. "Yes, Mr. Wagner life matters. Our lives matter. And your foolhardy attempts at being a hero put every man, woman, and child here at risk."

Wim caught sight of Ramey, her face panicked. She went to stand and Doc somehow sensed it. He stared her down. "No one is above the rules."

Ramey slumped back into her seat.

"That's why the council has decided that, as punishment for his reckless actions, his use of force against Ark residents, and his wanton disregard for the safety of this community, Wim Wagner must spend one week in the box"

The murmurs, louder now, returned and that time Ramey did jump to her feet.

"A week! That's too long!" She looked from her father to Wim. Back and forth. "Dad, he'll die!"

Wim wanted to tell her not to argue, not to get involved, but before he could do so much as nod his head in her direction, three members of the security force grabbed him by the arms and shoulders. Wim was bigger than each of them, but three against one wasn't much of a fight. Not that he intended to fight them anyway. Doing so would only make things worse, if worse was possible.

"Mr. Wagner brought this on himself. The decision has been made and it is final."

As the three men dragged him toward the rear exit, Buck whispered in his ear. "Yyyy- You done it now. Gggg- Glad I ain't you."

Wim ignored him and saw that Phillip had retreated to the exit. As Wim was pulled past him, the cop grinned revealing almost all his oversized teeth.

"That's a long time with no food or water. I don't think you can do it, big fella. I think we'll be pulling a zombie out of that box."

Wim considered doing the right thing and keeping his mouth shut, but then decided he may as well use his words, especially since they might be some of his last. "Either way, I'll be sure to look for you first."

Phillip's smile faltered and he raised his hand as if to hit him, then seemed to realize there was a roomful of people watching. Instead he leaned close enough for Wim to smell his breath.

"Just know that, after you croak in that hole, it'll be my shoulder Ramey cries on. That bitch wants me and I'm gonna fuck her raw."

The others dragged him away and Wim refused to look at anyone as he was shuffled out of the meeting hall, through the expanse of the courtyard, and toward the box.

CHAPTER TEN

Dr. Ellen Sideris leaned over the boy, who wasn't a boy at all. "No. I'd estimate his age at sixteen. Perhaps seventeen."

Doc peered over her shoulder and looked down. The boy was naked, revealing a body that was thin, almost undeveloped. "I would have thought younger. He doesn't even have pubic hair."

Sideris used a gloved hand to shift the boy's penis from side to side. "He shaves them off."

"You don't say." Doc took a closer look and saw she was correct. "Boys do that too now?"

"I'm no expert on adolescent male grooming trends, but this one does." She pushed a scalpel into the young man's festering, decayed flesh and sliced hunks of it free from his wounded face. Sideris kept her salt and pepper hair pulled back in a practical bun. She had small, deep-set eyes which were, at best, muddy brown in color. Her face was plain, long, and devoid of emotion, which Doc felt was her best trait aside from her intellect.

"Don't feel obligated to devote too much of your time on this one," he said. "He appears beyond saving."

Sideris glanced up at him but didn't remove the blade from the boy's skin. "I've always appreciated a challenge." Her eyes returned to the boy as she trimmed off a quarter-inch thick section of necrotic skin. Blood oozed from the wound, trickled down the contours of his head and neck, then pooled on the metal table upon which he laid.

Doc had met Sideris at a medical conference in Atlanta four years earlier where she was giving a lecture titled, 'How Extinction Events Benefit the Planet'. What it lacked for in creativity, it made up for in substance. Afterward, he approached her in the hotel lobby and offered to buy her a drink. She requested a gin and over the next four hours they became fast friends. He didn't reveal his plans that night. That came later, but when it did she became an eager member of the growing cabal.

"What have you been up to in that dungeon of yours?" She asked.

Doc hesitated. It was only a beat, but long enough for her to catch.

"Keeping secrets again, I see."

Sideris was one of his closest confidants, but he wasn't willing to divulge his plans just yet and decided to change the subject. "What do you believe happened to him? Was he attacked?"

"By a zombie? Certainly not," Sideris said. "I suppose this could have occurred in some sort of accident, perhaps being ejected through a car windshield. But the injuries are contained to his face. I'm relatively certain someone did this to him."

"Tragic. It makes you wonder just how bad things have become out there." Doc lifted one of the boys closed eyelids. The pupil constricted under the room's bright fluorescents.

"I'll take him when you're done."

She cast a brief dismissive look his way. "If he dies?"

"Dead. Alive. I'm not particular."

Doc thought she sneered, but pretended not to notice. He motioned to a silver bowl where she'd deposited the patient's excised flesh. "I assume you have no further use for this?"

Sideris didn't answer and Doc scooped up the bowl while she took out a suture needle and thread and began closing the wounds. It wasn't a pretty job. Sideris was no plastic surgeon, but Doc didn't think it mattered.

CHAPTER ELEVEN

W im had no watch so he had no idea how long he'd been in the box but small cracks that had previously allowed light to spill inside had gone dark so he supposed it was five hours at least. Only 140-some to go he thought.

It was cold, but not unbearable. Not yet anyway. He debated whether he might have preferred being confined here in the heat of summer versus the cold of winter and decided the latter was for the best. In the summer, he'd have already been desperate for a drink.

Part of him thought it was a bluff. Surely, they knew he could've live seven days without so much as a sip of water. He thought there was a fair chance he'd be let out on the morning, a sort of early parole that came with a warning that the next time the punishment would be for real. He didn't know if he really believed that a possibility, but the thought kept his mind at ease even as the temperatures fell and the cold metal against his back had shifted his skin from numb to a constant, throbbing buzz. He tried to alter his position, to keep himself away from the metal, but the box was too small. It's barely bigger than a coffin, he thought, then tried to chase away that image.

He drifted to sleep sometime through the night and was awoken in the morning not by the light of day but by an explosive banging against the thin walls. He jolted into a sitting position. He'd been right after all. They were letting him out.

"Rise and shine, Wim, No sleeping on the job."

It was Phillip's voice, tight with angry, mocking glee. "Get your forty winks in?"

Wim knew he wasn't getting out from Phillip's tone. He thought about going with the silent treatment, then decided that was no fun. "Fifty, actually."

"Oh yeah? I guess the box is probably a step up from whatever shanty shit hole you grew up in. Did you even have indoor plumbing?"

"We did. Color TV too."

Phillip gave another smack against the metal siding and the reverberations rang through Wim's eardrums like thunder.

"You stay awake now. I'm going to get breakfast. Pancakes, grits, and a ham steak. Might eat your helping too while I'm at it."

Wim felt his belly tighten and give a greedy rumble. Don't be a traitor, he told it. He'd get through this, if for no other reason than to look Phillip in the face when he got out and act as if he's just spent a few days in the Ritz Carlton and not a box too small to stand up or turn around in.

* * *

EARLY ON THE THIRD DAY, LONG BEFORE THE SUN HAD RISEN, WIM WOKE with a jolt that sent a searing flash of pain down the left side of his face. He'd been dreaming about zombies, about being attacked. Eaten. And in his barely awake stupor he thought he'd been bit. His hand shot to his cheek and he found wetness and when he drew back his fingers he saw the tips were stained black.

As his bearings returned, he realized he hadn't been bit, that he was still very much alone inside the box, but he still wasn't certain how he'd been injured. That answer came as dawn's first bits of light seeped into the box and Wim saw a thin strip of flesh clinging to the steel wall. He knew that skin was a jigsaw piece that fit perfectly against his face and, coupled with the nonstop shivering, he solved the mystery. His face had frozen to the box through the night and his sudden movement as he escaped his nightmare had ripped the two apart like halves of heavy duty Velcro. He made a mental note to try to keep his exposed flesh to a minimum from here on out.

By the end of the day he'd completely abandoned any remnants of hope that he'd be sprung early. His throat felt like he'd swallowed a mouthful of sandpaper and every time he managed to conjure some spit, it burned like fire when he swallowed it down.

The pain sapped any hunger he'd been harboring. Even if someone had set a double decker hamburger in front of his face, he'd be afraid to eat it. He imagined his throat had shrunk to the size of a drinking straw and couldn't even imagine trying to get anything down. It wasn't food he wanted, it was liquid. Any liquid. He hadn't pissed since early on day two and he knew that, if he did work up the need to go, he'd have to find a way to catch it and consume it. The thought would have nauseated him before but now he prayed for it.

Phillip's taunts came several times a day and Wim got the feeling the man was never more than a few yards away. He let him talk but had mostly given up on responding. Tempting though it was, he thought it best to conserve his strength,

The muscles in his legs seemed to have locked up and gone limp at the same time. He tried to keep his mind occupied, to think about taking Ramey and leaving the Ark behind for good, but as the hours past, staying positive became an impossible cross to bear.

When night came and the temperatures dropped even further, he understood he was probably going to die. The thought bothered him more than he expected because there were days back on the farm, when he thought death might be a blessing as he'd go into God's paradise and see his family again. See mama again. On many days, that sounded just fine. But things had changed. Wim didn't want to die even though the world around him was on the edge of extinction. He wanted to live. He wanted to see what was coming and what remained.

CHAPTER TWELVE

The recent nights had been full of tossing and turning but little sleep. Hal couldn't stop his mind from churning the events of the last few days repeatedly. Damn, Wim, he thought. This was all his fault. But if that were true, why did Hal feel so guilty?

Wim had threatened him. He knew it by the tone of his voice but he also knew Wim wouldn't have shot him unless Hal had tried to kill him first and maybe not even then. He worried that maybe he'd made it sound a bigger deal than it was. That it was his recollection that had sent Wim to the box where he might - probably would - die. And damn it, he didn't want that on his conscience. He liked Wim, even if he was just about as quiet as a monk. He'd often thought the Ark could use more men like Wim and less Phillip's. And now Wim could - would - die and he'd be responsible. He didn't like that one bit.

I should tell someone.

But who was there to tell? No one talked to Doc unless he spoke to them first. Phillip? That was a joke. That would be like telling a bear why he should take mercy on a salmon. No, there wasn't anyone to tell. This bed was made and all that was left was waiting to see how it ended up.

I never should have come here. It was a thought he'd had dozens of times, especially after they got word of the zombie apocalypse that was going down outside their walls. He'd initially been recruited by Doc to head construction, as Hal had overseen building a new wing onto the Cunningham/Miner Research Center. It all sounded good. He'd get to do what he loved, which was build things, and do it in one of the most beautiful damned places in the country. Maybe even the world. Sure, the hippy let's all live in harmony nonsense they preached got a little on his nerves, but the longer he worked and was away from civilization, the more he realized he didn't miss it. So, when they asked him to stay on permanently, an affirmative answer came quick.

They got word of the zombies from Phillip and a few other men who had gone to buy supplies. At first Hal found it hard to believe, but the look he saw on the faces of those men was impossible to fake. When the entirety of the Arks population came together for a meeting later that night, Doc informed them that similar results were coming in from all across the globe. He told them that this was the type of cataclysmic event they'd been preparing for and then he said something that still gave Hal chills whenever he allowed himself to think about it.

"The world is over," Doc told them. "Everything and everyone you knew before is gone. All that remains is the Ark."

Hal tried again to sleep and even dozed off for a fast hour, but woke himself up coughing around the time the first light of the day began to chase away the dark. He took a few swallows of water from the glass he kept on his nightstand but that didn't seem to help and, when the second wave hit, he had to lean forward in bed just to catch his breath. As the room slowly brightened, he saw specks of red spittle marring his bedsheets. That's not good.

Hal wondered if it was 33 years of smoking catching up to him. He hadn't had a cigarette since arriving at the Ark (they were on a long list of banned items) but he doubted a couple years made up for the previous decades. He thought about going to see Dr. Sideris but, truth be told, that woman gave him the creeps and he wouldn't trust her to treat a hangnail. Well, if it was the big C, he supposed waiting a few hours, or even days wouldn't make a whole lot of difference. He flopped back in bed, pulled the blankets over his head to block out the light and tried to fall asleep but sleep wouldn't come.

* * *

HAL'S COUGH EARNED HIM A FAIR SHARE OF ASKANCE GLANCES AT breakfast that morning. He got so self-conscious about it that he gave up halfway through his scrambled eggs and pushed his plate aside. He wasn't very hungry anyway.

After leaving the mess hall he made a detour which took him within twenty yards of the box. He'd pocketed a piece of bacon that he couldn't bring himself to eat and thought maybe he'd be able to sneak it to Wim. Hal had built the box, just as he'd built most of the structures on the Ark and he knew where all the best cracks and crevices were located. But, when he was close enough to see the box, he also saw Phillip sitting Indian-style, a rifle resting in his lap. The man just sat there staring straight ahead. Like a zombie, Hal thought and almost smiled.

He must have made a noise or maybe Phillip caught him in his peripheral vision, because the young man swiveled his head in his direction.

"You need something, Hal?"

Hal felt another coughing jag coming on and simply shook his head.

"Move on then."

Hal did and when he was confident that he was out of Phillip's sight, he let his chest muscles do what they'd been longing for and choked and coughed until he was so lightheaded that he had to take a knee in order not to fall. Near the tail end of it, what little he'd eaten for breakfast ended up on his shoes along with heaps of yellow bile and bright, crimson blood. The pile of it looked a little like an abstract painting.

Hal's head felt like a balloon at the end of its tether and he grabbed onto his ears to stop it from floating away. The world in front of him spun and twirled and then went black.

* * *

IN HAL'S DREAM, HE WAS EATING MEAT. IT WAS THICK AND RUBBERY AND red and with every bite blood squished out like jelly from an overfull PB&J sandwich. It was warm as it trailed down his chin and neck before getting caught up in the webbing of gray hair that covered his chest. The meat itself was flavorless. All he could taste was the coppery flavor of the blood and, as it plunged down his throat, all he could think was 'More. I want more.'

Hal came awake feeling stiff, frozen. The sun was high overhead but it gave off no heat. It must be noon. I've been laying here for hours.

He rolled onto his belly then worked his way up to his knees. His face felt tacky and wet and it reminded him of the blood in his dream. When he reached up and felt his skin, he came away with a handful of sticky, semi-congealed vomit. He swiped at it with his fingers, trying to clean it away before someone saw.

But, as he scanned the area around him he realized his worries were for naught as he was alone. Thank God. He thought again about going to Dr. Sideris and that time the idea didn't seem too bad. But first he wanted to clean himself up.

As he worked his way back to his cabin, he kept far enough away from the others so as not to draw their attention. Almost there. Another hundred yards.

His belly tightened and growled. The nausea was gone and, in its place, hunger that bordered on famishment. He remembered the bacon in his pocket and shoved it into his mouth. His cheeks puffed up like a chipmunk gathering nuts for winter and he thought he must be quite the spectacle as he chewed. No one seemed to notice. As he swallowed it down, his body gave no signs of satiation. He was still hungry. So hungry. He felt like his internal organs were devouring themselves in a tearing, raucous rumble and knew the only way to stop the pain was to eat.

CHAPTER THIRTEEN

The fourth and fifth days inside the box were a nightmarish jumble of cold, delirium, and thirst. Wim felt dried out as a scarecrow. He could barely move and his body was contorted into a fetal shaped ball on the floor of the box. Once, he thought he saw frost on the steel wall and went to lick it off. As soon as the tip of his tongue touched the frozen metal it stuck like glue.

Double dog dare you.

He quickly jerked his head back and the pink tissue stretched, then tore. There was no pain. No blood. Only cold.

Later he scratched loose a few handfuls of dirt from the floor of the box, then shoved it into his mouth and he tried to suck whatever moisture it contained. He repeated that every few hours and each time it gave him enough wetness to be able to swallow again. He never thought such a simple act could be so blissful.

He dozed off, or lost consciousness briefly and when he awoke the world was dark.

You've fallen down the well, you damn fool. How'd you manage that?

I'm gonna have to climb out.

He tried to stand. Couldn't. Aw heck, I broke my legs. Or my back. Maybe I'm paralyzed.

Wim tried to scream out for help but no words came. It was just as well because there was no one around to hear him. He had no neighbors and even the mailman only dropped his delivery at the end of the lane, far out of earshot.

He attempted to move his arms and at first, they too wouldn't cooperate. He tried again and that time they moved, slowly at first, painfully. He reached out, trying to grab hold of the walls of the well but when his fingers touch them they slid down helpless, unable to get a grip.

He stared up and saw nothing but darkness. How did he get down here? Was he sleepwalking? Or did he get into the apple pie moonshine his pa kept hidden in the root cellar behind the preserves? Damn fool, Wim. You damn fool.

Hours passed. His fingertips had gone bloody from trying to climb the walls to no avail. He sucked on the blood that oozed from his battered digits and didn't even mind the penny-like taste of it. Somehow it soothed him.

He must have drifted to sleep, or lost consciousness, but her voice brought him back to the world.

"Wim?"

His eyes fluttered. Opened.

"Wim? Are you all right?"

"Mama?" He stared up again but everything was still dark. "Mama, I'm down here. I fell into the well. I'm sorry I'm such a klutz."

"Wim! It's Ramey!"

Who? "Mama, you've got to get me out. It's so cold down here."

"Wim, listen to me. This is Ramey. You're not in a well. They're keeping you prisoner inside the box. It's been five days now."

The box? That sounded familiar and so did the voice. He shook his head in an attempt to clear away the cobwebs.

Think, you big oaf.

"Wim, come back to me, please. I need you."

Ramey. That was Ramey's voice. His fog dissipated and his sad reality came back to him. The box wasn't much better than the well but it was a moderate relief to have a mostly clear head.

"Aw, shoot. I'm sorry, Ramey. I think my marbles got scattered a bit in here."

"That's okay. I just needed to hear your voice. To know you're okay."

He thought he heard relief in her voice, but he heard sadness too. Not sadness, tears. He didn't think you could actually hear tears, but he knew she was spilling some. And he wished he could drink them.

"Where's Phillip? You can't let him see you here."

"He's asleep. It's fine."

But it wasn't fine. They both knew that.

"Wim, are you really okay?"

"How many days did you say it's been?"

"Five."

"Is it nighttime?"

"No, just before dawn."

Aw, heck. He was sure it was night. That meant he had almost two full days remaining.

"Wim, don't you lie to me. Are you really okay?"

His head had that taking on water feeling again. It made it hard to concentrate but he tried to push through.

"Will you make me a promise?" He asked her.

"Anything."

"No matter what happens, you'll still leave this place."

"We're going together. In the spring. As soon as the weather turns for the better. Did you know it's snowing now?"

Stop talking, he thought. Answer my question. I need to know you'll be gone from here. "I'm saying, no matter what. And that means even if you have to go without me."

"That's not gonna happen, Wim. I won't go anywhere without you. We're in this together. Have been since you saved my life back on that Pennsylvania road. You remember that, right? Poor Stan the truck driver almost made dinner out of me. But you didn't let that happen. We're always going to be together."

"Promise me Ramey."

She didn't. He could tell she was trying to prevent him from hearing her sobbing. It sounded like she'd moved a yard or so away. The soft hitching sounds passing through the wall caused him far more pain than the deep, frozen aches that assaulted his body.

"I need you to promise."

More crying and some sniffles. Then finally, "Promise."

She didn't say anything else. He heard her leave. Then Wim waited to die.

PART TWO

Six Months Earlier

CHAPTER FOURTEEN

The tomcat was old. This was his seventeenth summer and his once jet-black fur was now dotted and dashed with bits of gray. His eyesight was still admirable though and he watched the robin digging away at the wet soil, attempting to unearth a worm, with rapt, ravenous attention.

Hunting had been a challenge the last few weeks. The chipmunks, mice, and birds that usually fell prey to his still deadly sharp claws had seemingly gone away. And the humans, some of which used to set out dishes of milk or hard, tasteless kibble, were either gone or dashing around like animals themselves. Either way, they weren't feeding the old tom.

He took two slinking steps closer to the robin, trying to remain unseen in the cover of the unmown, foot deep grass. His movements were just a shimmery wave of green against the foliage and soon he was close enough to the bird to smell its moldy aroma. The tom's belly spasmed. It had been days since his last meal.

When the robin pushed its face into the dirt, its beak grabbing hold of a long, fat earthworm, the tom sprung. His old body crossed the yard-long void between them fast and silent and when he came down, he was atop his prey.

He sunk his teeth, what remained of them anyway, into the feathers. Their buttery texture tickled his tongue as his jaws closed. He felt hot blood flood his mouth and he felt more alive than he had in days, maybe weeks. Since everyone and everything went away.

The robin struggled, its wings fluttering furious and panicked. But even though the tom was old, he was still strong. There came a muffled crunch as its teeth smashed the bones in the bird's neck and then it went limp.

The cat savored his meal, devouring everything edible. Afterward he took a long nap, enjoying the warmth of the sun as it baked his ancient bones. Later, when it awoke, he felt renewed, almost young again. He wished some of his friends were still around so they could romp and jump and play together, but they were all gone too.

He spied the robin's severed head resting in the grass and he grabbed it between his paws, tossing it into the air and batting it to and fro. The game lasted for five or so minutes before the head went careening down an embankment and onto the road below.

Before everything went away the tom was cautious about roads. He'd seen too many of his own kind lying flat and dead upon them. But there hadn't been a vehicle in weeks and he bounded down the bank, his eyes locked on the robin's head, his new play toy.

The tomcat was old. He'd lost his hearing more than three summers before and now that became his undoing. As he sat on the road, rolling the head back and forth, he didn't hear the roar of the approaching engine. And by the time he felt the subtle vibrations through the pads on his paws, it was too late. He turned around just in time to see the orange monstrosity barreling down upon him.

The tom tried to flee, but it was far too late. The oversized wheels of the truck were the last thing he saw and then he joined his feline friends and the chipmunks and mice and birds in wherever it was that animals went when their days on Earth came to an end.

* * *

"Splat! Got to be quicker than that, pussy cat. Quicker than that if you want to avoid my truck," Solomon Baldwin cackled.

He checked the rearview mirror and saw a wet stain on the road behind him. That was all that remained of the old tom. He grinned and punched the horn.

"Saw one. Pussy none."

He'd been on the road for days, running down anything in his path. That was mostly zombies. Seemed they were just about all that was left. But he'd taken out a groundhog earlier in the week and a squirrel a day ago. This was his first cat and that delighted him to no end.

Gonna have to start me a log book, he thought.

He caught his reflection in the mirror. The bullet hole in his forehead had scabbed over and turned black. He thought about picking it off, God knew the fucker itched like a dirty asshole, but remembered how his brains had poked out of that hole, like a gopher popping its head out of its burrow, and decided to let the scab alone. Might be keeping me brains from leaking out, he reasoned.

He'd been driving for hours and needed a rest. Shortly after he passed into West Virginia he saw road signs declaring "Scenic Overlook" and he decided to see what the fuss was about.

After passing through a thicket of oak trees, he emerged at a wooden platform which overlooked a sprawling lake.

Not that special.

Still, he needed to work the cramps out of his legs and arms so he paced back and forth for a while. As he prepared to leave, he saw a gleaming white dot reflecting atop the water. It moved fast and even, making a direct line toward the island.

"Well I'll be..."

Saw realized the dot was a boat. He sat down and watched until it reached the island where movement ceased. He assumed that whoever was driving it docked the boat and got off, but he was at least three miles away and seeing those kinds of details were impossible. Nonetheless, his curiosity had been piqued.

After returning to his truck, Saw drove until he found an outdoor hobby shop a few towns away. There he gathered together some supplies, like hatchets, knives, and maps, but the prize he sought was a telescope.

He loaded up the biggest one he could find and returned to the overlook. After setting up the scope, he could clearly see the island and what he discovered changed everything. Up until that moment, he'd thought that the world had ended, that he was the only one left alive. Those thoughts had turned his normally jolly mood sour. Saw couldn't imagine living out the rest of his days all alone, without anyone else around to taunt or torment. That would be the most boring thing he could imagine. And a bored Solomon Baldwin was very dangerous.

Now, on this island, he saw not just a person or two, but a veritable town filled with them. Saw unfolded a map and marked his current coordinates, as well as those of the island. He also highlighted all the roads leading to the lake. He wasn't going there today or tomorrow, or even next week, but he'd be back. This looked like too much fun to pass up.

CHAPTER FIFTEEN

After fleeing The Greenbrier and the chaos that broke free from the underground bunker, Aben let Juli drive. Every now and again he directed her to make a right or left but he mostly sat in the passenger seat and allowed her to choose their destiny. The dog sat in the foot well alternating between curling up on his feet and sitting on its haunches and resting its head in his lap. Scratching the mutt's tan ears took his mind off Bolivar's death, at least to some extent. He couldn't shake the feeling that it should have been him. Bolivar was a good guy. Smart and calm and resourceful. A man with a purpose. This world needed men like him. Not homeless bums with one hand and a sour attitude.

"Where should we go now?"

Aben glanced over at Juli when he realized the voice was hers. She looked exhausted and a decade older than her 40-some years. He felt guilty for making her drive all this time, but not guilty enough to take over the duties.

"Huh?"

Juli pointed to the road ahead and Aben realized they were stopped at a Y intersection. A road sign informed them one fork would take them south, the other west.

"You don't have an opinion?"

Juli shrugged her shoulders. "I've never been further south than Myrtle Beach."

"You didn't miss much."

"So, west then?"

"Seems as good a choice as any."

It turned out not to be.

They were halfway across a bridge the signs had labeled the New River Gorge. It was one of the longest, and highest, bridges Aben had ever seen. A Chevy pickup had collided with a tour bus, blocking their lane and Juli stopped the car a few yards before it.

"Now what?" She asked.

"Turn around, I suppose."

In the back-seat Mitch popped his door open. "Bullshit. All we got to do is move one of 'em. I need to stretch my legs anyway."

And with that he was out of the car. The dog bounded after and Juli looked to Aben for an opinion he didn't have. She sighed and followed the others. Aben stayed behind and watched.

Mitch jumped up on the running board of the pickup and climbed into the vacant driver's seat. He looked down, then yelled out, "No keys!"

Juli was halfway between their Saab and the truck. "Shift it into neutral and I'll try to push it with the car."

Mitch did so, but when he exited the truck he peered over the hood to where the body was pinned against the concrete median. "Fucker's wedged in pretty tight. Let me check the bus."

Aben watched him but lost sight when Mitch disappeared around the front of the extra-long vehicle. As he tried to find the kid, he saw movement behind the dark, smoked glass windows of the bus.

Did I really see that? He couldn't be sure. The windows were almost black. He strained his eyes, squinting. And then he saw it again. Someone was in there. Or something.

Aben jumped out of the car and jogged toward the bus just in time to see Mitch slam his shoulder against the inward folding door.

"Wait!"

Mitch glanced his way but the door had already opened. "What?"

A silver-haired zombie tumbled down the steps and out the door, hitting Mitch in the back as she fell. The boy crashed to the ground, the woman on his back. He rolled onto his side knocking her off then jumped to his feet and backed away. As he did, he peered into the bus.

"Oh, fucking shit..."

Juli had been focusing on the truck and the sound of the commotion drew her toward the men. "What's going on?"

She got there just in time to see a small horde of zombies streaming out of the bus. All of them were sixty plus years old and Aben realized it must have been a sightseeing tour, silver riders or whatever the hell those things were called. What a shitty road trip they ended up with. Talk about deserving a refund.

"Juli, get back to the car!"

She hesitated, took another look, then ran. Aben was already there when she got back, but he didn't plan to stay. He grabbed his hammer. Juli caught his sleeve as he moved past her. "You're crazy if you try to fight them with that. There's too many."

Aben didn't respond. After all, she was right. Instead he returned to the bus where five of the zombies had Mitch surrounded.

He swung the maul hammer and crushed the head of a woman whose perm was so tight it probably doubled as a face lift. Then he smashed in the face of a man who sported the kind of flat top crew cut only worn by old veterans.

Mitch grappled with a skinny broad who wore a "Ask grandma, she'll say yes" t-shirt. The kid grabbed her by the hair, which proceeded to pop off her head. He stared at it quizzically, not realizing it was a wig. Aben brought the hammer down on the back of her nearly bald skull.

More zombies had bunched around them. Fifteen, maybe sixteen. Aben knew the only reason they were still alive was because they were of the slower, clumsier variety. But even with that advantage, they were far outnumbered.

Two of the creatures grabbed his good arm. Mitch snatched the maul from his hand and used it to smack one of them in the face. Its upper lip folded inward with a wet, stomach turning crunch and it lost its grip on Aben. Then, Aben spun sideways, grabbed the other creature and threw it over the edge of the bridge. The almost 900 feet fall was long and he didn't watch all of it. Immediately, he turned and grabbed the maul back from Mitch. More zombies had arrived on the scene.

Aben heard an engine roar, then looked past the zombies and saw Juli leaning out the car window.

"Get back!" She screamed.

Aben turned to Mitch. "Go on three."

Mitch nodded and Aben held up one finger. Then two. Mitch ran. Little prick. Aben followed, dashing head and shoulders down pushing through the pack of zombies. Just as they cleared them, they heard the tires squeal as Juli laid rubber and vaulted the car forward.

It plowed into the old, undead travelers. Most bounced off like tennis balls. Several fell and the car rolled up and over them, the tires spinning as they ripped away their flesh and sent black blood spewing. The car rocked and bounced and by the time it hit the bus, its forward momentum had almost ceased.

Juli climbed out the door and looked back to where a trail of destroyed and wounded zombies laid in the wake she'd left behind. Some were missing arms and legs, but still crawled toward a potential hot meal.

Aben made quick work of them. The maul crumbled their heads like empty soda cans and within a minute he'd finished them off.

Juli grabbed his hand as he led her across the carnage, her feet sliding in the gore like she was trying to walk on ice.

"Holy shit, lady! That was awesome!" Mitch said as he looked at the bodies. He didn't notice the zombie coming up behind him. It was a tall, gaunt man in a Cincinnati Reds hat and his hands grabbed hold of Mitch's greasy mop of hair before he even knew it was happening.

The boy struggled to break free but the zombie had a solid grip. It leaned down, its mouth open and drooling saliva which spilled onto the teen's head. Aben was fifteen feet away, too far to get there before the zombie would have already sunk its teeth into him. He was ready to try anyway when he saw the dog bounding toward them. He had an idea.

"Duck!"

Mitch stared at him, his wide eyes full of fear. "What?"

"I said duck, you dumb son of a bitch!"

Mitch dropped to his knees and between his unwashed oily hair and the zombie's own drool, he slipped free just as the dog hit the creature's chest. The Reds fan stumbled back one step, then another. That's when it hit the barrier. It was far too tall and top heavy to recover its balance and the zombie did a backward swan dive off the bridge.

Mitch turned to watch it fall. When it hit, a crazed grin spread across his face. "Take that motherfucker!" His words echoed through the chasm. The dog licked at Mitch's hands in a 'hey, don't forget me' gesture and the teen scratched its neck, almost giddy. "Good dog. That's a good fucking dog!"

There were a few zombies left and Aben took care of them. Juli had been trying to start the car with no luck and Mitch's examination of the bus found no keys.

"So, what do we do now, man?" Mitch asked.

"Walk," Aben said.

He helped Juli get Grady out of the car and over the bodies, then they crossed the remainder of the bridge on foot. Aben knew the others weren't fond walking, but he much preferred it.

CHAPTER SIXTEEN

The trio and the dog had walked five or so miles when Juli smelled it. She told herself it was her imagination, but the more time past, the worse it got. The smell, was shit and it was coming from Grady.

The small, silent man had kept a steady pace as long as Juli led him by the hand. When the smell became too strong to ignore, she risked a glance at the tops of his shoes, crisp white sneakers that she had found for him at the Greenbrier a few days earlier, were covered in brown liquid with small chunks mixed in for good measure.

Aben had taken the lead and was five yards ahead. She thought it strange but the man seemed different now, more confident. Like somehow being inside a car handicapped him. Mitch was beside him, as was the dog.

"Aben," she said, the word coming out as a whisper. He didn't respond and she repeated herself, louder. "Aben?"

He looked back this time. "What is it?"

Juli turned to Grady. "Wait right here." He didn't respond as she let go of his hand and moved toward the others. She beckoned Aben closer with her finger. She didn't want Mitch to overhear this. There was something cruel about the boy. Maybe it was just the cocky arrogance of adolescence, but she knew he'd howl over Grady's predicament if he found out.

"He…" She glanced back at Grady who stood exactly as she'd left him. "He had an accident."

Aben looked at him, curious. "What kind of accident?"

Juli saw Mitch looking at them and leaned closer to Aben. "The kind that happens in your pants."

Aben furrowed his brow at first. Then it hit him. "Oh. Oh!"

"He'll need cleaned up. Can we stop at the next house we come to?"

"Of course."

Aben returned to the lead. Juli heard Mitch ask him, "What was that about?"

"None of your concern," Aben said.

She appreciated that and had a feeling Aben was a man she could trust. At least, she hoped.

* * *

THE NEXT HOUSE WAS ALMOST HALF A MILE AWAY. IT WAS A RAMBLING, unkempt ranch with blue shutters and dirty yellow siding, but it would do. Aben took it upon himself to see whether the house was empty. It was.

Juli took a bowl from the kitchen cabinets and there was enough water remaining in the lines to fill it. She led Grady into the bathroom and undressed him. Juli had raised two children and changed more than her share of dirty diapers along the way. But she'd never had to clean a man before. The experience was more embarrassing than anything else. Fortunately, Grady sat there, motionless and silent as a statue, while she scrubbed the feces from his cracks and folds, out of his fine, almost white pubic hair.

"There," she said upon completion. "All better. You were a good boy."

She was aware that she was treating this man like a child, but didn't know how else to behave. She wondered if he'd ever speak to her. Or speak at all, for that matter. Who knows, maybe he's better off like this, not having to remember what he's lost and see what's become of the world.

Juli raided the bedroom closet and found pants and shirts that didn't fit well, but were close enough for him. She dressed him like he was her very own life-sized Ken doll, then fed him some of the baby food they'd taken from the car before abandoning it.

Aben and Mitch slept in separate rooms, while Juli put Grady to bed in the master. She considered leaving, but thought it safer to stay close. She laid beside him, their bodies fitting together like stackable Tupperware. Only $39.99 on the Home Shopping Network. She wondered if Donald had survived the plague. As she drifted to sleep, she hoped so.

CHAPTER SEVENTEEN

An overturned pick up blocked the road. Saw considered ramming it out of the way but knew it would get caught up on the rebar spikes and he'd have a hell of a time getting free of it. He grabbed a tow rope from the rescue kit he kept tucked under the seat and jumped down from the cab.

As he looped the rope around the axle, he heard the shuffling feet on the roadway.

Bugger me.

He'd left the sledgehammer, along with his pistol, in the dump truck and didn't have any weapons on him. If it had been just one set of feet dragging he wouldn't have been as concerned but there were several.

When he turned around, he saw four zombies between himself and his dump truck. There was one woman and three men, including one rotund, football-shaped fellow who looked to be half again Saw's size.

The idea of running didn't occur to him. Solomon Baldwin wasn't a runner, he was a fighter. As they closed within ten feet of him he removed the tow rope from the crashed pick up and held it in his hands, the metal hook dangling from the end. He rocked it back and forth, building up momentum.

"Come closer, mates. Saw's got a surprise for you."

The zombies did close in. The first in line was a teenage boy who had the long, lean body of an athlete. He was two yards away when Saw swung the rope. The metal hook arced through the air and slammed into the boy's face, destroying a set of teeth so perfect they could only have been shaped with the help of braces. The teen went down in a heap and Saw slammed a booted foot on the back of his neck. He felt the ensuing crunch all the way up his body and that set his pulse racing.

He pulled the tow rope in close again, twirling it round and round. The next zombie in line was the lone female of the group. She had a Pittsburgh Pirates baseball cap pulled down low on her forehead, almost covering her dull eyes. Her strawberry blonde hair was pulled into a ponytail which poked free from the back of the hat.

Saw thought about saying something he perceived as clever. Maybe 'batter up', but that seemed a little too much. Instead he swung the rope overhead like it was a lasso. It whipped through the air and the metal hook smashed into the side of her face, knocking the cap askew. Saw thought she looked a bit like a wannabe rapper. A rapper with her head crumpled inward just above her ear. She took two staggering steps, then hit the ground.

He'd been so busy watching the end of her that he didn't realize the other two zombies were on each side of him. To his left was an old man in a canary yellow button-down shirt and green polyester pants. The football-shaped giant was to his right.

Saw tried to use the tow rope but they were too close to build up any momentum. He choked up on it, grabbing the hook in his fist like it was a sixth finger. He spun toward the giant and lashed upward with the hook. It poked a hole in the soft flesh under its jaw and the hook curved out its open mouth like a metal tongue.

Saw grabbed the rope in both fists and jerked it with all his considerable strength. The giant's jaw tore loose and skittered down the street like a kicked can. Its tongue dangled unrestricted, black blood dripping from the wounds.

That's when the old zombie grabbed him. It smelled like Ben Gay mixed with death but the old bastard had a hold of Saw's arm and he wasn't letting go. As he tried to pull free the giant zombie was back for round two. It grabbed Saw's head in its oversize hands and caught hold of his ears, twisting them like it was trying to tune in a weak radio station.

The old man was leaning in for a bite of forearm a la Solomon when its face exploded from the nose up. A spray of bone and blood and chunks of flesh soaked Saw's upper body. Even the giant zombie seemed shocked, peering over at its brethren like it was trying to figure out where its head went.

Saw used the distraction to tackle the zombie to the ground. It tumbled head first to the pavement where he stomped on its skull, over and over and over again until it was nothing more than a pile of chunky gore.

With the zombie finished off, he spun around trying to figure out from where the gunshot had originated. He saw nothing at street level and raised his gaze skyward. That's when he saw the flash as the glass of the scope reflected the sunlight.

Are you going to shoot me too?

Saw raised his hand in a half wave, half surrendering motion. "Hello up there."

The person peering out from behind the scope shifted it a few inches to the side, revealing a feminine face. "Hello down there."

"Thanks for the good shooting," Saw said.

She laid on her stomach, in a sniper's stance, and she'd yet to set the rifle aside. "How do you know I was aiming for him?"

"Wishful thinking." He couldn't see her well, but she had a heavy mop of black hair and Saw thought she might be Asian.

"If I come down there are you going to kill me?"

"I hadn't planned on it."

Her name was Yukie Endo. She was Japanese in name but born and raised in America and she seemed fascinated by Saw's Birmingham accent. She was plain with a wide, doughy face and short, even by Saw's standards. Despite her unimpressive physical attributes, she kept the rifle slung over her shoulder and Saw had a feeling she could handle herself.

As far as she could tell she was the last person alive in her Western Maryland village. She'd been working on clearing out the zombies over the last few weeks and, along the way, had amassed a sizable collection of firearms, one that impressed Saw. He knew how to use a pistol but his aim was for shit and he'd never fired a rifle or shotgun in his life.

Yukie was equally impressed with Saw's dump truck. She peered up at it in a kind of awe and, when she reached up and plucked a chunk of flesh free from the razor wire, he knew she was a keeper.

* * *

SAW SAT ON THE TOILET INSIDE A CRAMPED BATHROOM STALL. AS HE emptied his bowels, he passed the time by reading graffiti scrawled on the walls.

50 yards to the outhouse by Willie Makeit.

Call BJ Betty for great head - 130-4984

This place smells like ass.

He was disappointed there wasn't anything more creative. Then, after scanning the scribbles, he found a multi-verse poem.

People who write on shit house walls, roll their shit into little balls.

People who read those lines of wit, eat those little balls of shit.

Saw burst out laughing upon reading it. "A regular Robbie Burns that one is."

He grabbed a handful of toilet paper, wadded it up and reached under his bum to wipe, making sure to dig around for a few moments. He dropped the used paper into the bowl. He tried to flush but it only swirled lazily around twice, just enough to stir up the smell. Saw wasn't too concerned. It wasn't like he'd be returning any time soon. Or ever, for that matter. He closed the lid.

Let it be a surprise for the next bastard.

When he exited the restroom, he emerged into the dreary light of an overcast, gray afternoon. And into the company of more zombies than he could count.

There had been none when he went into the loo and he wondered where they'd all come from. Certainly, he hadn't made that much noise. He tried to look over and around them, searching for Yukie, but there were too many to see past. The door banged closed behind him, and every zombie there turned their heads toward him.

"Bugger me."

He had no weapons on him, a mistake he told himself he'd never make again if he got out of this.

Where the fuck is Yukie?

The closest zombie wore a highway worker's uniform, its neon green reflective vest was stained with blood. The man in the uniform looked to be around forty with salt and pepper hair and a cigarette still tucked behind his ear. He pushed toward Saw who backed away until he hit the restroom door.

Saw reached behind himself, feeling for the doorknob and got it. The construction worker was almost on him and two others - a fit young woman in a spandex outfit like bicyclists wore and a middle-aged woman in mom jeans and a blouse with a pink rose print - were on its heels. Saw knew he was walking into a trap, but he couldn't see any other option. He jerked open the door and dove back into the restroom, slamming it shut behind him.

He checked the cinder block walls, hoping he'd missed seeing a window on his first foray into the room, but there was none to be found. He could hear the zombies outside. Their bodies hitting the door. Their undead hands scratching and clawing in a desperate attempt to get him. To eat him.

Saw needed something he could use to fight but the room was almost empty. A dirty sink stood in the corner and under it, an over-flowing trash bin. He upended it, sifting through used paper towels, cigarette butts, a used condom, but found nothing useful.

At the other side of the narrow room a mop leaned against the wall. Saw grabbed it. The handle was wooden. This might be something. He snapped off the mop end with his foot and the wood splintered into a jagged shard. He held it before him like a five-foot-long spear, poking and jabbing with it. As weapons went, it was rather pathetic but under the circumstances, it would have to do. He felt a little like a medieval soldier, ready to rush into battle and almost certain death. All he was missing was his shield. That gave him an idea.

The door to the restroom opened slowly. The nearest zombies had piled against it and they stumbled backward. The cyclist fell and a few others toppled over her. That allowed the door to open far enough for Saw to emerge. In his right hand, he brandished the mop handle turned spear. In his left, he carried the lid to the toilet tank. His own porcelain shield.

He charged forward like a bull, holding the lid in front of him and knocking zombies to either side. A gangly teenage boy in a plaid shirt and skinny jeans grabbed onto the mop as Saw passed him. Saw jerked it from the lad's grasp and then thrust the spear forward, puncturing the teen's skin just below his eye socket. The boy careened backward and the spear pulled free. Saw kept running.

He muscled by a fat man in a tank top and jean shorts, then came upon a skinny woman in bunny rabbit scrubs. She avoided the end of his spear, so Saw slammed her in the face with the lid. He felt her nose and cheek bones shatter under the force of the blow but, before he could even take a moment to enjoy it, he was grabbed from behind.

Whatever had him was tall and heavy and it had a hold of his shirt and wasn't letting go. Saw lurched forward and heard his shirt tear, then felt it come free of his body. His chest, which was covered with hair so dense it almost looked like he was still wearing clothes, was cloaked in sweat. He saw the man that had grabbed him, a policeman that must have been six and a half feet tall, staring down at the now empty shirt it still held in its hands.

Saw stabbed it with the mop handle, catching it just below the breastbone. The spear went in deep, poking out the other side. The zombie staggered a step back, but recovered in an instant and came at

Saw again. He tried to get the spear loose but it had impaled the zombie like a shish kabob skewer.

"Fuck it then."

Saw spun away from it and came across a woman who didn't have a spot of skin remaining on her face. He could see up the holes where her nose had been, her teeth biting up and down with no lips or cheeks to conceal them. Saw raised the toilet lid and brought it down over her head. She collapsed.

Ugly bitch. Did you a favor, I did.

But there were more zombies ready to take her place. Dozens of them. Each time he turned in a different direction there were more and more and more. They had swarmed like bees and he had no way out.

Solomon Baldwin wasn't the type to go down without a fight. He destroyed two more zombies with the toilet lid and was swinging for the third when he was hit in the back. The lid fell from his hand and broke into three pieces on the pavement.

He grabbed the biggest piece - it had a nice, sharp point - and used it to puncture the eyeball of an elderly woman with her hair rolled up in curlers. He was about to stab a boy who looked to be no more than four years old when he heard the horn.

It was loud, aggressive, and very familiar. The zombies looked toward the sound of it. Saw did too.

His dump truck came barreling in. The first of the zombies were punctured by the steel rebar he'd welded to the front end. More followed. And more after that. They were stacked on the long poles five or six deep by the time the truck was within ten feet of Saw.

He found Yukie behind the wheel. He could see her plain, round face was full of determination even though blood had splattered the windshield. He was so caught up in the sight of her that he almost let himself get run down. He dove to the ground at the last minute, making himself as flat as possible.

Christ, I hope that bird can drive a straight line.

The engine of the dump truck roared as it rolled over him. He covered his head, not that it would do a bit of good if Yukie was even one foot too far in either direction, but he could still hear the bones being crushed under the oversized wheels. And then it was past him.

Saw didn't waste any time. He jumped to his feet and found a clear path behind himself, like the red sea after Moses had parted it. This path too was very red, very bloody. Several smashed corpses littered the path, but Saw ran over them, paying them no heed. He almost slipped in the gore but kept moving.

The beeping that signified the truck had shifted into reverse began. Saw turned back and watched with admiration as Yukie made a three-point turn, running over more zombies and catching others in the razor wire that lined the vehicle's sides. She steered the truck a few feet to the right, widening the path, then stopped when she reached him.

Saw jumped onto the sideboard, flung open the door, and joined her in the cab.

"I sure am happy to see you, love."

She grinned, her chipmunk cheeks puffing out with glee. "Bet you'll be more careful where you take a shit from now on."

"Hell, I might never shit again."

There was no great hurry now and Yukie took her time running down the rest of the zombies, leaving behind a new kind of red sea, this one comprised of mangled and smashed bodies.

Yukie looked downright gleeful throughout the process and Saw thought again how glad he was that he'd found her. He even thought he might love her a little and hoped she'd end up being more loyal than his slag of a wife, but that was a low bar.

CHAPTER EIGHTEEN

The sun was hot on his back and Aben could feel sweat soaking his shirt. He wanted to move into the shade, away from the rays that beat down on him, but first he needed to get the dog to come to him.

"Come on, dog. Let's go inside and get you some water. Some for me too."

The dog ignored him. It was more interested in sniffing around a hedge of mountain laurel that was so thick it could serve as a wall. He'd been trying to get the dog's attention for almost ten minutes and his patience was almost up.

"Damn it, dog. Come here!"

The dog's only response was pushing its upper body further into the bushes.

"Son of a bitch!" Aben kicked the ground, splashing up a cloud of dust that rose and hit him in the eyes, further annoying him. "God-damn!" He wiped at his face with his remaining hand.

"Smooth move."

Aben turned and through bleary eyes saw Mitch watching from a few yards away. He wondered how long the kid had been spying on him.

"What are you doing?"

"Watching you make a fool out of yourself."

Little smart ass. Aben didn't like him much but had a modicum of admiration in the way the kid so clearly had no respect for anyone.

"How about helping me instead?"

Mitch strolled toward him but rather than lending a hand, he sat down in the grass. In the shade.

"Thanks," Aben said.

"Sit down. The dog isn't going anywhere."

Aben wondered what made the teenager an expert on canines, but his own attempts to cajole the animal were doing no good so he followed suit, moving into the shade where he flopped down beside Mitch. "So, what's your plan?"

"Don't have one," Mitch said as he watched the dog. Only its hindquarters were visible now against the sea of green foliage. "How long has it been with you anyway?"

Aben did the math in his head. "Three weeks now."

"And you're still calling it 'dog'?"

He shrugged his shoulders. What was the big deal about names anyway? The only thing names were good for were remembering people when they were gone. While they were alive, you didn't need to use their name, you just looked at them and spoke.

"How about Prince?"

Aben raised an eyebrow. "Seems a little pretentious. It's just a mutt, after all."

"When I was around ten, me and some friends were playing kick-ball at the playground. One of them kicked it into the woods at the far end of the field and I went in to find it. But before I found the ball, I almost tripped over a little black dog. I think it was a cocker spaniel. It had those long, floppy ears. It had its foot stuck in a rabbit trap, the snare kind. I thought it was going to bite me when I set it loose but it didn't. It hung around and watched us and seemed kind of lost so when we were done playing, I went back over to it and petted it for a little while."

Mitch reached into his pocket and pulled out a bag of mostly smashed cheese curls. He took one of the more intact ones and lobbed it toward Aben's dog. Soon after, the dog popped free of the mountain laurel, its nose twitching. In less than two seconds it homed in on the orange treat and gobbled it down. Then it looked to the men and began to amble toward them.

"It stank bad. Like old potatoes when they go bad. You know the smell?"

Aben nodded.

"Looking back, I guess it had been eating out of trash cans, getting by on whatever it could find. Its fur was all knotted and clumpy and as I tried to get my fingers through it I found its collar. It was just one of those cheap plastic ones, the ones that are supposed to keep fleas away, and there wasn't a license or vaccine tags or one of those 'If lost, please return to 123 Elm Street' badges. But someone had written on the collar. It was so faded out I could barely read it. But I worked it out anyway. It was his name."

Aben watched as Mitch tossed another cheese curl toward his dog. It wagged its tail as it ate the snack.

"I pulled one of the shoelaces out of my shoes and tied it around its collar and used it as a leash as I took it home. I was all excited because I'd always wanted a dog but my parents were totally against it, especially Senator SOB. He always said, 'You're not responsible enough to care for a dog, Mitchell. I don't believe I'd entrust you with a gerbil.' But I figured, if I found a dog, not just found but rescued one, saved its damn life probably, how could they say no? I was practically a hero after all."

Aben's dog lumbered into the shade and Mitch fed it another cheese curl, scratching its ear with his free hand. After eating, the dog licked orange coloring from Mitch's fingers.

"No one was home when I got there so I filled up a bowl with water and another bowl with some leftover chicken alfredo and we sat in the kitchen playing and eating all afternoon. And when my father got home I was a proud little fucker. I was all, 'Sir, I found this dog on the playground. I saved him from a bear trap' because I always tended to bullshit a little and I don't know why but I really expected to get a pat on the head like I was a good boy. Like I'd done something he'd approve of for once. Something moral and noble. The kind of shit he always preached."

"Instead he flipped his fucking lid. How dare I bring some bug infested stray dog into his home? How could I be so careless? All that horse shit. He drew back his hand and I knew he was going to smack me. It wasn't like a rare occurrence or anything. But when he pulled back, that dog must have known what was coming too and it ran over on its little legs and can you believe that dog chomped down on Senator SOB's ankle?"

Aben could believe it. From the look on Mitch's face, the boy took great joy in remembering the event.

"Bit right through his fucking cashmere dress socks and drew blood. And my father squawked like a baby. You'd of thought he got bit by a timber wolf. Fucking asshole."

"Well, he started screaming about rabies and grabbed the dog and took off for the garage. I watched him drive away and saw the dog standing up on its hind legs and looking out the window like it was going for a ride. All excited. And that was the last time I ever saw it. Don't have to be a rocket scientist to know what happened, right?"

Aben wasn't sure, but he thought Mitch's eyes looked wet but he only saw then for a moment because the teen looked down and dumped the remaining cheezies onto the ground for the dog to eat. When it finished, it looked up expectantly and Mitch held up his empty, orange hands.

"Sorry, pooch. I'm all out."

"So that dog's name was Prince, huh?" Aben said.

"No, it was Jerome. Now that's a stupid fucking name for a dog."

Aben couldn't help but laugh. Mitch grinned too. Maybe the kid wasn't so bad after all.

"Prince is a much better name."

"I still think it seems a little pretentious."

"Maybe. But have you seen any other dogs?"

Aben shook his head.

"Exactly. Makes this guy pretty damned special then, doesn't it?"

"What about us? Are we special too?"

Mitch stood up, clasped his hands together and raised them over his head while he stretched. "Shit yeah we are. Look around this world, man. We're not princes, we're fucking kings!"

Mitch jogged away, toward wherever he'd come from. When he disappeared, Aben returned his attention to his dog.

"Prince? You like that name?"

The dog stared at him and panted.

"Prince," Aben said, raising the pitch of his voice to an almost cartoonish level. The dog's ears perked up. "Prince! You want that to be your name? Prince?"

The dog cocked its head sideways. Aben would have preferred a bark but supposed that would have to do.

CHAPTER NINETEEN

"Stop the car, please."

Juli almost ran off the road upon hearing the voice from the back seat. It was too light, too gentle to belong to Mitch. Aben was beside her and it certainly wasn't the dog. That left but one option.

Grady. The man who hadn't said a word the entire time she'd been around him. The man who was as close to catatonic as she'd ever seen in person. She spun in her seat and looked behind her. Grady's eyes were no longer the empty pools that looked ahead but saw nothing. Now, they were alert, focused.

She felt the car swerve and realized she was still driving.

Shoot!

She smashed her foot against the brake pedal, thrusting them all forward in their seats as the car came to a sudden halt. The dog flopped off Aben's lap and landed on the floor with a 'woof' that sounded startled, if a dog can sound startled.

Aben had found an old rust bucket Impala while looking for guns in a storage barn behind the house. He'd said it probably wouldn't run, but it did. Then he said the tires were probably dry rotted, but they weren't. The car looked like a jalopy, but as far as Juli was concerned, it beat walking. They'd been on the road for about an hour, when Grady interrupted the drive.

"Thank you," Grady said.

"Holy shit! You said the gork couldn't talk!" Mitch said, his voice high and excited. Juli really didn't like the teen. His presence made her think of her own son, Matt, who she'd left locked in their perfect, suburban home. Matt was a zombie but he was still better than this foulmouthed, self-involved young man. But she couldn't allow herself to be concerned with Mitch now, not when Grady had seemingly returned to the land of the living.

Grady paid little attention to his companions in the car. Instead he opened the door and stepped outside. Juli quickly followed and heard the other doors open too. The dog bounded out, ran a few yards then stopped to urinate.

"That looks like a good idea, boy," Aben said, then he turned his back toward the others and did the same.

Juli ignored them both. All her attention was focused on Grady who strode softly almost like he was floating, toward a small, clapboard building. The paint peeled off the walls in thick chunks and the setting sun transformed it from white to a brilliant orange that almost made the building look like it was on fire. Faded block letters above the door labeled the building "Church of God with Signs Following." Grady pushed open the door and stepped inside.

"Wait." Juli chased after him but he continued.

She looked back to Aben who had zipped back up and looked on. "Help me, Aben! There could be zombies in there."

Aben snapped to attention. He grabbed his maul hammer from the car and chased after.

Sunlight spilled through the windows, drawing irregular rectangles across the dusty interior. Juli's eyes scanned the building, scared and nervous, but it appeared empty. More than empty, it looked like it had been abandoned since long before the zombies.

There were no ornate stained-glass windows, no murals of Christ and his disciples, no oversized crosses mounted on the walls. It looked as simple as a summer camp mess hall, with six rows of flat benches for seating and a small lectern which looked as if it might have been fashioned out of used barn wood front and center. Grady stood at that modest pulpit.

"God is in this house. He's called us here."

Julie went to him. She couldn't believe what she was seeing. He seemed completely normal. Like someone had flipped a switch and brought him into the light.

"Please sit, Juli. And you as well, Aben."

Juli turned and saw Aben standing in the open doorway, half in, half out of the church. He stayed there, but Juli followed instructions and sat in the first row of pews.

"How do you know our names? You've been in… something like a coma, since they found you."

"I was with God. And he told me everything."

Grady looked toward Aben who remained on the precipice of the sanctuary. "Thank you for caring for me during my time away."

"Don't mention it," Aben said.

"This is our home until God instructs us otherwise," Grady said. "Here, we will be safe in the arms of our Lord."

Juli heard the door close behind her and when she looked, Aben was gone.

"He'll understand, in time," Grady said.

"Will I understand too? Because right now this looks like— "

"A miracle." Grady's lips turned up in a serene, almost angelic smile. "It is. The first of many to come."

Grady picked up a bible from the lectern and opened it sending a cloud of dust soaring into the air. The light caught it and made it look like a million diamonds glistening around his head.

"Let's start with the book of Isaiah, chapter 26. 'Your dead shall live; their bodies shall rise. You who dwell in the dust, awake and sing for joy! For your dew is a dew of light, and the earth will give birth to the dead. Come, my people, enter your chambers, and shut your doors behind you; hide yourselves for a little while until the fury has passed by.'"

Juli had questions too. So many questions that she didn't know where to begin, but she had a feeling now was not the time to speak. It was the time to listen.

CHAPTER TWENTY

Aben cooked Spam on a propane grill and he was certain it was one of the best damned things he'd ever smelled. He'd put on four cans, which he felt would be more than enough for them and the dog.

Prince, his name's Prince. He had to keep reminding himself.

He wasn't certain but he believed Spam was already precooked so once it had sufficient grill marks to give it character he slid if off the grates and onto a serving tray which he then carried into the church.

Grady was in his usual spot at the pulpit. Juli sat in the front row. Mitch and Prince were nowhere to be seen.

Aben wished he had a bell to ring signifying dinner was ready but he didn't so he had to settle for clearing his throat. That didn't make it over Grady's blathering. He was ready to speak up, but something Grady said caught his attention.

"Last night, as I prayed, God told me how the plague started. How all of this misery began."

He's got a direct line to God now? This is new. Aben leaned against the back wall and listened.

"It was not He who punished mankind. He played no part in the death and destruction we all have witnessed."

'We all?' Aben glanced around the room to verify that it was only the three of them. It was.

"One of the Devil's disciples started the plague. Together, Satan and this man did their best to destroy God's greatest creations - Earth and its inhabitants, both man and animal. God played no hand in their evil plot, but he did ensure that some of us were spared. That some of us remained behind to restore humanity and spread God's love."

"And lest we begin to fear that the dead who now walk the Earth are our enemies, God has assured me that is not the case. Those men and women are but victims - pawns in the plot to undermine our Lord and Savior. The dead are not to be feared, they are to be loved. They are not to be slaughtered, they are to be saved."

Aben had heard enough. He liked Grady much better when he was catatonic. "I hate to interrupt, but I made dinner."

Juli looked back at him and gave a slight wave. She stood up and moved to the rear of the church, but then returned her focus to Grady who had not moved. "Come now, Grady. You have to eat."

Grady held on to his bible like a man cast adrift in the ocean clinging to a life preserver. "I shall not. I need to keep my mind clear so that I can hear God's voice."

She gave Aben a pained, confused - I don't know what to do - look.

"Let him go. He'll eat when he gets hungry enough."

Juli took another look at Grady who'd turned his attention to his bible. His lips moved soundlessly as he read. Julie followed Aben out of the sanctuary.

* * *

THE SMELL OF THE SPAM BROUGHT PRINCE RUNNING AND MITCH wasn't far behind. Aben had spread out a few plastic plates on a picnic table and Juli opened an extra-large can of mixed fruit and the three humans and one dog ate together. The food was nearly all when they heard a vehicle in the distance.

Mitch jumped to his feet and started toward the road.

"I wouldn't do that," Aben said. "You don't know who's coming."

"Someone alive, that's who. And we haven't seen anyone since leaving the Greenbrier so I'd say that makes whoever it is pretty fucking interesting."

Mitch was off. Prince looked at Aben as if asking permission to join him.

"Stay," Aben said denying him. The dog hung its head and pouted.

Juli watched the teen dash toward the road. "It sounds big," she said.

Aben nodded. The engine rumbled along indiscreetly. It was diesel, that was certain. Probably a tractor trailer. It made him remember Jay or Ray, the trucker who'd been his final ride before the apocalypse. Wouldn't it be a crazy coincidence if Jay or Ray was behind the wheel of whatever was rolling toward them? Now that would be a miracle Aben could get behind.

But it wasn't Jay or Ray. It wasn't even a tractor trailer. The vehicle that approached the church was a blaze orange dump truck that looked like something out of a *Mad Max* movie. Only this was real life and Aben had to admit that he was damned impressed. Steel spikes jutted from the front end and the exposed sides were cloaked with razor wire. This was a vehicle made to kill zombies. Or anything that got in its path.

Mitch stood at the edge of the road jumping up and down and waving like a—

"Goddamn fool," Aben muttered. "You stay back," he said to Juli. "You too," he added to Prince who gave a little whine as Aben stomped away.

The brakes of the dump truck screamed as it rolled to a stop five yards past the church. Mitch ran up to it, well ahead of Aben who found himself more worried about the teen than he'd expected himself to be.

"Mitch, hold back."

But the driver's side door of the dump truck was opening.

"Wotcha!" A voice called out. It was gravely and hoarse. The man to whom it belonged followed a moment later. He dropped down from the cab and Aben was surprised he wasn't as large as his voice.

He was five and a half feet tall at the most but wide. Aben could tell he had the type of muscles that weren't built in the gym but the kind earned in real life. He was an ugly son of a bitch too and a quarter-sized black spot in the center of his forehead didn't help matters. When he smiled at them, his mouth was filled with brown and black teeth that looked broken, or perhaps rotted.

Mitch ran up to him like a kid meeting Santa Claus. "I haven't seen anyone else in weeks. Thought maybe the whole rest of the fucking country was dead." He thrust his hand out. "I'm Mitch."

The man took Mitch's hand in his own. Aben thought it looked exceptionally large for his height.

"Solomon Baldwin. And I'm very much alive. So's me friend here." He banged on the side of the truck. "Come on out. They don't seem like the types to rape and kill us to me."

The passenger door opened and an even shorter Asian woman emerged. The drop down from the cab was a big one and she hit the ground with an 'oof.'

"You okay?" Aben asked her.

She nodded. "First step's a doozie. I'm Yukie."

"Aben."

Mitch headed her way. "And I'm— "

"Mitch. I heard."

Saw looked from the men to the church. He spotted Juli in the distance. And the dog. "Looks like we interrupted a family gatherin'. Sorry if we're intruding."

Aben wasn't sure what to think of these new arrivals but, considering how other people were in such short supply, it seemed pointless to be rude without cause. "Not at all. We just sat down for a bite to eat. Want to join in?"

Saw smiled again. Aben wished he'd stop that as the sight of his mouth sapped much of his appetite.

"I reckon we would. Eh, Yukie?

Yukie nodded. "I can always eat."

"So, what's on the menu?" Solomon asked.

"Spam and fruit," Mitch said.

"Sounds delicious!"

"I made it though, so I wouldn't get your hopes up too high, Solomon," Aben said.

"Don't imagine a man can fowl up Spam. If he did, it would be a first. And please, call me Saw. All me friend do."

* * *

THE FOOD WAS GONE IN SHORT ORDER BUT THE CONVERSATION CARRIED on into dusk when everyone was little more than a dark outline in the diminishing light. Aben surprised himself by how much he enjoyed the company of the new arrivals. It was a delight to hear fresh voices, different stories. It felt almost normal, or as normal as life could be in this new world.

The only light was the orange flicker at the end of Juli's cigarette. Even she seemed happier than she had in days, maybe weeks. Aben supposed it was good for her to have another woman around, some estrogen to balance out the testosterone.

Juli finished off her cigarette, blew out a mouthful of smoke then stifled a yawn. "I hope you two will stay the night."

"We got no place to go," Saw said.

She led them to the church and pulled open the metal door. Grady had lit dozens of white candles and, as their eyes adjusted, the details of the simple sanctuary came into focus. As did Grady who sat in the front pew, his back turned to them.

"Grady," Juli said. "We have guests."

There was a muffled thump as Grady closed his bible and set it down beside him. He stood and turned to the men and women at the back of the church, a small smile on his thin lips.

"Welcome. Welcome friends."

He moved down the narrow aisle, seeing Yukie first. She put out her hand but he ignored it and gave her a gentle embrace.

"Hello, Miss. And welcome.

Yukie gave him an awkward hug in return. Aben thought, if he didn't know how pious Grady was, he might have been flirting with her.

When they separated, Grady looked past Aben and Mitch and Juli until he found Saw. His smile vanished. Saw appeared not to notice the change in demeanor and strode forward.

"'Ello, mate. They tell me your name's Grady. I'm Sol— "

Grady took a step backward. He turned his face like he couldn't bear the sight of the man before him. Like Saw's very presence caused him pain. "Get out of here!" His voice rose above its usual whisper, but was still breathy and quiet.

"Pardon?" Saw asked.

"You shouldn't be here."

Saw looked toward Aben with a bemused smile, one that thankfully didn't show his teeth. Aben shrugged his shoulders.

"And why's that? Do I got B.O. or something?"

His attempt to defuse the situation failed. Grady managed to look at him again and Aben thought the diminutive, fragile man looked almost fierce.

"You're of the Devil!"

Juli gasped. Aben had almost forgotten she was there. "Grady! How could you say that?"

Saw put his hand on Juli's shoulder. "It's aw right miss. I been called worse."

Juli ignored him. Her focus was on Grady. "You apologize."

"I will not. Get that man out of here. This is a holy place and his very presence is a desecration."

Juli reached for him but Grady pulled away.

"Noffin' to worry about," Saw said. "I can sleep in me truck. Or in the grass for that matter. It stays nice and warm at night in these parts."

Saw exited the church. Aben decided to follow, leaving Juli alone to deal with Grady and Yukie.

The Brit had made it a few steps away when Aben caught up to him. For a moment, he thought he saw something like anger on the man's face but Saw's quick grin made him think he imagined it.

"I'm sorry about that. About Grady. He's a little…" Aben twirled his finger around his ear, hoping that sign for 'crazy' translated to the UK too.

"Chap's fucked in the head. Anyone can see that. I'll stay out of his little chapel if it keeps the peace. I'm not one to go looking for trouble."

Aben appreciated that. He liked Saw and Yukie and found them far more pleasant company than Grady.

"Tell you what, I'll crash out here with you. That'll give us two sets of ears in case anything should wander in."

"You don't have to do that."

"I don't mind. I've slept in far worse places than the grass on a summer night."

"You and me both mate. You and me both."

CHAPTER TWENTY-ONE

The town had two prizes - a supermarket and an army navy surplus store.

"Want to flip for it?" Saw asked Aben and Mitch.

Aben shook his head. "We'll hustle for supplies. I never did much enjoy grocery shopping."

Saw agreed to take the supermarket. He had a feeling that bringing back a truckload of food might win them over. It wasn't that he felt the need to prove himself - they'd be lucky to team up with him, not the other way around - but he knew that, should he ever return to the island he'd uncovered earlier in the summer, he'd need an army of sorts. And men like Aben and even Mitch seemed to hold potential and could be valuable assets down the road.

They thought the market was empty. From the outside, all they could see through the plate glass windows were row after row of shelves full of food waiting to be scavenged. Not a person, or zombie could be seen.

The doors to the supermarket were locked but a good hit to each of them with Saw's sledgehammer fixed that. He and Yukie climbed through the now empty metal frames, grabbed shopping carts, and began loading them up.

As Saw examined a shelf of boxed cupcakes, donuts, and other treats, it amused him how, before the plague, so many people had lamented artificial preservatives. They worried that they'd cause cancer or make your ticker explode or cause your balls to shrivel up to the size of peas. But now artificial preservatives were pretty much the greatest things ever created. All those little old ladies with root cellars full of that shit could be laughing their way through the apocalypse, if they weren't dead.

Saw swept an armload of desserts into the cart, then he moved on to the canned good aisle where the bounty was equally plentiful. He'd filled his first cart and was on his way to retrieve a second when he heard Yukie scream.

"Yukie!"

She sounded far away, near the back of the store. He abandoned the shopping carts and ran toward her voice.

As he zigzagged through the aisles and end caps, her screams drew nearer. Then he heard a gunshot. And another. He was close now, an aisle away, maybe two.

He smelled the dead before he saw them. Their roadkill on a humid day aroma was impossible to mistake.

Saw rounded the corner and ran smack into a zombie wearing an olive-green janitor's uniform, knocking the dead man backward where he toppled into a display rack of cheese puffs. The air-filled bags exploded underneath him in a series of forty or more pops. All combined they sounded almost like an explosion. Saw looked up and found ten more zombies surrounding Yukie, all sporting varieties of grocery store uniforms. He spotted two dead zombies on the floor, black blood dribbling from bullet holes in their heads. But it was the ones up and walking that he was worried about. Most of them were within arm's reach of Yukie who was pinned against a shelf filled with kitchen rolls and toilet paper.

Yukie aimed the pistol at a pimple-faced, scrawny teen who looked like just about every bagboy Saw had ever seen. She pulled the trigger. The gun clicked. She looked to Saw, her eyes pleading.

"I forgot to reload," she said.

Saw had left his pistol in the truck and the sledge setting beside the entrance. He scanned the area around him, looking for something to use but there was nothing close by except laundry detergent and cleaning supplies.

A short, fireplug of a zombie in a butcher's coat grabbed on to Yukie's arm. She tried to pull herself free but a woman in a blue vest sporting a name tag reading "MaryJo" joined the fray.

Saw knew it was now or never and he'd grown rather fond of Yukie. He grabbed a gallon jug of Tide off the shelf, popped the top and tossed the blue detergent over the floor. Then he grabbed another.

"Hey, you ugly bastards!"

Their heads swiveled toward him, almost in unison.

"Least you know you're ugly. Now how about we play a little game of cat and mouse?"

Saw stepped toward a zombie whose gray hair was concealed under a black hairnet. He grabbed hold of it and plucked it from her head. Then he ran.

The zombies stumbled toward him. As soon as they hit the detergent their feet slipped and skidded out from underneath them. Some managed to stay upright for a moment, their arms flailing, their hands grasping at the air, but soon enough they hit the floor too.

Zombie MaryJo had released Yukie and joined the others on the slip and slide, but the butcher zombie still struggled with her. Yukie held it off with a stiff arm as Saw circled back, avoided the flopping, struggling mass of the monsters, and went to her. He grabbed the zombie by its apron, pulling the white straps tight around its throat. The monster was half a foot taller than Saw and considerably heavier. The Brit had to jump onto the butcher's back before it released her.

The butcher fell sideways, crashing into the shelves of toilet paper which rained down on them like oversized marshmallows.

"What the hell's this mess?"

Saw, still clinging to the butcher's back, looked up and saw Aben standing at the edge of the skirmish. Mitch was close behind.

"'Ello there, lads." He looked around, at the flopping mass of zombies. "Got ourselves in a bit of a sticky wicket we did."

Aben looked around, nodded. "Appears so."

"Think you could lend a hand?"

"Well, I've only got one."

Aben took his maul and moved to the first zombie, a chubby man with a bad comb over. He used the maul to smash in the top of his mostly bald pate. The maul pierced the skin, then the bone, sinking deep into his brain tissue.

Mitch tiptoed through the spilled detergent, a pistol in hand. When he reached Saw, he pressed the barrel against the side of the butcher zombie's head and fired. The zombie, and Saw, went down in a heap.

When Mitch went to shoot another, Aben shook his head and issued a curt, "Nope!"

Aben finished them off with the maul, leaving behind a scattering of corpses with black brains and gore seeping from their caved in skulls.

"Toss me some paper towels."

Saw did and Aben caught it between his stump and body. The big man set the maul on a shelf then ripped off some kitchen rolls and used them to wipe it somewhat clean before returning it to his belt.

"Told you I didn't like grocery shopping.," Aben said, then turned and marched away from them.

"Thanks anyway," Saw called out.

"Any time."

* * *

BACK AT THE CHURCH THE QUARTET UNLOADED THEIR HAUL. SAW carried two cases of canned meat toward the entrance and was half way through the door when Grady appeared.

"Afternoon," Saw said as he tried to push past him but Grady refused to step out of his path.

"You're not welcome in the house of God."

"Heard that before. How about this food? Is it welcome?

Grady eyed the cans. "Hand them to me."

"Alright, but they're pretty heavy."

He passed them to the little man who struggled to keep from dropping them. It was clear it was almost more than he could handle and Saw tried to assist but Grady turned away.

"I'm fine. I have His strength inside me." The man wobbled inside, almost falling twice before disappearing around a corner.

CHAPTER TWENTY-TWO

Rain trickled down, enough to soak the ground and be an annoyance but not enough to keep everyone inside. Juli pulled weeds from a patch of flowers that had sprouted up at the front corner of the chapel. She thought the color combination of the red and pink impatiens wasn't the best, but she enjoyed seeing them anyway. They made her think about her rose bushes and she wondered if they'd blossomed yet. Probably not without someone around to fertilize and prune. Oh well, she supposed they weren't her concern any longer.

There was a steady drumbeat of hammers as Aben, Mitch, and Saw worked at replacing some of the rotten clapboard siding around the corner from her. Grady was inside, probably reading the bible or writing another sermon that no one but Juli would hear and Yukie was making everyone lunch.

It was an ordinary, if somewhat boring day, the kind of day Juli had grown to appreciate in the aftermath of the plague, until the girl showed up.

Juli heard branches snapping in the nearby tree line. It sounded light, almost airy, and she assumed maybe a gray squirrel or chipmunk was hopping around out of sight. She didn't give it any considerable amount of thought until Prince began to bark.

Juli peered into the trees but saw nothing. She glanced toward the men who continued sawing boards and nailing them fast. Prince continued barking and Juli set the dandelion digger aside and rose from her knees to her feet. She took two steps toward the woods, trying to spot whatever the dog could see or smell or somehow sense.

Prince moved to her side and Julie leaned over to scratch its head. She realized the dog's hackles were raised. "What is it, buddy?"

While she looked at the dog, she caught sight of something out of the corner of her eye. Something pink. She spun back toward the woods and saw movement and more pink.

A dress. A little girl's dress.

She moved through the trees like a ghost, there one moment, gone the next. Juli took another step toward her, trying to see her better. She was small and thin to the point of being frail.

How long have you been alone?

Another step. She was only a few yards from the edge of the trees.

The girl also came closer. Juli could see her pink dress was tattered and dirty.

You poor thing.

Juli crouched down. She wanted to be at eye level to put the girl at ease. To show her there was nothing to fear.

The girl pushed through the last of the trees. And that's when Juli realized she was a zombie.

She looked to be five or six years old. Along with her torn and stained pink dress, her light brown hair was littered with twigs and leaves giving it a wild, bird's nest appearance. But the worst part of this creature before Juli was her face. The girl's bottom lip, along with most of the flesh from there to her chin, had been eaten away. The white of her baby teeth stood out in stark contrast to the black, scabby tissue around them.

Juli inhaled sharply and the girl's dead eyes homed in on her. Her mouth fell open and a soft, barely audible growl emerged from her ravaged mouth. She sounded like a small, wounded animal.

"Oh, God. How could this happen to you?" Julie felt her tears start to flow. The unfairness, the tragedy of it, it was too much.

The little girl stumbled forward, only a few feet away now.

"Juli, step aside"

It was Grady's voice. Juli turned and saw him striding forward his hands empty, weaponless. When he reached Juli's side, the dead girl was almost within arm's reach.

"What are you doing, Grady?"

Grady ignored her. He took another step toward the child and laid his hand atop her head. The zombie looked up at him, her upper lip pulled back in a snarl. "This is where you're supposed to be. God has sent you here."

The little girl's arm swung out, slashing at Grady but catching only the air. He never so much as flinched but Prince's barking recommenced, only more agitated, more angry.

Grady put his free hand on the back of the dead girl's neck. She struggled and squirmed but he held fast. "Be calm."

Juli thought this was crazy. Did he really think his words made a difference? As much as it pained her to see what happened to the girl, she knew there was no hope for her. Whatever had made her human was gone now. This was nothing but a vicious, hungry shell.

Grady pushed the zombie toward the church. As Juli turned to watch them, she saw Aben approach.

"What's got Prince so worked— "He stopped when he saw the child, staring, examining. Juli could see his gaze change from curious to bewildered when he realized the child was dead.

"Get away from it!" He screamed.

Grady shook his head. "Do not fear this child. God has sent her to me."

Juli caught Aben's gaze. He raised his eyebrows. 'What the hell?' Juli shrugged her shoulders. 'Your guess is as good as mine."

They watched Grady and the zombie approach the church, the child fighting to break free as they walked. Neither of them realized Saw was coming until he was just a few steps away, a claw hammer in hand.

"Fucking shit, man! Get away from it!"

Grady spun around, startled by Saw's booming voice. When he turned he lost his grip on the zombie and she lurched away, tottering toward Saw and Saw was coming for her.

"Don't you hurt her!" Grady yelled, but it was too late.

Saw brought the claw end of the hammer down on the child's head and buried it handle deep. A squirt of black fluid jutted up like water from a drinking fountain. The girl took a step. Another. Then fell face first onto the wet ground.

Grady stared down at the girl. Juli expected the worst. She knew what happened to his son and how it had sent him into a catatonic state. She almost expected the same to happen now. His sanity seemed so tenuous. She didn't know if she could bear to see him regress back into that condition and she prayed that Grady's God, if he was really up there, would protect him.

Saw ripped the hammer free from the little girls' skull and wiped the black blood off on his jeans. He looked to Grady. "You can thank me later, mate."

Grady's head came up slow, like someone cranking an old manual window. But eventually his eyes met Saw's face. Juli could see them from her vantage point. They weren't broken or wounded or sad. They were enraged.

"You're no longer welcome here," Grady said to Saw.

The killer furrowed his brow. "What's that supposed to mean? I wasn't allowed inside your precious church anyway."

"That chapel and this ground is Holy. You have no purpose here. Tomorrow, I expect you to be gone."

Grady knelt at the girl's body and slid his arms under her. Juli could tell it took all his strength, but he lifted her. Saw twirled the hammer in his hand as if debating whether to use it again. After a moment, he turned away. "Man's off his rocker, he is."

Grady didn't say a word. He carried the girl's lifeless body to the church and disappeared inside.

"Can you tell me what that was all about?" Aben asked Juli.

She shook her head. His guess was as good as hers. "I have no idea."

The door to the church slammed shut. She jumped.

"Let me talk to him," Juli said.

"Good luck with that."

As Juli went to the church, she saw Mitch conversing with Saw, the older man gesticulating wildly while Mitch laughed.

* * *

As JULI APPROACHED FROM BEHIND, GRADY HAD THE DEAD GIRL'S BODY sprawled out on a pew as he used a wet rag to clean the death from her head and face.

"Grady, are you all right?"

He didn't look at her. "I'm fine."

"Are you really?" She moved in front of him into his eyeline. "What were you doing out there?"

Grady squeezed the rag. Black fluid dripped from it. When it stopped, he continued cleaning the body. He didn't answer Juli.

"Grady, you have to speak to me. What am I supposed to tell the others?"

"They're welcome to listen to the sermons if they care to hear God's message."

"I want to hear from you, not God."

He finally looked at her. "God speaks through me. His words are my words. Do you not know that?"

"Apparently I don't. I'm asking you Grady, why you risked your life out there."

"I was never in danger."

"Bullshit."

He flinched as if the word caused him pain.

"We were all in danger. The girl was a zombie. And zombies kill us. That's what they do."

"You don't understand."

"That's why I'm asking. Help me understand."

Grady set the rag aside. He moved to Juli and peered into her eyes. He reached out and took her hands and Juli felt her skin break out in goosebumps. It was almost as if she could feel a mild electrical current running through his hands, into hers. She nearly pulled away but stopped herself.

"You think the zombies are the monsters but they're not. We are. The zombies don't kill us for our flesh. They consume our sins and cleanse our souls so we're worthy of entering the Kingdom of God."

Juli didn't know what to say, so she said nothing.

"In John, Jesus said, 'Whoever feeds on my flesh and drinks my blood has eternal life, and I will raise him up on the last day. For my flesh is true food and my blood is true drink.'" Grady rolled up his sleeve to show the healed bite wound on his arm. "My Josiah didn't hurt me when he did this. He gave me salvation. So, do you understand now, Juli? We have nothing to fear from the undead for they were sent here to save us."

She could see the earnestness in his face, the belief in his eyes that he believed what he said. It was so raw and so real that Juli started to believe it too.

* * *

ABEN FOUND JULI CROUCHING BESIDE A SMALL GARDEN THAT GREW IN an open meadow behind the church. At the sound of his footsteps, she spun around, clasping a small pair of clippers in her hands.

"Only me," Aben said holding his hands up in submission.

Juli lowered the clippers and smiled.

"You were expecting someone more exciting."

She shook her head. "I've had enough excitement to last a lifetime."

Aben sat down beside her. "That doesn't exactly help my ego."

"Sorry, Aben. My manners are lacking. "

"Well, if my wounded self-confidence is my biggest problem, I'd say life has taken a definite turn for the better."

Silence fell between them. Aben knew what needed to be said but hadn't quite got there yet. He tilted his head toward the garden. "What you got there?"

"Someone was nice enough to plan a garden before the plague. I feel a tad guilty that they won't be able to enjoy the bounty."

She plucked a green tomato nearly the size of her fist from a vine. Aben looked at it skeptically. "Shouldn't you let it ripen up first?"

Juli looked down at the tomato. "I used to fry green tomatoes at home. Not for the kids, they turned their noses up at them, but for Mark. I'd coat them in some flour, salt and pepper then fry them in butter. Real butter, not margarine. Sprinkle them with some freshly grated parmesan cheese, not the canned stuff, at the end. Mark ate them like candy."

"Sounds like a way to take a healthy food and make it practically sinful. I approve."

Juli looked at him and he saw her eyes were misty.

"I'll make you some, if you want. We don't have any cheese and I'll have to substitute oil for butter but…"

Aben shook his head. He appreciated her kindness but it only made what he had to say more difficult. He considered saying nothing at all. To instead vanish like a coward in the night, which was pretty much all he was anyway. But he'd been with this woman for almost two months, a longer period time than he'd been around anyone in twenty or so years, and he felt he owed her his honesty, for what little value that held.

"I'm leaving with Saw. Mitch is too."

Juli's gaze fell from his face to the ground, but her expression remained unchanged.

"You don't seem surprised?"

"I'm not. I've felt it coming for a little while now. Can I ask, why?"

Aben had asked himself the same question and didn't have much luck coming up with a solid answer.

"What's so special about Saw and Yukie that you'd choose them over us?"

"It's not like that. I'm not choosing them." But he was.

"We've been here for going on six weeks. And it's the same thing day in and day out."

"So, you're bored? That's the only reason?"

"I don't like sticking around one place to long. Never have. Call it boredom or whatever you want, but it's time to move on. You can come too. We all want you to."

"You know I can't leave Grady alone."

"But he's better now." Aben took a glance at the church. "In a way."

"He still needs someone to look after him."

"Why does that have to be you?"

She looked at him again, her eyes narrowed. "Because there's no one else to do it, Aben. That's why."

"But he's off his rocker. Come on Juli, you see that don't you? You don't buy his holy roller 'I've been chosen by geeeee-zus to save the world' bullshit, do you?"

Juli rolled the tomato between her hands. "He was bit by a zombie— "

"You don't know that for sure."

"You told me that. You and Bolivar both. And I saw the bite wound. It was made by a child's mouth. So, don't try to rewrite history to fit your new agenda."

Ouch, that one hurt.

"Grady was bit and he didn't turn. Isn't that some kind of miracle?"

"We don't know how any of this really works. We're going off what we've seen in movies for Christ's sake."

"I'm going by what I've seen with my own eyes. Everyone I saw get bit by a zombie turned into one. Grady is still normal— "

Aben chortled, derisive.

"Relatively speaking. You asked me if I believe what he's preaching? The answer is, I don't know. But considering everything else I've seen the last two and a half months, things that seemed so impossible they were silly... Why is it so hard to believe that God is speaking to Grady?"

This was going nowhere. Aben had suspected it would go something like this, but it still disappointed him. "Alright then. We'll leave in the morning. If you change your mind before then—"

"I won't."

"I know you won't."

He strode toward the church ready to gather his meager posses-
sions his dog, and be done with this place.

* * *

THE DUMP TRUCK, WITH ITS BIZARRE, VIOLENT ARMOR, ROLLED AWAY
from the church and into a heavy fog that filled the valley. To Juli it
looked like it was being swallowed up.

She felt a deep ache inside as she watched it fade out of view. Aben
had become a kind of family. A brother she never had, maybe. And
even Mitch, for all his annoying faults, had been with her so long she
couldn't imagine what life would be like without his presence.

Part of her wanted to scream. 'Come back! I changed my mind!
Take me with you!' She could see herself running after them, her feet
smacking against the pavement as she gave everything she had to
catch them. Catch them and run away with them.

"I know you're sad," Grady said behind her.

She hadn't realized he was there and she quickly wiped away tears
that had whetted her cheeks. He'd remained in the church when the
others left and, as far as she knew, hadn't even said goodbye. That had
angered her and now she let the anger come back and push away
some of the sadness.

Juli turned to Grady. His face was so calm, so peaceful that she
almost wanted to hit him. She wondered how he'd react. Would he
even react? She could imagine him standing there with the same
maddeningly serene expression plastered to his face even after getting
blindsided.

"Aben did so much for us. He saved you, you know that don't you?"

Grady nodded. "The choice was his as we all have free will. In the
end, he turned his back on God."

"He turned his back on you."

"And I am God's vessel. He still has time to find salvation, but the
longer he sidles up with evil, the less chance he has. I wish I could say
I was optimistic, but considering his choices…"

Juli couldn't stand looking at him. She walked past him, toward the garden, but he grabbed her wrist. His touch was light and harmless, but she didn't pull away because she felt that same strange electricity she'd experienced earlier.

"We have to look at the bigger picture, Juli. We can't mourn one man when our mission is to save the entire world."

Juli glanced back at him. The rising sun poked through the clouds, spraying rays of light downward. One of them illuminated Grady's face and made him look like he was glowing.

It's just the sunrise.

But it felt like more than a coincidence or some happy accident. Grady looked like an angel or maybe some prophet straight out of the New Testament. John the Baptist maybe.

No, it's Jesus. He's getting lit up like Jesus himself.

She didn't believe Grady was the Second Coming. She wasn't even certain he was sane. But she'd made her choice.

PART THREE

CHAPTER TWENTY-THREE

Doc knew the sedation should be wearing off any time now so he sat by the young man's side and waited. Eventually his eyelids fluttered and a few small moans escaped his stitched-up face.

"Wake up, my child, and tell me your tale of woe."

It took a few more minutes, but the teen did awaken and as his eyes focused under the dull green fluorescents, he turned his mangled face toward Doc.

"Hello there, young friend."

"Hi." The boy winced as he spoke, as the pain coursed through his face. He reached up and his fingertips traced the sutures that lined his cheeks. "Where am I? Who are you?"

"You're on the Ark. A compound of sorts which I founded and which is safe. And I am Douglas Younkin, but you can call me Doc."

"Like the rabbit?"

"Pardon?" Doc thought the boy must be delirious from his pain medication.

"You know. Yabada, yabada, yabada. What's up Doc?"

"Oh!" Doc chuckled. "Well, yes. Like that. But the rabbit wasn't Doc. The rabbit was asking Doc what was up."

"Close enough."

Doc patted the boy's hand. "I suppose."

The teen pushed himself up in the hospital bed so he was sitting somewhat upright. "Can I have a drink or something?"

Doc nodded. He poured water from a plastic pitcher into a cup then dropped in a straw and handed it over. The boy sucked it down greedily. When he finished, Doc refilled it.

"Now it's your turn."

The boy finished off another cup of water. "I'm Wayne Supanek. I'm 17 and I was living in Harper's Ferry when the zombies happened. Everyone died. My mom. My dad. Even my gram. They all turned."

"Did you have to kill them?"

Wayne shook his head. "I just ran. Took my dad's Honda and drove away as fast as I could go. Made it a hundred miles or so before I hit a pileup on the interstate that I couldn't get around so I started walking."

Doc was already bored. The boy's story was the same as everyone else. Sickness. Death. Fear. Running. So sad. Blah blah blah.

"Yes, I understand. It must have been quite traumatic." Doc leaned forward, resting is hand on top of Wayne's. The boy wriggled his own away and Doc pretended not to notice. "One of our men found you. Your injuries were... severe."

Wayne averted his eyes and gave a curt nod.

"What happened? Who cut you?"

"The Devil did this to me."

"The devil? Red skin, pointy tail, pitchfork? That kind of devil?"

Doc thought he saw Wayne's pupils constrict, the muscles in his face tighten. The boy wasn't amused.

"No. He was a man. But he's a killer. He asked me to help but I wouldn't so he cut me. And left me to die. Told me the blood would attract the zombies like sharks to blood in the water. And they almost got me a couple times. I barely got away—"

Doc wasn't interested in how the boy survived. He wanted to know more about the person who cut him.

"Yes, I understand. But the man you mentioned. Who did he want to kill?"

Wayne lifted his face to look Doc in the eyes.

"Everyone who got in his way."

The boy's stare was so intense that Doc broke eye contact. "Well, you're safe here, Wayne. We'll take good care of you."

Doc stood up and walked, almost scurried out of the room. He turned back when he reached the doorway.

"And, Wayne?"

"Yeah?"

"I'd consider it a personal favor if you don't mention this devil of yours to anyone else. At least for the time being. The people here are… on the excitable side."

"No problem."

Doc didn't like this, not at all.

* * *

Thud, thud, thud, thud.

Thud, thud, thud, thud.

Thud, thud, thud, thud.

Doc drummed his fingers against the desk repeatedly. It was one of his nervous tics. Flaws he usually hid well, but which reared their heads under times of duress. Like now.

He checked his watch again. 6:38. The men were late. He despised tardiness in the best of times and this was far from that. It was still dark outside but that would be changing soon.

Thud, thud, thud, thud.

Thud, thud, thud, thud.

There came a knock at the cabin door. "Come in!" Doc said.

The door creaked, then opened. Phillip was the first through.

"What took so long?" Doc said as he climbed to his feet and stalked toward him.

Philip gave a sheepish shrug of his shoulders and tilted his head backward, toward the next man in line. That was Buck Prentiss, a former soldier who had yet to abandon his crew cut.

"I'm ssss - sorry, Doc. I ssss- slept in."

The stuttering was worse when Buck was nervous and it would have normally annoyed Doc, but right now it defused his temper, at least to some degree. He enjoyed seeing these younger men cow to him.

"I wwww - won't dddd- do it again."

Doc nodded. "I'd hope not."

Darry Skiver was next into the room. His thick, black framed glasses made him look like a nerd from the 1950s, but his body was fit and muscular. He was quiet and followed orders well. Last came Santino Espina, the oldest of the bunch at forty-eight. He was tall but quite lean and the combination made him look inconsequential, like a gangly teenager who'd never grown out of his awkward phase. However, Doc had seen him beat a man to death with his bare hands earlier that year.

The four of them watched Doc expectant, silent.

"It's been brought to my attention that there may be survivors in the vicinity. I need you men to go on a scouting mission and see if you can find any evidence of that."

The men cast furtive glances at one another, wary. Doc knew they had not been expecting anything along these lines. They hadn't been off the Ark in months. The last time they were, a fifth man, Kelvin, had been killed by zombies.

"What brought this on?" Phillip asked.

"The boy Wim brought in, Wayne. He said the man who cut him is some sort of killer. Now the boy could be mad with fever or simply an outright liar, but I want you to make sure the area is clear."

"And what if we do find someone?" Phillip's hand fell to the pistol on his waistband as if he knew the answer to come.

"If you find someone alive, anyone, kill them. I don't care if it's a man, woman, or child."

Santino was the first to nod in agreement. Phillip followed, then the others.

"Be back by dusk. I'll tell everyone you're out for supplies since William is incapacitated." He shooed them away with his hands and they retreated toward the doorway. Before they could exit, Buck looked back.

"Dddd-Doc?"

"Yes."

"Shouldn't we bring something back? I mean, in case anyone sees us. They'd wonder why we're empty-handed."

Doc considered this, nodded. "Yes, very true. I'll make a small list. But Buck?"

"Yyyy - yes?"

"If you want to bring me something, make it a zombie. Female. Late teens or early twenties if possible."

Buck's eyes grew so wide the eyeballs looked as if they might tumble free of the sockets. "A zzzz - zombie?"

"Yes, Bbbb - Buck," Doc said with a sneer. "A zombie. And I want her unharmed and with no prior injuries to her torso. Do you think you can handle that?"

Doc's gaze was harsh, unforgiving. Buck looked away. "Yes, ssss-Sir." Buck fled the room.

Phillip was the last out and Doc flashed a ghoulish smile at him. "Make her a pretty one, Phillip." He added a wink. Phillip didn't say anything as he left the cabin.

CHAPTER TWENTY-FOUR

No one realized Hal hadn't returned to his quarters the night before. No one missed him at breakfast that morning. No one saw him laying a hundred yards from camp, his body curled into a ball as the pain arced through him like electricity cooking him from the inside out. No one saw him die. And no one saw him come back.

He rose from the gulley in which he died, first climbing to his knees, then pushing his way onto his feet. Clods of snow fell as he swayed, took a step, then tumbled back to the ground. His second attempt was more successful and soon enough he was staggering toward the common ground.

Hal, or the thing that used to be Hal, came upon little Tommy Spielman first. The boy was about eight years old, skinny as a fence-post, and in the middle of building a snowman when Hal reached him.

The boy saw the shadow fall over top of him, turning the white snow a dirty gray. He looked up, squinting as his eyes adjusted to the bright, gun metal colored sky, but saw nothing. Tommy kept tilting his head back, leaning his whole upper body backward in the process. When he reached a 120-degree angle, he found Hal looming behind him.

It was hard to see Hal's face against the bright sky and, even if he had got a good look, little Tommy wouldn't have realized Hal was a dead man anyway. He only had two or three seconds to wonder why this man was staring down at him with his mouth open when Hal lurched forward and grabbed him by his ears. Hal used them like handles as he lifted the boy upward, raising him toward his gaping mouth. Tommy didn't even have time to scream before the zombie bit down on his face. The feeling of teeth shredding his tender flesh was unlike anything the boy had ever felt before. Soon, their teeth clattered together as Hal's mouth chomped through Tommy's lips and tore them free from his face.

"Tommy?"

As shock overwhelmed him Tommy managed to turn his head to see Pete Decker, one of his very best friends, staring at this strange, horrific scene.

Tommy tried to speak, but all that came out was a wet gasp as blood flooded his throat. "Hegrrahhhh."

Hal also had also turned to see Pete. The boy was almost as round as he was tall and he'd always reminded Hal of the fat kid in the *Little Rascals* movies. That thought didn't pass through his mind now though. All he saw in Pete was a fresh meal.

The zombie dropped Tommy who fell into the snow which gave a brief puff. Crimson blood quickly stained the snow red and, to Pete, it looked a little like a cherry snow cone.

Pete couldn't understand what had happened to his friend's lips and he couldn't understand what Hal, the nice old guy who sometimes gave him his leftover pudding at dinner, was chewing on. The way his jaw smacked up and down, up and down, Pete thought he might have a mouthful of bubble gum. Or maybe taffy. Pete remembered getting saltwater taffy at Ocean City a few years ago on summer vacation and he loved it even if it did take a long time to eat.

But taffy, or bubble gum for that matter, didn't leak red stuff and there was a lot of red stuff running out of Hals mouth as he chewed away.

"Mr. Hal? What are you eatin'?"

Hal didn't answer but he did swallow down little Tommy's lips. He was beyond thinking now, but the plump morsel that was Pete Decker was impossible to ignore. He stumbled toward the boy and Pete took a step backward. Hal matched that move and Pete again backed away. But that time Pete's foot hit a divot in the snow and he collapsed backward.

I could make a snow angel, he thought.

Hal dove on top of him. Unlike Tommy, Pete did manage a scream. Several of them. His high-pitched wails as Hal ate him alive assaulted the otherwise peaceful morning.

As Hal devoured Pete, little Tommy emerged from the snow, hungry, fast, and ready to eat. He sprinted toward camp.

CHAPTER TWENTY-FIVE

"I'm not the one who makes the rules."

Ramey stared at her father, so shocked her mouth would have fallen open if she'd let it. How could he look her in the eyes and lie to her like this?

"What are you talking about? The people here don't take a shit without your permission. Nothing happens without your approval."

Doc's eyes narrowed. Was he angry at her? She almost hoped he was. She was tired of the benevolent dictator act he'd been playing since her arrival.

She'd found him in his quarters, clutching a cup of coffee like it was lifeblood. She thought he looked small like this. So mortal and average and lacking in the swagger he carried when out amongst his followers. He seemed less like Doc and more like her father. Or maybe that was wishful thinking.

"The committee votes on every major decision. That's the way it must be, Ramey. You'll come to understand that in time."

"Fuck your committee. You know damn well that you can get him out of that box with one word."

He opened his mouth to speak but Ramey cut him off before he could get started.

"He'll never last two more days. "

Ramey expected to see something in his eyes. Remorse. Regret. Maybe compassion. Instead, she saw nothing but detached calculation.

He's looking at me like a lab rat. Not like his daughter.

She'd traveled hundreds of miles to find her father. She'd risked her life in the process. Others had lost theirs because they had tried to help her find him and his supposed safe haven. Was all of that in vain? It sure felt like it.

Ramey crossed the four feet gap between them and took her father's hand. She was surprised how cool it felt. What could she say to get through to him? To bring back the man he used to be?

"Please, dad. I'm begging you to do this. He saved my life out there, more than once. He's a good, honest man. He was only doing what he felt was right."

He didn't respond right away. She thought she was making headway.

"I can't lose him, dad. I love him."

As soon as the words spilled from her mouth she felt the muscles in his hand spasm and he slipped free of her grasp. His eyes shifted from being simply detached and became angry. Cruel.

"I thought I raised you to be smarter than that."

Ramey knew the words were meant to hurt her, but instead they only made her angry. "You didn't raise me. You abandoned me."

She spun on her heels and headed to the door. Pulling it open, she was ready to storm off when she saw the zombie. She knew immediately what he was. He had that fast but awkward gallop she'd seen so often outside these walls. But how was this possible? How did a zombie get onto the island?

Ramey didn't realize Doc was behind her until he grabbed hold of her shoulder and pulled her back into the confines of the cabin.

"What— "she couldn't get the words out before he slammed the door closed and locked it.

Ramey turned to her father but he wasn't looking at her. He was staring out the window.

"There's a zombie out there," she said.

"No. Not one. Many."

Ramey followed his gaze and realized he was correct. Ten or more of the creatures ran through camp, attacking and eating anyone they could catch. Their wounded, pained screams brought back a rush of horrible memories.

"Oh God no."

Ramey turned away from the carnage and saw her father flip a small, metal switch. Outside, an air raid siren, the kind she only knew from movies, began to wail. The sound was almost deafening and drowned out the screams.

CHAPTER TWENTY-SIX

"Wim? You alive?"

The morning sun spilled through the cracks in the box, painting pinstripes on his face, which had grown noticeably thinner. He hadn't fallen asleep since Ramey left but he was barely conscious. So, when he heard the siren blaring, he assumed it to be another hallucination. Nonetheless, he held his hands over his ears.

The noise ricocheted off the metal walls of the box, so loud he thought they were shaking. He closed his eyes, trying to shut it all out, but then he heard a voice yelling.

"I asked if you alive in there?"

The voice was familiar. Female, but husky and with a heavy Appalachian accent and sandpaper grit. But he couldn't pinpoint it. It wasn't Phillip though, so he dared to answer. "I am."

A gunshot rang out and immediately afterward light flooded the box, assaulting Wim's eyes which had grown strangely accustomed to the dark. He couldn't see anything but a black shape against the sea of white.

"Dere's trouble out here. We need you."

The shape pushed something toward him and as Wim's eyes

adjusted to the brightness, he realized it was a rifle. He looked past the gun, to the hand holding it, and saw Delphine.

"What's going on? Why are you letting me out?"

She again shoved the rifle at him, and this time he accepted it. Then she handed him something much more important, a gallon jug of water.

"I reckon you're parched, so drink up while you listen."

He did. He chugged the water so fast that his stomach spasmed and he regurgitated the first several swallows. It spilled into the snow, melting it.

"Dere's zombies in the Ark. Don't know how it started but people's getting bit and infected. I counted sixteen, mayhap seventeen."

Wim stopped gulping the water as he did the math in his head. That was about one fourth of the entire population of the Ark.

Ramey. God, don't let them have got Ramey.

Delphine must have seen the terror in his eyes. Either that or the old woman could read his mind.

"Ramey's all right. She's holed up with Doc in his cabin. But I haven't seen the other two you came in with. "

Wim tried to stand but his legs gave out. He didn't think he'd ever been so weak, so helpless, and it annoyed him to no end. Especially now when lives were at stake.

"Easy now," Delphine said. "You ain't no good to no one if you pass out."

"I'm fine."

Wim sucked down a few more swallows of water. The jug was half empty already and he wanted more but his stomach felt on the verge of bursting and he forced himself to stop. He set the butt end of the rifle on the ground and used it to steady himself as he worked his way to his knees, then his feet.

The world around him started to spin and he shut his eyes against it. In his head he counted to five, then opened his eyes again. That time all remained steady.

Keep it together.

"You okay with that rifle or you want a handgun?" Delphine asked and pulled aside her shawl to reveal two pistols in her waistband.

"I've always favored long guns."

"Good man."

Wim checked the rifle and saw a round was already chambered. "Where's Phillip?"

Phillip and his security crew were the only people that Wim knew of who were allowed to carry firearms on the Ark, which made Delphine's weaponry even more of a mystery.

Delphine shook her head. "Haven't seen him all morning. None of them."

A deep, masculine scream echoed toward them from the camp. Wim took a step away from the box. His head was still cloudy but he no longer felt like he was going to collapse.

"Take me to the zombies."

She did.

* * *

DELPHINE LED HIM A FEW HUNDRED YARDS TOWARD CAMP. ALONG THE way they passed several spots where the snow was disturbed and red, but there weren't any bodies. Wim knew why. Because the dead were coming back.

The first one he saw was Amy Orlean, a hefty woman on the downhill side of middle age who served as the Ark's cook. Wim and his friends usually ate out of cans but on the rare times where they were welcomed into the mess hall, special occasions mostly, to eat with the others, he often thought that Amy's peach pie was the best he'd ever tasted. Even better than what his mama had made, although he'd never have told her that if she were still alive.

Now, Amy wasn't baking up something sweet. Now, she straddled a man Wim only knew as Stevie. He seemed to recall the twenty-something year old jeering at him the other day, before he was sent to the box. He had little memory of the beanpole of a man aside from that and he didn't pause before he shouldered the rifle and sent a bullet zipping through Amy Orleans' head.

The woman toppled over, landing chest down atop Stevie who desperately, and unsuccessfully, tried to push off her corpse.

When Wim and Delphine reached the scene, Wim grabbed hold of Amy's denim jacket with his left hand and hauled her off the struggling man. Blood dripped from the bullet wound above her temple but also from her mouth and, when he looked closer, Wim saw a masticated wad of flesh jutting from her clenched jaws. His eyes moved from her to Stevie and he saw a missing hunk of skin about the same size where his shoulders met his neck.

Stevie stared up at them, his eyes so wide Wim could see white all the way around the irises. "Oh shit man thanks. Thank you. That fat bitch was trying to eat me! Can you believe that?"

Wim had liked Amy and it made him wince to hear her called such names, but he supposed a man who had just been attacked by his first zombie might have a right to be crass. He didn't have a chance to respond before another gunshot rang out and Stevie's face collapsed inward as a bullet tore through the bridge of his nose. The snow under his head exploded in a crimson burst and then Stevie went limp.

When Wim looked to his side, Delphine was already lowering the pistol. She raised her wiry eyebrows at him.

"He got chomped. That meant he was gonna turn into a zombie, don't it?"

"Yep. That's usually how it works. But maybe you should have asked that question before you shot him."

"Mayhap I should. Too late now though."

They continued. Wim shot three more zombies by the time they reached the outskirts of camp and Delphine one. All were dashing about like wild animals stalking prey but there wasn't any prey to be found. Wim hoped everyone had the good sense to lock themselves inside somewhere but whatever optimism he held on that matter vanished when he saw five zombies all huddled around some bodies on the ground. They look like pigs at a trough, he thought.

He recognized them but didn't know any of them well when they were alive and that made it easier to pick them off one by one. When he finished he turned to Delphine.

"Have any more ammunition for this?"

She nodded and passed him a box of bullets. Wim reloaded while Delphine stepped into the fray and looked to see who they'd been eating.

"Aw, dammit," she said with a sigh. "They got Marty Knecht. We used to play chess outside the dining hall when the weather was hospitable. Always suspected the scoundrel of cheating when I went into a daydream, as I'm apt to do on pretty days."

Delphine stared down at dead Marty Knecht. His face looked like a pile of partially chewed, raw hamburger with two big, white eyes plopped haphazardly in the middle.

What remained of Marty's mouth fell open and his tongue lolled out. Those eyes somehow moved within the pile of gore and locked on Delphine. She didn't hesitate and shot him in the head. "Guess he won't be cheatin no more."

Wim's rifle was reloaded and ready to go. He rubbed his palms against the denim of his jeans, using the friction to bring some feeling back into his cold hands, which were well on their way to being completely numb.

As they rounded the corner, nearing the door to the clinic, Wim saw a woman running. He assumed she was a zombie and raised the rifle but when he saw six undead monsters chasing her, he realized she wasn't the hunter, she was the hunted. Her name was Barbra Lowe and she was a nurse who'd stitched up his calf when he'd ripped a ragged, five-inch gash in it early last the summer. She'd done a good job and it left just a thin, milky streak of a scar.

Wim shot one of the zombies pursuing her, then another. Delphine fired, hitting one in the back but that didn't do so much as make it stumble. Wim shot the one she'd wounded, then aimed at the fourth. Just as he shot, the zombie dipped to the right and the bullet whistled by harmlessly.

The creatures were close to Barbra now and the pale, golden-haired woman kept looking back. As they neared her, her rearward glances became longer and longer.

Wim shot again, dropping the zombie he'd earlier missed. As he went to take aim at the fifth, Barbra fell. Between the snowfall and her constant, fearful looks behind her, she hadn't seen the circle of rocks that stood guard around the fire pit and, when her foot hit them, she did a forward somersault before crashing to the ground. Her back hit the rocks and Wim heard something break. That sound was immediately replaced by Barbra's screams. And then the zombie pounced on her.

It chomped a mouthful of flesh off her forearm before Wim could fire. Delphine beat him to the punch sending a bullet through the zombie's head, but it was too late. Barbra tried to push herself up as blood gushed from the wound but her legs were immobilized from the fall and Wim knew it didn't matter anyway. He was glad her face was hidden when he shot her in the side of the skull and prevented her inevitable transformation.

* * *

"LET ME GO!" RAMEY TRIED TO FREE HERSELF FROM HER FATHER WHO had a vise grip on her wrist. She was surprised he was so strong.

"You're staying in here. Where it's safe."

"People are dying out there. Your people. Don't you care?" She saw the truth in his face. He didn't care. She wondered if anything she'd ever believed about her father had been real.

"It's too dangerous, Ramey."

"I can help them. I've seen this before. I've fought them, remember?"

There came a crash at the window and both of them flinched. They turned to see a woman just a few years older than Ramey banging against the glass.

"Let me in, Doc! They're right behind me!"

Ramey again tried to free herself, but couldn't.

"No. It's too late for her."

Ramey saw three dead children running for the woman and realized her father was right this time. Within seconds they were on her. The first one latched onto her, biting a small mouthful of flesh from her side. The next got her forearm, its tiny teeth sinking in to the bone. The third jumped onto her back and started chomping on her head. Ramey saw it pull back with long, bloody strands of hair caught in its teeth.

It didn't seem possible, but the woman's screams were even louder than the siren. She flailed and thrashed, knocking the child at her arm to the ground. It jumped back up and buried its teeth into her stomach, excising her belly button in one extra-large bite. Her strength gave out and she fell against the window, smearing blood against the glass as she slid down the slick surface. Ramey turned away, unable to watch any more.

"Give me a gun and let me go help."

"I told you— "

"Do it!"

Doc's eye twitched. Ramey didn't know if it was anger or shock.

"I don't keep any guns here. Besides, you know how I feel about firearms." He looked beyond her, grimaced.

Ramey turned to see what he was looking at, but before she could find anything, her vision went black.

* * *

Wim saw the zombies first. There were a half dozen of them, mostly children, all clumped together. He only saw their backs as they squatted down on their haunches their faces hidden, but he had a good enough idea what was going on. They were eating.

"Think that's the last of them?" Delphine asked.

They hadn't seen any other zombies in more than ten minutes. He hoped this was indeed the last of them, that they'd eliminated all the others. He was tired of killing, but even more so, he was just plain tired. Five days of not eating or drinking was catching up to him, leaving his legs weak and eyesight bleary.

"Might be."

They got within eight yards of the zombies before opening fire. In under half a minute the creatures were dead. Or dead again, Wim supposed. Their bodies half sunk into the fallen snow, strewn atop each other in a haphazard pile, but all Wim cared about was finding who they'd been eating when their ends came.

He grabbed the shirt of one, lifted it free of the mass and tossed it aside like a sack of feed. Then the next. Delphine watched with her gun raised, ready to shoot if the need arose.

After Wim had moved the fourth zombie, he saw a thin, chocolate colored arm poking out from under the pile. The site of it caused his stomach to tighten up.

"Get on with it," Delphine said, making Wim realize he'd been staring, motionless, at the arm, which had several bites taken out, and made him think of a partially eaten ear of corn.

He grabbed the zombie, which he recognized as Vince, the frequent gatekeeper and one of the men whose testimony sent him to the box. Despite that, Wim loathed seeing what had become of him.

After casting Vince's body aside, Wim's eyes went to the person at the bottom of the pile. He fully expected to find Emory or Mina. His gut told him to prepare for it but he still didn't know how he'd deal with seeing another of his friends dead.

But the brown arm didn't belong to Mina or Emory. The woman who had been breakfast for the cadre of zombies was Ellen Sideris. Her body had been protected by a heavy parka, leaving her face to bear the brunt of the assault. A good seventy percent of the skin was gone, along with all her nose, her lips and her right eye.

"Oh, Lord," Delphine said as she peered over Wim's shoulder.

At the sound of the voice, Sideris's remaining eye opened and, after lolling around momentarily confused, settled on the two of them. Wim knew his rifle was empty as he reached out and pressed against the zombie's chest to hold her to the ground.

"Hand me your pistol."

Delphine passed it to him like a distance runner handing off a baton. Sideris's head darted forward, lunging at him with her skinned mouth, her teeth smashing together as she bit and missed.

Wim pressed the pistol against her temple, keeping it flush as she tried to bite him, and squeezed the trigger. Sideris's brains blew out the opposite side of her skull, spraying the white snow like red water from a hose. What remained of her head fell against the ground and her struggling ceased.

CHAPTER TWENTY-SEVEN

The cold air made Emory's bones hurt. He'd been hurting a considerable amount of the time lately, to the point where thoughts of long, painful illnesses taunted and harassed him. It's just the cold, he told himself. He wasn't sure he believed that any more but knew worrying was pointless. Besides, at his age and under the circumstances, he knew the overwhelming majority of his life was behind him and each additional day he was given was a bonus.

The Ark's population had been more than halved that day and that meant every man, woman, and - no children, they're all dead now - was on deck. Emory's job was of the janitorial variety. After the bodies were gathered, he was to clean up whatever bits and pieces were left behind, depositing them into a heavy-duty garbage bag. He scooped up a piece of skull the size of a salad plate and took a moment to stare at the long, blood-stained blonde hair that sagged off it, wondering to whom it might have belonged. Whoever it was certainly didn't need it now and he added it to the gruesome collection.

The bag was growing heavy, a stress that made his hands ache even more, so he set it aside and pulled them inside his jacket sleeves, clenching and squeezing them in attempt to increase the blood flow.

It worked to some extent and he lifted the bag with both hands, slinging it over his shoulder as he trudged toward the next bloody scene to continue his work. Doing so, he felt a bit like a hobo carrying all his belongings in a sack, perhaps running for a train car, hoping to ride the rails to greener pastures.

As he stepped around the corner of one of the out buildings, he saw Phillip and Buck, two of the Ark's police force, carrying a body. It took him a moment to realize what was different about this scene, which he'd seen occurring all day long, then he realized the arms and legs weren't hanging limp and useless. Whoever the men were carrying was tied up.

Buck walked backward as they moved and he caught his foot on something, dropping to his knee. When he stumbled, the body jerked and the head swiveled side to side, purposeful. Emory could see it was a woman.

"Watch it!" Phillip barked and Buck jumped to his feet.

"Ssss- Sorry."

"Sorry my ass. I've got the danger end."

They disappeared around a motorhome.

Emory had been clustered together with all the other survivors when orders had been given out. He'd heard first hand that all bodies were to be taken to the field at the north end of the Ark to be burned. He could already smell the smoke, and the awful, acrid aroma of charred flesh and hair that came with it. And he knew that no one had been injured and survived. So, who were these men carrying?

I've got the danger end.

They've got a zombie, Emory realized. But why hadn't they destroyed it?

He set the garbage bag aside and followed, keeping a healthy distance and making certain no one was watching him being a nebby nose. When he reached the travel trailer, he peeked around the corner and saw the two men approaching the medical clinic. Emory also knew that, somewhere in that building, were Doc's private labs. Scuttlebutt around camp, into which Emory was always eager to insert himself, was that he was doing research for a cure inside there. Emory had his doubts.

From his vantage point twenty yards away, Emory couldn't discern if Phillip used a key or a card, but a door opened and the men disappeared inside. It banged closed behind them, the sound so loud it made Emory flinch.

Emory crossed the gap to the building. He knew it was pointless, but tried anyway. Locked. He then moved to the front where the entrance to the medical clinic was located. That door was unlocked and he leaned halfway inside where the office appeared empty.

"Hello?"

No response came. He considered continuing in but thought that unwise. Tensions were at an all-time high on the Ark today and 80 plus years of life experience was more than enough for Emory to know that there were times to keep your head down.

CHAPTER TWENTY-EIGHT

The female zombie laid on its back atop the gurney, naked save for an opaque hood which was pulled tight around her neck and shrouded her head. Her arms were bound behind her back, unseen under her pallid flesh. Her legs were tied to stirrups, spread far apart to put her crotch on display. Black fluid, the consistency of cool honey, seeped from her vagina, a fetid ooze that Doc sponged away with the same amount of concern he'd have shown dusting off an end table.

"I don't think I can do it Doc."

Doc looked to the edge of the lab where Phillip waited. The man was naked except for a pair of boxer briefs and his skin had broken out in gooseflesh. Doc realized Phillip was shivering.

"I can turn the heat up a bit if that will make you more comfortable. I'm quite used to the cold down here myself and I forget that others aren't."

Phillip stared at him, his beady eyes wide. "It's not the temperature. It's…" His eyes drifted back to the dead woman who laid spread eagle before him.

"Oh, come now. We've had many discussions about this. You know how important this experiment is. You assured me you were up to the task, Phillip. I put my trust in you."

"I just don't know. This is gross as hell. I mean, she's dead, Doc."

Doc had been sitting on a wheeled stool for his up-close examination of the zombie's nether regions. Now he spun and used his feet to move himself toward Phillip. "But is she? Perhaps by conventional standards. Yet, she breathes. She eats. She moves. Is that not life?"

Phillip looked from Doc to the zombie, then back. It was clear he wasn't convinced.

"Yeah, but you can shoot her in the heart and she'd still be able to walk around. Live things don't do that."

"That's true. But you act as if that's a flaw. Phillip, that makes them better than us! Humans like you and I are dependent on our variety of organs. If one fails, the whole ship goes down. Yet these creatures, they don't require a liver or kidneys or a heart. All they need is their brain. It's astounding! Miraculous even!"

He couldn't understand why Phillip was being so uncooperative. The dead woman had a fit, toned body. He'd even taken the time to put a bandage over the ragged hole in her shoulder where she'd been bitten.

"I understand you find yourself in a quandary, Phillip, but she is perfect for you." Doc pivoted on the chair and glanced at the dead woman. "When I first saw her, I suspected she had breast implants but that assumption was incorrect. Check for yourself."

Phillip hedged.

"Do it, Phillip."

Phillip crept closer to Doc and the zombie. Doc nodded approvingly and Phillip stepped to her side. He reached out, slow, cautious, and rested his bare palm over the woman's breast. Doc thought he saw some relaxation come over him. Phillip even gave her partially erect nipple a flick with his index finger.

"There. See."

Phillip flashed a weak smile. He ran his hand down her breast, across her concave abdomen where a belly button ring, a fake diamond butterfly, decorated her naval. Then, southbound progress ceased. He glanced at Doc, his eyes flitting away.

"This is of the utmost importance, Phillip. It will raise our experiments to the next phase."

"Can't I just jizz into a cup or something? And you could use a turkey baster to shoot it inside?"

Doc bit his lip to stop himself from saying something overly cross, but his ire had been raised. "No. We won't be performing some bizarre redneck artificial insemination. The odds of conception are greatly increased during coitus. And we can't delay any longer."

Doc stared him down and Phillip seemed to shrink before him. "Close your eyes, Phillip."

Phillip did.

"Now who do you see? Who do you want to be on this table before you? A Playboy bunny, maybe? Perhaps a porn star even?"

"No..."

"Who then? A high school crush. Someone here on the Ark?"

Phillip didn't respond. Doc had long suspected this.

"Ah, I see. You want this to be Ramey, don't you?"

Even with his eyes closed, Phillip dipped his head to the floor in shame.

"It's fine. I've seen the way you look at her. The way most of the men here look at her. And I understand. She's young. Innocent. I'd wager to guess there's a good chance she's still a virgin. What's that term you fellows used - barely legal? If you play your cards right, you could be the one to deflower her. Imagine that, Phillip. You could be her first lover. Her only lover. She'd be an awe of you."

Phillip's lips parted and a small gasp escaped.

Doc moved closer to him, examining the young man. The bulge in his underwear hadn't changed and Doc was growing weary of this. It was time to speed things up.

"Keep your eyes closed, Phillip. Now picture Ramey here before you. Not a speck of clothing on her tight, flawless body. Her breasts pert, perky, practically begging you to touch them. Caress them."

Doc took Phillip's hand and placed it on the zombie's gray, cantaloupe-shaped breast.

"What do you want to do? Squeeze it? Suck it? Taste it? You can do anything your heart desires."

Phillip pulled his hand back and Doc thought for a moment that he'd lost him. But then Phillip's palm flashed forward and smacked the breast with an open palm. The sound of it echoed through the small, enclosed room.

"You want it to hurt?" Doc asked.

Phillip nodded, his eyes still closed.

"That's fine. You can do anything to her. I won't judge you. And no one will stop you."

Phillip hit her again. The iron-colored skin flared white.

Doc saw Phillip's crotch swell. He reached out and placed his gloved fingers into the man's waistband and slowly pulled them down whispering into Phillip's ear as he undressed him. "This new world belongs to us. Everyone in it is ours for the taking. No one can stop us. Not anymore."

Doc grabbed Phillip's cock. It felt like an uncooked sausage in his fingers. He gave it a light squeeze then pumped his fingers up and down. Up and down.

"Together, we've brought down the civilized world, Phillip. Now we're rebuilding it to be whatever we want. In this new world, we're Gods."

Doc's fingers worked faster as he spoke and Phillip's uncooked sausage grew and hardened.

"If you want Ramey, she's yours. If you want to hurt her, you can. I won't stop you. All that's standing in your way is Wim. Remove him from the equation and you can do anything you want."

He steered Phillip forward and guided his hardness toward the zombie's rotting, seeping vagina. Doc lined up the two and pushed Phillip into her.

"Take her, Phillip. She's yours. Ramey is all yours."

Phillips hips thrust like pistons. The wet, smacking sounds filled the room and Doc turned back to his notes and added the date and time.

After a minute or two, the sounds came harder, faster. Doc glanced back and saw the zombie thrashing on the gurney as Phillip pounded away, merciless. Under the hood, she gasped and growled. Her dead flesh jiggled

Soon, Phillip's buttocks spasmed, clenched, then quivered. He moved to pull out.

"No!" Doc ordered. "Stay with her."

Phillip laid atop the dead woman, their groins still locked together. Phillip's entire body rose and fell with each exhausted breath. His face laid against the sack that covered her head and, although beneath it the zombie's sounds were of rage, Phillip kissed the covering like a man in love.

Doc watched as more black fluid seeped from the woman's vagina, now intermixed with white opaque semen. Doc believed that, from this new primordial ooze a new species would emerge. That this was the next step up the genetic ladder. He'd destroyed life. Now he was ready to create it.

CHAPTER TWENTY-NINE

"Everyone might have died if it weren't for Wim."

Phillip flinched at the fury in her voice. He'd seemed more on edge than usual. He wouldn't look her in the eyes, keeping his face turned downward. He looked sweaty and paler than normal. Ramey wondered if the recent zombie attack had him behaving and looking this way, or if something else was going on. Maybe he's getting sick, she thought. If so, what kind of sick was it.

"Well, the way I heard it was that Delphine was the one who saved everyone."

"Delphine did what you wouldn't and let him out. Where were you anyway?"

"We had to go for supplies since Wim didn't bring back half of what we needed the other day."

"Because he was fighting for his life. Just like yesterday. While you were out there having a circle jerk with your buddies."

Phillip kicked the wood floor and turned away from her. He clasped his hands together behind his neck, elbows parallel to the floor and paced. He was angry and Ramey enjoyed bringing that out in him.

"Look, I don't know what you expect me to say. Doc sent us out first thing in the morning. How was I supposed to know all hell was gonna break loose 'til we got back?"

"How about saying you're sorry."

"I am. I never wanted you— "

"Not to me. To Wim."

Phillip left his arms drop. Now his face wasn't angry, it was bemused. "For what?"

"For almost killing him!"

"I was doing what I was told."

"That's the problem around here. No one thinks for themselves. They just listen to my father like a bunch of brainwashed imbeciles."

Phillip's arm darted out fast and before she even realized what was happening he'd grabbed hold of her shirt. He pulled her in close to him, so close that his tuna-scented breath assaulted her nose.

"Don't you talk bad about Doc!"

She slapped him, her fingernails tearing across his cheek and leaving thin ditches that weren't quite deep enough to bleed.

Phillip jerked his hand, ripping open her shirt, then lost himself staring at her exposed bra. The distraction was enough for Ramey to slip free, leaving him with just a handful of blue material.

Before she could decide whether to run or to fight back, Doc stepped into the doorway. He looked from Ramey to Phillip, then back. His face emotionless.

"The meeting is ready to start." He turned and left them without another word.

Phillip took a step toward Ramey who backed away. "I'm sorry."

"Yeah, you are. You're really fucking sorry, Phillip."

She fled before he could respond but she heard something in the room shatter.

* * *

BARELY THIRTY PEOPLE REMAINED ALIVE ON THE ARK AND ALMOST ALL of them were at the meeting. Doc stood at the front, but the adulation his followers had shown him days before, when Wim was on his way to being condemned, was missing now. Now most looked at him with apprehension. To Ramey, that was a relief.

"Before the bodies were destroyed, we examined them carefully. Only one had not been bit, which makes it clear where the infection originated. The person who first became ill, who first became a zombie, was Hal Dade."

The crowd murmured amongst one another.

Beside her, Wim held Ramey's hand. Emory was next in line. Only Mina was missing - too afraid to leave the trailer. Ramey looked at the men and was proud to sit with them. She wouldn't distance herself from them now and regretted ever doing so. These people were more humane, more brave, than anyone who'd been riding out the apocalypse on the Ark.

"I'm left to deduce that Hal became infected when William Wagner brought the boy to the Ark. Because they hadn't been properly decontaminated before contact was made, Hal was exposed to the virus and regrettably, succumbed."

Ramey squeezed Wim's hand and leaned in closer. "Don't listen to him."

"Are we all in danger now?" A man with long, black hair that framed his face like a china doll, shouted.

That raised the decibel level of the other murmurs.

"The short answer is, I don't know. After the meeting, everyone will receive medicine and vitamins to boost your immune systems. But if the disease has evolved... become more virulent, as I suspect it has, then we may need to take extra precautions."

"Like what," a woman shouted out as if on cue.

"Starting immediately, no one will be allowed outside the walls of the Ark. We will be instituting a ration system to get us through the winter. Details on that plan will be forthcoming."

The murmurs reached an almost frenzied pitch. This isn't going over well for him, Ramey thought.

"I understand this will be a challenge for us all. And if there were any way to avoid it, we would. But after today's tragedy, we must take every precaution to ensure our safety and survival. Not to be grandiose, but the future of mankind may depend on us."

"Oh, Heavens, if that's true I pity future generations," Emory said. Ramey couldn't suppress a smirk. He had a point.

"It's now more important than ever that everyone cooperate and obey." Doc folded up a paper from which he'd been reading. "Now are there any questions?"

There were dozens but Ramey and her friends didn't stick around to listen to all of them. Emory went back to the trailer and Ramey was invited along but she wanted to talk to Wim first.

She told Wim about the experience with her father in the cabin, about how she'd realized he wasn't the man she'd built him up to be. All through the conversation, Wim kept himself at arm's length and the longer it went, the more frustrated she grew. It was like she didn't understand anyone anymore. Finally, she'd had enough.

"Wim, all I want is to be with you. But since we've been here, it seems like you don't even want to be alone with me. I don't know what I did wrong but I want to fix it."

"You haven't done anything wrong."

"Then what is it?" She didn't give him an excuse now. She pulled him in close and pressed her body against his. "Why won't you touch me? Why won't you be with me?"

Wim pulled his hands free and Ramey thought he might push her away.

"Tell me, Wim. Please."

"I... I don't know how to say it."

"Just spit it out. Whatever it is, I can take it." Even though she knew that wasn't true. If he had something bad to say, to tell her he'd changed his mind and didn't love her any more, she didn't know how she'd react but it wouldn't be well.

He risked a glance toward her and Ramey thought she saw something new in his face, something she hadn't ever seen in him before. Fear.

"It's nothing you've done. I want to be with you so bad that some-times I feel clear sick about it. But it isn't right."

"Why?"

"When I'm with you, heck even when I'm not, I feel like I found a piece of my puzzle that's been missing all my life even though I thought it was whole. I didn't think I needed anything more than what I had. But now I know better. And at the same time, I feel like I'm too dumb and too old and that, when you get out of your teens and experience more of life you'll realize that too."

"I'll never— "

"You don't know. You can't know. It could happen. And I don't want to be someone you regret."

Ramey grabbed his coat and leaned into him. She thought his eyes looked wet and she wanted to kiss him so bad it hurt but she could tell he still had words to say.

"I haven't been to church since about the time my mama died. But I got enough of it growing up that I know right from wrong. And I know it wouldn't be right for me to be with you, the way a husband and wife are meant to be together. Not until you know you want to spend the rest of your life with me."

She felt a tear hit her cheek and thought it was Wim's until she rubbed her face and realized she was the one crying. "You won't sleep with me because you think we should be married first?"

Wim nodded. She thought she could feel his heart beating even through multiple layers of clothing.

"Then marry me, Wim."

He cast quick glances down at her, like he was trying to get a peek at an eclipse, then stopped and finally looked her in the eyes. She didn't realize she could love him even more but in that moment, it was so strong that she felt like a bomb was going off inside her.

"What?" He asked.

"I don't need a ring or a church or a piece of paper. I need you. So, marry me."

"Are you sure? I don't want you to just say it."

"I want to be with you forever. I'm as sure of that as I am my own name. Marry me."

"But, how can we?"

"I might know someone. You let me take care of it."

She pulled his face down to hers and kissed him. The rough stubble from almost a week of not shaving scratched at her face like sandpaper but she didn't mind. She didn't mind at all.

CHAPTER THIRTY

Mina stared out the kitchen window as she washed dishes in lukewarm water. She hadn't stepped foot outside the Airstream since the zombie outbreak. Maybe it was a glorified tin can but she was safe there.

"You ain't safe in here either, Birdie. You ain't safe nowhere," her daddy's voice said. And she knew he was right. She wasn't safe inside. She wasn't safe outside. She wasn't safe on the Ark. She wasn't safe anywhere. She understood that now. And what made that even worse was that Mina also knew she'd never be safe again.

Why'd you leave me alone, Bundy? You could have blown the both of us up in that ambulance and saved me all this misery.

He thought he was saving her, but in the process cursed her to a life alone with nothing but her fear and her father's voice to occupy her mind.

Outside the trailer a man stumbled past the window. Mina immediately knew his gait to be that of a zombie. She'd seen it too often to mistake it. He lurched along the dirty pathway that was half snow, half mud.

Mina backed away from the window.

Don't see me.

But she bumped into the table, knocking a cup to the floor. It exploded.

"Way to go, Birdie. You can't do nothin right."

The man's head slowly turned in her direction. Mina dove to the floor, landing on the broken glass. A thick shard of it buried itself in her knee, hitting bone. Mina ignored the pain. She needed a weapon because she knew the zombie was coming.

She crawled on her knees, the glass grinding itself into more pieces as she moved. She pulled open a cabinet filled with pots and pans. They banged and clattered as she rummaged through them and she heard the zombie at the door. Hitting the door. Trying to get in.

Mina took the handle of a heavy cast iron skillet and turned toward the entrance. She gripped it in both hands like she was holding a ping pong paddle. It wasn't much as far as weapons went, but she'd killed her own father with a bedpan so she suspected she could make do.

The door handle clicked and slowly came open. Mina squeezed the skillet's handle so tight her black knuckles turned white.

"Get away from here!"

The movement stopped.

"Mina?"

Holy shit, it knows my name!

"I said get away!"

A shadow fell into the doorway and then the zombie moved into the frame. Only it wasn't a zombie. It was Nestor Campagna, a man who was assigned to keep watch at the gate during the last meeting.

"Everything okay in there, Mina?"

She realized what a spectacle she must be. Skillet raised, ready to strike, blood pouring from her knee. If everyone here didn't already think she was a crazy black woman, just wait until this story worked its way around camp.

"Nestor?"

"I heard a noise. Sounded like something broke."

Mina set the pan aside. She went to stand but the glass in her knee made her rethink that. "I dropped a mug. It broke."

"I see that. What's with the skillet?"

Nestor stepped into the trailer but remained in the door way. His big, dark eyes were wide.

"He's scared of you, Birdie. He can tell you're crazy as a June bug."

"I was..." She couldn't come up with a lie quick enough and decided to go with the truth. "I thought you were a zombie. Saw you walking by looking funny."

Nestor offered a guilty smile and raised up his foot. "The sole came off my boot. Kept filling up with snow and I kept trying to kick it out." He took another look at her bloodied knee. "I'm really sorry I gave you such a scare."

"It's not you. I'm half crazy."

"No. After last week, everyone's nerves are shot." He grabbed a dishcloth off the counter and handed it to her. "That looks like its gonna need stitches. Why don't you let me help you up to the clinic? Get it disinfected and cleaned out good. Last thing you need's an infection."

The clinic. Doc's clinic. He was about the last person Mina wanted to see. She took a look down at her knee and saw the mangled mess of flesh plus the glass extruding from it. The wound would certainly require stitches but Mina could sew in a pinch and thought she'd prefer doing the job herself to letting Doc anywhere near her.

* * *

DELPHINE HANDED EMORY A BAGGIE OF MARIJUANA AND A SMALL STACK of thin papers.

"That's the last of it until next summer so you best make it last."

"Much obliged, Madame."

"I ain't no Madame."

Delphine had been his supplier since they arrived at the Ark. Well, since a month after they arrived. When he wasn't doing whatever task he'd been assigned for the day, Emory enjoyed wandering. On one of his walks he'd seen the ten feet by ten feet patch of plants soaking up the sunlight. It was a mile or more from camp, near the isolated north end of the island and he'd wondered who had taken the initiative to plant them.

He decided to play detective and make it a point to visit the garden daily. About a week in to his stakeouts, he saw Delphine staggering toward it, a five-gallon bucket of water clutched in her hands with plenty sloshing out as she walked. He didn't confront her about them that day. In fact, he waited almost a week. Then, one day in the mess hall he casually commented, "Mary, Mary quite contrary, what makes your garden grow?" in a singsong voice. Delphine's head snapped around so quick he thought she might sprain her neck. He flashed a reassuring smile and took a seat beside her and their friendship had begun.

They sat in front of the remnants of that garden now. The plants had been cut to the ground, revealing the nearly frozen lake that stretched out before them.

"It's quite lovely, isn't it?" Emory said.

"Prettiest place I ever did see. But I ain't seen many."

"Well, I have. And it's certainly near the top of the list."

They were silent for a minute, taking in the view and enjoying the cool but not quite cold air that blew by. It was hard for Emory to stay quiet for long though.

"This is going to sound selfish, coming from someone who survived the plague when so many did not, but I do wonder if this might make the people who survived change for the better."

Delphine narrowed her eyes which turned into black slits. "How's that?"

"People, not everyone certainly, but most, seemed to have forgotten that life is a gift. Living became something that happened in between working and driving and shopping and playing games on your phone. It was an afterthought. Maybe this will make people appreciate it again."

He thought Delphine looked skeptical or confused, or both. She didn't respond for a long while but when she did she surprised him.

"You think people here appreciate it? Running around like drone bees, doing their part to keep the hive going?"

"I think there are many flaws here."

"You got that right. There's many a day I wished I'd have told Doc when he showed up here and told me about the commune he wanted to build, that he could stick it where the sun don't shine. But at the time, the way he told it, it sounded good and almost Christian. After all, I didn't need all this land for myself." She paused to sniff and clear her sinuses. "But the way I imagined, in a commune all's equal. That ain't the case here."

"Certainly not."

"But now the doing's done and I'm stuck with him. Guess that's my penance for him keeping me alive."

Emory watched her. There was frustration and sadness in her eyes. He wanted to keep her talking but was wary about pushing it too hard. "I understand. It's almost miraculous that he could prevent the plague from reaching the island. Out there—" he motioned to the air beyond them, "It seemed virtually no one was spared."

Delphine gave something like a snort or a "Hmpf" but didn't respond further.

Emory pocketed the marijuana and decided not to pursue the issue. Not now, anyway. He stood and stretched. Joints in his lower back snapped like dry twigs.

"Well, my friend, I must head back lest the others worry I've fallen into a ditch or perhaps got kicked in the head by one of Wim's cows and am now wandering about dimwitted and lost."

Delphine shook her head. "You're an odd duck."

Emory smiled. As an old, gay, black man he'd been called many things in his life. An 'odd duck' was a compliment in comparison. "And you are a splendid horticulturist."

He gave a little bow and left her. As he strolled away he thought his friendship with Delphine had the potential to produce much more valuable fruit than cannabis. He thought that, in time, Delphine might be the key to unraveling this mysterious world Doc had created.

CHAPTER THIRTY-ONE

The news ripped through camp like a tornado. The boy Wim had brought into the Ark was not simply alive, but up and walking around. Mina saw him when she went to collect their rations. It was her first foray outside the trailer and she saw the boy sitting in the mess hall, eating breakfast with a few of the others. Harsh, black stitches that reminded her of railroad tracks curved up from each side of his mouth, but he seemed fine aside from the cosmetic damage. She even saw him laugh when Phillip tried, and failed, to balance a spoon on his nose. The boy saw her too and Mina could feel his eyes on her as she waited in line.

She asked around and found out his name was Wayne Supanek. No one knew why he'd been sliced up, but Doc had assured them that he was no longer contagious, if he'd ever been so in the first place. And apparently Phillip had been put in charge of acclimating him to camp. That alone made Mina hope to avoid him, but after she was handed her box of canned and dried food and bottled water, Wayne caught her as she hit the exit.

"I'll get that for you," he said as he held open the door.

"Thanks, but I could have managed."

Mina passed through into the cold daylight.

Stay away from me.

But he didn't.

"You're one of the outsiders, aren't you? Phillip told me about you."

"My name's Mina. And I'm sure he did."

"He told me how Doc's people saved you and your friends. How'd you get here?"

"In a car."

"But like, how'd you find it? Does Doc let anyone who survived in?"

"Nope, we were the last. Until you. And I bet your new pals didn't tell you this, but they didn't exactly welcome you with open arms."

"Why not? You'd think they'd be happy to find survivors."

Mina didn't need any more friends, especially ones who'd been vetted by Doc and Phillip, but Wayne followed her like a lost puppy all the way to the trailer, peppering her with questions the entire time. She tried to be curt, bordered on rude even, but he refused to take a hint.

When they got within ten yards of the trailer, the door pushed open and Wim leaned out. Mina could see the surprise on his face when he spotted the kid. He bounded down the steps and into the snow.

"You're— "

Wayne cut him off. "Holy shit, man. You're the guy who saved me. Wim, right? I'm Wayne."

Wim pushed his hand forward and the kid took it between both of his, pumping up and down rapid fire. At the sight, Mina's frost thawed, just a little.

"I thought for sure you were gonna die," Wim said.

"I almost did, from what I've been told. I sucked up the antibiotics like a motherfucker, but I made it. Beat the odds all over again. Wish there was still a lottery because I'd sure as shit be playing it."

"How about you get out of the cold and come inside?" Wim said.

Wayne nodded and raced up the steps. Wim took the box from Mina, a big smile on his face. She hated to do anything to change that expression, but he needed to know.

"Doc and Phillip are already in his head. So just be careful what you say, okay?"

Wim's smile did falter and Mina immediately felt guilty. "I will."

* * *

MINA WATCHED AS WIM AND WAYNE SHARED STORIES ABOUT THEIR lives and the days after the plague. Mina found the kid to be a little too excited about the whole ordeal, but tried to write it off as the follies of youth.

"You ought watch that one, Birdie. He worms his way into the group and next thing you know, they won't have no need for you," her daddy's voice said inside her head. She thought he might be right too. Wayne was young and bound to get bigger and stronger. He'd certainly be more of an asset than herself.

It was clear Wim liked him and now that bothered her. And it bothered her more that the boy was so doggone happy. What gave him the right to be so happy?

"You've got a pretty sweet set up here though. I mean, an island? Doesn't get much safer than that," Wayne said.

"I suppose," Wim said.

"Suppose? Do you know something I don't?"

Wim opened his mouth to respond but Mina cut him off. "He means that, on an island, we run out of supplies. Then people like him have to go risk their lives so everyone else can wipe their butt."

"Oh." Wayne giggled. "I never thought about that part." He turned back to Wim. "But anyway, thanks for saving me. I'd have died for sure without you."

"I'm glad I found you."

"I am too man. I think I'm gonna like it here."

Mina had liked it on the Ark too, at first. That changed over time but she wasn't going to tell Wayne that. He could find out what Doc and his allies were like all on his own.

CHAPTER THIRTY-TWO

"She's correct. Although I might be a little out of practice." Emory grinned, a delighted smile if Ramey had ever seen one.

"How did you know about this?" Wim asked Ramey.

"We talk, Wim. Not everyone's a glorified mute like you."

Wim's cheeks brightened and Ramey gave him a pinch in the side to show she was kidding.

He still feels thin, she thought and shivered a little because of how close she'd come to losing him forever. "How many ceremonies did you say you performed? Twenty?"

"Heavens no. Twelve at the most. Ten is more likely though. Perhaps even as few as eight. Weddings all tend to blend together after a while so it's difficult to keep track.

"But how are you allowed to marry people? You're not a reverend," Wim said.

"That's correct. I am an ordinary citizen. Albeit a very gay one. When marriage between people like myself became legal, I had a myriad of friends who wanted to make their love official but they desired something a touch more intimate than standing in a court-house in front of some stranger. So, I took a few courses on the internet and a few weeks later, wah-lah. Emery Prescott, Licensed Minister at your service."

"Ain't you just full of surprises? Full of something, anyhow," Mina chimed in from the stove where she added tea bags to a pot of boiling water.

"I'll disagree with neither assertion," Emory said to her, then turned back to the others. "Now, pray tell, why are my extracurricular activities of such sudden interest to you both?"

Ramey almost blurted it out, but she wanted to hear Wim say it. She wasn't upset that she hadn't received an actual proposal, but she wanted to hear the words come from his lips this time.

Wim hemmed and was on the verge of hawing too when he finally managed to say it. "I plan to marry Ramey. I want her to be my wife."

She didn't care if he wasn't eloquent or that there was nothing poetic about his plain, just the facts ma'am, manner of speaking. It was what was behind the words that mattered and she knew that, when Wim said something, it was the truth and that was all that mattered. But then he surprised her.

"I didn't think it was possible to love someone the way I love her. And I don't intend to ever let that go."

Ramey grabbed hold of his arm and pulled herself into him. She wanted to kiss him but knew doing so in front of Emory and Mina would make him uncomfortable, so she stopped herself. That's okay. There will be time for that, and more, later.

"I must say, that's the best news I've heard in nearly forever," Emory said and Ramey saw his eyes shining, wet with tears. She thought he looked equal parts happy and proud and then came a pang in her chest because she thought this man who had been such a father figure to her during their time on the road, was far happier over this news than her real father would ever be. She pushed that thought out of her head as quick as possible, not wanting to ruin the moment.

"Is there a time-line that we're dealing with? Christmas nuptials, perhaps?"

Ramey hadn't given that part any thought and when she looked to Wim she saw he was equally clueless. "What do you think?" He asked.

"I don't like waiting. I'd marry you this very second if Emory's up for it."

"Oh no. No, no, no," Emory said as he stood up. "I'm going to need some time to prepare. To write something worthy of two of the best people I've ever known committing themselves to one another." He grabbed a notebook off the counter.

Ramey thought she could almost see the gears spinning in his head. "When then?" She asked.

"Would two days be sufficient?"

"Do we have a choice?"

"Of course not."

"Then two days it is."

Emory extended his long, thin arms and wrapped them around her, the notebook clanging awkwardly against her back. She was shocked at the strength in his embrace. Over his shoulder, she saw Mina pat Wim on the forearm and try to smile. Ramey suddenly felt guilty for being so happy while Mina was still adrift in a sea of depression over losing the man she had loved.

When Emory let go, Ramey went to her. She had never gotten to know Mina as good as some of the others, but she couldn't imagine the pain she had endured.

Mina gave a tight smile. "Congratulations."

Ramey put her arms around the frail woman and felt her go as stiff as a board. She put her lips close to Mina's ear and whispered, "I'm sorry you didn't get to be happy too."

Mina softened. Just a bit. So slight that Ramey might have missed it if she hadn't been paying attention. "I was. It just didn't take."

Ramey released her and their eyes met for a flitting moment before each looked away.

Wim spoke up and broke the strange silence that had momentarily overtaken the trailer. "I want you there, Mina, if you don't mind."

"Of course. You're my friends."

"Who else will be attending? Emory asked. "I don't imagine your father."

Ramey lost her smile. Her father was the last person she intended to tell, let alone invite. The very idea made her feel ill. "No. Not him. The four of us came here together. That's enough for me."

"There's someone else I'd like to be there," Wim said. "If you don't mind."

"Who, Wim?" Ramey asked.

"Delphine. She saved my life. And she's not like the others here."

"Indeed, she is not." Emory said.

"Is that all right with you?" Wim asked.

"Of course. You don't have to ask for permission."

"Very well then. Now, I must get to work." Emory slipped out of the kitchen, to his bedroom.

"Will you both have some tea?" Mina asked. "It's generic, nothing fancy, but I make it sweet."

"That sounds good to me," Ramey said.

As Mina took a pot from the stove, Ramey thought her life was almost as perfect as could be under the circumstances.

CHAPTER THIRTY-THREE

The snow came down fast in big, fat flakes that took a full three seconds to melt after landing on Wim's face. He didn't mind the snow. He suspected his heart was beating so quick and pushing so much blood through his body that it could have been negative twenty degrees and he still wouldn't have felt the cold.

Emory stood to his left and Mina and Delphine waited a few feet to the right. There was no music but that didn't matter. Emory had picked out this spot, a little bluff overlooking the lake at the north end of the Ark, one of the few borders unmarred by a fence or wall.

The water, which would have normally been lapping at the rocks, was mostly frozen, leaving just a sea of white ice stretching out as far as he could see. Wim had never imagined a wedding day that required him to be the groom, but he doubted he could have dreamed up anything more perfect.

He caught Emory staring at him and wondered if he'd done something dumb like forget to comb his hair or buttoned his shirt unevenly.

"How do I look?"

"Like one of the happiest men I've ever seen." Emory placed his hand on Wim's freshly shaved cheek and caressed it with his thumb. "I couldn't be any prouder if you were my own son. Thank you, Wim."

Wim furrowed his brow. "For what?"

"Never mind. You might want to look the other way."

Wim turned to look down what passed as an aisle. Ramey appeared through the blowing snow, slowly at first like a TV signal on a stormy day, and he could only make out bits and pieces of her. As she neared him, he saw more clearly. She wore a white sweater and blue jeans. She didn't carry any flowers - it was December, after all - and she kept her hands clasped in front herself while she walked to him. When she got close enough, Wim saw she was crying. Her cheeks glistened with frozen tears.

"You're so gorgeous, it took my breath away," Wim said to her and he meant it. He took her hands in his own and hoped his weren't sweating from the nerves that threatened to overtake him.

"And you look so handsome. You even have your shirt buttoned up all the way," she said, squeezing his hands and grinning.

Wim turned from her to Emory. "Now what?"

Emory unfolded a piece of notebook paper. "I've prepared a few remarks. If I would have had more time, I suspect I could have been more eloquent, but hopefully I did a satisfactory job."

"I'm sure you'll do fine," Wim said.

"Alright then. Without further ado." Emory turned is face downward, toward his notes. "I met Wim almost seven months ago as I sat on a park bench and contemplated whether there was a point to going on in this new world. I was leaning toward the answer being no when Wim pulled up in his Bronco."

"I still miss that truck," Wim said and everyone chuckled.

"As do I," Emory said and continued. "That very first day, Wim told me about Ramey. How she was the person who made him leave his farm and venture out into the world with the rest of us. As we traveled south, I felt the odds of locating her were slim, but he kept going on and on about her and I sensed there was something very special about her. I could tell how important she was to Wim and I was more than willing to go along for the ride. In the end, it was Ramey that found us. And as soon as I saw them together, I had a feeling it would be permanent."

"This is the part where I'd usually talk about the future and ups and downs, trials and tribulations, and leaning on each other rather than letting the hardships in life tear you apart, but I suspect that, for the most part, those missives are not necessary. The two of you have been through enough challenges for several marriages and even though there are bound to be more, I believe you'll be even stronger together."

Emory pulled out a crimson, silk handkerchief and held it up. Wim thought it looked vaguely familiar and he seemed to recall Emory holding it once or twice in the past.

"Grant gave me this many decades ago." Emory unfolded it and reveled white embroidery at the bottom. It read, 'And now two become one.'

"I've had this in my pocket every day since. It's been on every continent on the planet and more countries than my tired old brain can quite remember. When Grant gave it to me he said, 'I chose red, because red is the symbolic color of love. But I decided on a handkerchief because I know life is never as perfect as we'd hope and sometimes the need to wipe away our tears arises. When that happens, even if you're in pain or lonesome or angry, remember that you have my heart."

Emory's eyes glistened. Wim saw him swallow hard and then he continued. "Ramey, Wim is my very best friend. I'd be lying if I didn't admit a part of me is reluctant to hand him over to you, but I know you'll take good care of him."

"I will." She looked at Wim as she said it.

"And Wim, I know you frequently lament the age difference between the two of you. But as an octogenarian I can assure you that age is only a number. One thing I learned through my life is that it is meant to be shared. Both in the good times and the bad. Having someone at your side with whom you can experience the highs and lows is God's greatest gift. I suspect that is even more true now. And the fact that you two managed to find each other not once, but twice, like you each held magnets pulling you toward the other, well that my friends is the very definition of kismet. So, I'm giving you this handkerchief to remind you to always share not only your hearts, but your tears."

He extended the cloth to Wim. Wim took his hand, the old dark skin feeling as soft and fragile as velvet, and gave it a light squeeze.

"Thank you."

Emory nodded but Wim thought he seemed ready to change the subject.

And that's what he did. "Ramey, would you like to say anything?"

Ramey nodded. She pulled an index card from her pocket but rarely needed to look at it while she spoke. "Wim, I was a total shit to you the last few months. I'm using the excuse that I'm young and dumb but that doesn't make it alright. Because you've been nothing but good to me since the day we met. You saved me then. In more ways than one. And you keep saving me. I hope you never get tired of me being me, because I don't know how to stop."

"And I don't want you too."

"That's good. Because you're stuck with me now. At least, you will be in a few minutes. And when we can get out of this place and really start our lives together, I have a feeling that I'm going to be happier than I ever thought possible. I want to be your wife because you're the best man I've ever known. A better man than I might deserve, but I'm glad you're mine."

She grabbed his belt buckle and pulled him in close. He shivered as she looked up at him, smiling big and looking like the most beautiful woman he'd ever seen in his life.

"Wim, do you have a few words to say?" Emory said.

"Only a couple. I'm not as good with them as you," Wim said to Ramey as he took her hands. He thought they felt so soft and warm and perfect in his own. "I spent the last ten or so years of my life all alone. It never bothered me all that much, and I grew accustomed to it. But now that I know what it's like to love you, I can't imagine my life without you. And I promise you, Ramey, that I'll love you every day for the rest of my life."

He saw a tear slide down Ramey's cheek and wiped it away with the back of his hand. Then he looked to Emory. "That's all I got."

Emory was crying too, more than Ramey even. "That's more than enough, Wim." He took a moment to compose himself.

"With that, I think it's time to wrap up this ceremony so these two amazing people can begin their lives together. I now pronounce you husband and wife."

Wim watched him. A second passed. Then two. Then three.

Emory leaned in to him. "Now is when you kiss her."

"Oh." Wim grinned, a little embarrassed. He put one hand on Ramey's waist and the other on her neck and pulled her in to him. He thought her mouth tasted sweeter than honey and he felt her hands in his hair as she held on to him. He half hoped the moment would never end and, for once, didn't even mind being the center of attention.

When they separated, he whispered in her ear. "Promise me you'll never leave me. That we'll always be together."

"There's nothing I want more."

That wasn't really a promise. He realized that later on, but in the moment, it was what he needed to hear.

* * *

THEY LAID IN BED, PRESSED TOGETHER, ALMOST MELDED INTO ONE form. Ramey could feel Wim's heart beating as his chest pressed against her. It was fast. Strong. He held on to her so tight that she thought she might break but she'd never imagined anything could feel that good.

Their bodies were drenched in sweat from the recent consummation of their marriage and now the cool night air felt even colder. Ramey shivered.

"Are you all right?" Wim asked, his voice full of concern.

Ramey turned her face up toward his, smiling. More than smiling. Glowing. "I'm not alright, Wim. I'm wonderful."

"You still want to leave here in the spring, right?"

There was almost nothing she wanted more. "Of course."

"Is there somewhere you want to go? Because I'll follow you anywhere."

She hadn't given it much thought. "Not really. Just far away from here."

"I was thinking about finding us a little cabin somewhere. Maybe in North Carolina or Tennessee. Where the winters aren't so long, but you still get the change of seasons."

"That sounds nice."

"It won't always be easy. But I have faith we can get through anything that gets tossed our way as long as we've got each other."

She felt him give her another squeeze, and wasn't sure if he'd realized he'd done it or if it was his subconscious way of saying he'd never let her go.

"We could clear off a section of land for a garden. Take in any livestock we come across and raise them up. Not for eating, just for the noise and company"

She thought that sounded good. She'd grown skeptical of people after her time here and had no great desire to live amongst them again. Animals would be nice though.

"I can picture it in my head already. You'll be running around, chasing the chickens back into their pens when they get out, because they always do. Gathering eggs for a late breakfast because I got distracted talking to the cows while I milked them. You're wearing a pretty little dress— "

"I'm not really the dress type, Wim," she said with a lazy, contented grin.

"That's all right. You'd be beautiful in anything. Even one of those old flour sacks. But I can see you sitting on the porch of our very own home and me sitting beside you. Maybe I'll make us some of those tilted back chairs, Adirondack's, I think they're called. Or maybe a swing. Yep, it'll be a swing so we can sit side by side. And because it'll be up in the mountains we'll get to see the prettiest sunsets ever."

Ramey could picture it too. It sounded perfect.

"And afterward, we'll look up at the stars and there'll be so many and they'll be so bright, that it won't even feel like we're on the same planet anymore. It'll be like we found ourselves a whole new world. A better one."

Until that day, Ramey never thought it was possible to love someone so much. She laid her head against Wim's chest, her ear over his thudding heart, and thought they should leave the Ark at that very moment. That the two of them could disappear into the night. Run away and find a new place where they could be happy together forever. And later, when she looked back, she realized that maybe they should have done just that and avoided the carnage that was to come, but instead they made love again and dreamed about a future.

PART FOUR

CHAPTER THIRTY-FOUR

Saw loved watching Yukie dress after they fucked. She wasn't much to look at, a right munter really, but the bird had a way about her that he found almost irresistible. And she was fun in the sack too. He hadn't had his balls drained so often since he was a lad.

"What are you staring at?" She asked.

"I like the way you jiggle."

A lesser woman might have been offended, but Yukie grinned. She held her arms out at her sides and shook her body, sending her flesh shaking like a mild earthquake was taking place.

Saw went to her and grabbed her flabby belly in his hands. Then he kissed her.

Yukie's hand squeezed his crotch which was swollen, eager. "Again already, big man?"

Saw pushed himself against her. "Saves you the trouble of getting dressed."

"That's true."

Yukie rolled his balls in her hand like they were two big marbles and kissed him back.

Yeah, he liked this one. He liked her a lot.

* * *

ABOUT THE ONLY THING OF INTEREST SAW COULD FIND IN LONDON, Kentucky was a huge banner spanning Main Street which read "World Chicken Festival." Nonetheless, he found it far preferable to London, England and all its toffee-nosed wankers.

Paramount on his mind now was finding a hospital. It wasn't a life and death situation, but for the last few days, every time he pissed he felt like his cock had been doused in petrol and set aflame. In between pisses, oily white goo seeped out his dick hole almost constantly. He was no doctor but he knew a dose of the clap when he saw it. And even though they'd assembled a small arsenal of firearms and enough food to last for weeks, they were woefully unprepared for medical issues that didn't involve slapping a bandage on it. It was time to fix that.

He sent the men off to search the town for anything of interest. He didn't want them to be aware of his plumbing issues so he didn't tell them why he and Yukie were headed to the hospital.

Getting inside was easy enough. The sliding double-doors were wide open. In the lobby, a zombie with a cast extending from its foot to above its knee flopped on the floor. When it saw them, he grabbed at the tile, trying to crawl toward them. Its bloody fingers were worn down, allowing the glistening, white bone to poke free of the destroyed skin. The bones could gain no traction on the floor, clawing across the tile with a sickening screech. Unable to make any forward progress, it gasped at them.

"Look like you need someone to put you out of your misery, mate," Saw said as he stepped forward raising his sledgehammer overhead. The zombie reached for him and Saw responded by beating its skull in.

They didn't encounter any more zombies as they traveled down the halls. After a few turns and detours they came to a door with a sign reading. "RX - Authorized personnel only."

Saw glanced at Yukie. "Uh oh, love. Looks like they're trying to keep the likes of us out."

"I won't tell if you won't."

He tried the door. It was locked. A blow with the sledge did little to change that situation. Saw tried again. And again. And again. After a dozen or so hits the handle and lock tumbled free. Saw struggled to catch his breath and sweat had soaked through his shirt. That was more of a workout than he'd expected. He pushed the door open and extended his hand. "After you."

Yukie stepped into the room and he followed behind. "What are we looking for again?"

"Start with anything ending in 'cilin,'" Saw said as he scanned the almost endless rows of shelves. "Or 'mycin.'"

Their search proved quite productive and yielded two plastic bags full of antibiotics of various varieties. Saw was pleased with the haul and popped a handful of the pills into his mouth, then dry swallowed them. He tilted a bottle toward Yukie. "Your turn."

"How do you know I need them? I don't have any symptoms?"

"Well, I sure as shit didn't catch this sitting on the loo."

Yukie took a few pills and swallowed them with a grimace. Saw noticed that she'd pilfered a bottle of pills from the narcotics section, but he decided to let that slide for the time being.

"Time to move on, don't you think?"

She nodded and they headed toward the doorway. Saw got there first and what he found in the hallway hit him like a punch in the gut. "Bugger me."

Yukie pushed in beside him and together they looked out upon a hallway filled with zombies. They rolled in from both sides, dozens of them. Yukie barked out a short, piercing scream which seemed to fire up the monsters even more. They moved in faster, their hungry groans echoing off the walls and ceiling. The stench of their death was almost overwhelming in the small space.

"Where'd they all come from?"

"Must've heard me breaking down the door. Christ, we should have checked this place out first."

Yukie tried to pull him back into the room. He resisted. "Come on."

"I beat the fookin knob off. They'll push the door straight open."

"We can block it."

"With what? A bunch of shelves? That wouldn't buy us two minutes."

"Then what?"

Yukie clutched his arm, her fingernails digging into his skin. He felt it pop and warm blood trickled down his flesh. Saw realized they only had one chance. They needed a distraction. He pointed to their right. "There are less that way. See?"

Yukie looked. There were less, but the numbers were still overwhelming. Saw knew he had a full magazine in his pistol. Eighteen rounds plus one in the chamber. He didn't know for certain what Yukie's gun held but imagined it was in the same vicinity. That gave them less than 40 bullets for at least that many zombies.

"We have to shoot our way out," he said.

"It's too many." Yukie chewed on her lip but she was already pulling her pistol from its holster.

"All's we need's a clear path, love. Shoot up the middle and we make a mad dash the hell out of here."

Her big, brown eyes met his. He saw worry in them. Fear. He lifted his hand and took her chin between his thumb and index finger, then gave her a quick kiss. "We'll be just fine. We've got out of stickier spots than this." That was a lie but in the moment, it sounded good and she didn't correct him. Saw didn't wait. He stepped into the hall and started blasting.

Solomon Baldwin was a lot of things, but a marksman was not one of them. Most of his shots hit, but landed in the zombies' chests, arms, stomachs. He got in a few headshots but by the time he'd fired fifteen rounds he hadn't dropped more than three.

Yukie, on the flip side of the coin, was damned near a pro. She only missed two headshots and a narrow but almost clear escape route had started to form.

Saw shot again and the head of a zombie nurse in Hello Kitty scrubs blew into pieces. Yukie took out an orderly who had his long, gray hair pulled up in a man bun. Saw's next shot went wide, sending bits of white tile flying as it ricocheted off the wall. He shot again and sent a bullet into the chin of a Japanese woman in a doctor's coat. Her jaw split in half but she kept coming. Yukie finished her off.

"I'm out," Yukie said, holding the pistol up as if to show him it was empty.

Saw was almost certain he had one round left but there were still two dozen or more zombies bearing down on them and that slim path to freedom was shrinking by the second.

"Run!" He said and she did. She dashed up the channel their shooting had created. But Saw knew it wasn't enough. The horde was closing in. He'd never make it through. One look behind him revealed even more zombies following.

He wasn't getting out of this one alive. That was plain as day and the thought infuriated him. He'd been built for a scenario like this. The world in chaos. No arbitrary rules to follow. This was his destiny. A world where only the strongest would survive. It couldn't end like this. Chomped to death in a hospital hallway all because some slag had given him a dose. Solomon Baldwin's fate wasn't to end up as zombie chow.

Yukie glanced back to check his progress. She was five or so yards ahead of him now.

"Keep going!"

She did. He followed. Yukie was a better shooter, but Saw was a far quicker runner. He'd closed the gap to a few feet when he put his last bullet to use.

He shot Yukie in the back of her chunky thigh. He'd been aiming for her knee, but this did the trick just as well. She collapsed on the floor, skidding across the tile and into the oncoming zombies.

As they began to tear her apart, Saw caught her staring at him, her eyes wide and confused. He thought about apologizing, but he'd been quite fond of her and didn't want his last words to her to be lies. He wasn't sorry. He'd done what was necessary.

Yukie's agonized shrieks filled the halls and drew even more zombies toward her, making it easy for Saw to maneuver past the few remainders. He used the sledge to crush the head of an elderly man in a hospital gown, hitting him so hard the man's scrawny neck opened and his skull almost came clear off. After that he had smooth sailing. He'd even managed to keep all the antibiotics. All things considered, it wasn't a bad afternoon. Not bad at all.

CHAPTER THIRTY-FIVE

It had been almost two months since they left Grady's church. Along the way they'd picked up a few new arrivals. Jimmy Hetzer was the first. They were somewhere in East Tennessee raiding a gun shop for arms and ammunition when Aben heard a roaring sound coming from a back room. He motioned for Saw to have his back as he approached the closed door from behind which the noise emanated.

Aben held the maul in his lone hand and used it to smash apart the doorknob rather than waste time turning it. Then he kicked the door open, ready to bludgeon whatever or whoever lay behind it. Before that could happen, he found a fellow who looked almost as bad off as the homeless men and women Aben had slept beside in alleyways and gutters in the days before the plague.

Jimmy Hetzer was pushing sixty with male pattern baldness that looked even worse because his remaining hair was long and gray and hung in unwashed clumps to his shoulders. He was a few weeks into growing a sparse beard that made his face look even dirtier than it probably was. His head was tilted back and his mouth hung agape revealing pink gums with no teeth in them. And he snored like a motherfucker.

A three fourths empty bottle of scotch stood on the desk in front of him and a few empties littered the floor. It wasn't hard for Aben to understand why the old man hadn't reacted to the office being broken into.

Jimmy's feet were propped up on the desk. Aben returned the maul to his belt and grabbed hold of Jimmy's foot, an act he immediately regretted because his sock felt so stiff and hard that it could have stood up all by itself. He shook the foot back and forth and after the third shake Jimmy woke up.

"Holy jumped up Jesus!" He said and he would have tumbled backward out of his chair if Aben wasn't still holding onto his foot.

"Calm down, buddy." Jimmy breathed so hard and fast Aben thought the man might have a coronary. "I'm not gonna hurt you."

Jimmy collected himself, as much as was possible. The first thing he did was take another hit off the bottle. The second was reach for his false teeth that were sitting on the desk and teeming with flies. He swatted them away and shoved the hunks of plastic into his mouth. Aben thought they looked too big for his face and made him look like an old man version of a ventriloquist's dummy.

"Who the hell are you?" Jimmy asked.

Turned out that Jimmy had been living in the store in between trips to the local liquor shop. He'd been on a mostly liquid diet since the plague and, when Saw offered him a can of spaghetti, the man didn't bother with a fork or spoon and had it all gobbled down in under a minute.

"Got another one?"

Aben was surprised when Saw asked him if he wanted to join them. He didn't see much value in an old drunk, but then again, five months ago the high point of his day was finding a half-eaten eclair in a dumpster so he supposed he had no right to judge.

* * *

LONNIE DRAPER FOUND THEM OUTSIDE OF CAMBRIDGE, OHIO. THEY'D stopped at a fuel depot to top off the tanks of Saw's dump truck and fill two 55-gallon drums he'd added to the back for reserves. Jimmy had been put in charge of starting the siphon and, in the process, ended up spilling almost a gallon onto his faded Metallica t-shirt. Aben worried the man would catch them all on fire unless that was taken care of, so while Jimmy filled the tanks, he went into the shop.

He found an XXL uniform shirt with a name tag reading 'Pedro' hanging in a locker and thought it would do. As he was on his way back outside, he discovered a man aiming a bolt action rifle at his three companions who all stood with their hands in the air.

"I said I don't want your food, I want your truck," the man said in a calm, detached voice.

Aben thought he looked about thirty and in good shape. He had a crew cut and a sleeve of tribal tattoos on his left arm. He had a heavy bottom lip that sagged down to reveal brown, tobacco stained teeth.

Although he knew his aim was shit, especially at a distance of twenty or so yards, Aben hoped he could bluff his way through the situation so he pulled out his pistol and aimed it in Lonnie's general direction.

"The truck's the one thing you can't have, mate. How would you expect us to get where we're going without it?" Saw said.

"And where are you going?"

"Haven't decided yet. Expect I'll know when I get there."

"Yeah, well I don't give a shit. I want that truck."

Aben could see in Saw's face that he was close to doing something rash - something stupid. It's now or never.

"Hey there, pal," Aben said. Lonnie's head snapped in his direction. The rifle barrel wavered as he tried to decide whether to keep it aimed at the three men in front of him or the man with the gun beside him. "How about you put down that rifle and we have a conversation."

Aben could tell the man was scared. Four against one were bad odds, even when you had a gun. "You do that and I promise none of us are going to hurt you."

Lonnie's head swiveled back and forth so many times that Aben thought it might break loose and fall off. Instead, he tilted the rifle to the ground.

Lonnie Draper had been a member of the Ohio national guard and was on emergency call up in Cincinnati when everything went down. He didn't provide many details, and that was fine. There was only so much talk of death a person could absorb before it became as tedious as listening to the weather during a stretch of sunshine and no chance of rain.

Saw's dump truck was getting cramped so Aben and Lonnie scouted the town until they came across a Cherokee with a key above the visor. Aben let Lonnie drive.

* * *

THEY DIDN'T FIND ANYONE ELSE ALIVE OVER THE COURSE OF SEVERAL weeks and Aben began to wonder how devastating the plague had been, about whether mankind could be on the verge of extinction. It seemed impossible, but then again, almost everything he'd experienced the last few months would have seemed impossible in his life beforehand. He was surprised to realize he hoped his most dire thoughts were untrue. He hadn't had much need for people for the last twenty or so years, but thinking that he might be one of last the few hundred, or even thousand, people alive was too damned depressing to consider.

In Western Pennsylvania, as they trekked up and down the mountains, Saw stopped his dump truck in front of a five-foot-high wooden sign reading, 'Higgins Haven Scout Camp & Recreational Area.'

"What do you say, boys?" Saw asked them.

It didn't seem like anything special to Aben and the other men didn't tender an opinion, but Saw assured them it would be a good place to hunker down and prepare. He didn't say what he was preparing for, not then anyway.

"It's good and remote so there won't be many zombies in the immediate vicinity. And I don't imagine it would have much appeal to any groups or individuals passing through looking for places to raid.

Lotsa cabins so we can have as much privacy as we each desire. Seems like a peach of a place to me."

And it was settled.

All they had to do was kill a dozen or so scouts and another four troop leaders that had turned into zombies. After that, Higgins Haven became their new home.

CHAPTER THIRTY-SIX

"Give it, Prince!"

The dog dropped the tennis ball and Aben caught it before it hit the snow. Prince jumped up lunging for the ball but Aben pulled it back just in time. When the dog landed, his feet crunched through the icy glaze that covered the recently fallen snow.

Prince gave an excited bark and Aben lobbed the ball extra hard down the hill where it rolled and ricocheted through a maze of trees. The dog sprinted after it, just the hint of a limp on the leg that had been injured when Aben found it - or when it found him - months earlier.

He didn't like to think about those first weeks. About men like Bolivar and Dash who had been lost along the way. Even now, amongst this new group of survivors, of fighters, he missed them.

Aben thought it seemed to be taking longer than normal for the dog to return and wondered if the ball had gotten lost somewhere down the hill. He couldn't see Prince from this vantage point and moved closer to the trees. With every step, his feet fell through eight inches of hard snow. It didn't take long before he was out of breath.

"Prince! Come back, boy!"

He waited, watched. Thirty more seconds passed with no sign of the dog.

"Damn it."

Aben trudged through the snow, taking extra caution as he moved downhill. The dog's footprints were easy to follow but going was slow and knowing that he'd eventually have to climb back up the hill made the trek even more annoying.

By the time he reached the bottom, he was breathing heavily and sucking in mouthfuls of the icy air made his lungs feel like they were full of glass. He saw the tracks leading through a copse of pine trees and followed.

It was a scraping sound that caught his attention. The noise came fast, frantic, frenzied. Instinctively, Aben's hand dropped to the maul which was holstered in his belt like a gun. He didn't pull it free, the feel of it was enough to calm him. Somewhat.

Aben continued forward, along the dog's trail. The sound grew louder with every step. He realized it wasn't scraping. It was scratching.

When he broke free of the trees, Aben saw Prince. He only realized he'd been holding his breath when it came out in a sudden rush. The dog stood atop a frozen pond, clawing and digging at the ice with its front paws. Aben grinned at the sight.

"I send you after a ball and you come up with a couple fish?"

Fish sounded pretty damned good. Aben hadn't eaten fresh meat since a turkey sandwich more than half a year earlier and he missed it. He moved to the edge of the pond and surveyed it but he couldn't see anything through the thick, opaque ice. As hungry as he was, he had no pole or net and couldn't see any sense pursuing the matter.

"How about you come back here and we'll look for the ball?"

The dog ignored him as he kept scratching.

Aben's curiosity was piqued and he rested one booted foot atop the ice. He stepped down, putting a quarter of his body weight on it, then half, then all of it. It held. Aben moved onto the pond, the ice suspending him above the water below. He scooted across, careful not to slip on the slick surface. Within half a minute he'd reached Prince.

The dog continued to pay him no heed and when Aben rested his hand on Prince's back the dog jumped back like it had received an electric shock. Aben couldn't stifle a laugh and that seemed to snap the dog out of its obsession, at least momentarily. It pushed its muzzle against Aben's bearded neck and gave him am eager lick.

"That's my boy. I was starting to think you didn't like me anymore."

The dog licked him again then turned its face back to the ice. He'd cleared away the snow and its toenails had carved a half inch trench into the glassy surface. Prince stared at it and whined.

Aben eased down onto his knees and he could feel the cold stabbing through his pants. He leaned forward, onto his elbows and hoped none of the others were watching because he imagined that he looked quite the spectacle.

He leaned in closer, but no matter how hard he tried, he couldn't see through the ice.

The dog gave another whine then recommenced its digging. Aben realized his hands were going numb in the cold and wondered if dogs could get frostbite. He suspected they could and decided this had gone on long enough.

"That's enough now, Prince. Let's head back to the camp."

He grabbed the dog's collar and tried to pull it away but Prince gave a low growl and he pulled his hand back. In all these months, it had been rare to hear the dog growl, and never at him.

"All right then. Have it your way." He stood up and shuffled away from the dog, a few feet at first, then a few yards. He expected the dog to follow. It did not.

Aben turned back, his patience thin. "Prince!" The tone in his voice made the dog look in his direction. "Come!"

Prince turned back to the ice, gave another whine, but finally moved toward Aben.

About damn time.

The dog crept in his direction, almost belly crawling on the ice. Aben took a step backwards. Then another. When he went for a third, he heard the groan.

At first, he wasn't sure where the sound originated. It sounded human, pained. He began to turn around to see if someone, or something, was watching him after all and when he moved there came another groan. This one was followed by a crack and a pop. Aben barely had time to think, 'all that's missing is the snap' before the ice beneath him gave way.

The plunge was so fast he didn't have time to take a breath and the next thing he knew he was falling into a frigid chasm. The freezing water hit him like a truck and he instinctively gasped, sucking a mouthful of fluid that tasted like mud and rotten seafood into his throat and lungs.

He choked on it, his diaphragm spasming as it tried to expel the water. In the process, his body tried to breathe again but he stopped himself from swallowing in more.

Within seconds, every part of his body was numb. His scraggly beard floated up, into his face and in front of his eyes. Looking through it was like trying to peer through a patch of seaweed. Aben tried to push it away as he kicked to propel himself upward, but he still couldn't see and he slammed his skull into the ice.

His vision went blank for a moment and when it returned he thought the water around him had taken on a deep red color. He reached up and examined his head and could run his fingers underneath a large gash that had opened above his hairline. He knew that would have hurt like a son of a bitch if he had any feeling left.

Despite being submerged, Aben heard a high pitched, frantic barking from above.

Sure, bark. You got me into this mess.

He tried to follow the noise, to move closer to it hoping the dog would lead him to the hole. As he did, his eyes began to adjust to the dim conditions underwater and he caught movement in his peripheral vision. He turned to look, but lost it.

Just a fish.

Despite the cold, his lungs were burning. He wasn't sure how long he'd been under but he knew he needed to get air now, not later.

Focus on the dog. Listen.

Prince sounded close, just to the right. Aben swam toward the noise, staring up, hoping to see the hole, to see freedom, but seeing only more ice. More movement stole his attention. It was ahead of him, but lower, camouflaged amongst the weeds and muck that filled the bottom of the pond.

Forget about it and get the hell out of here.

He pushed himself upward, against the ceiling of ice and tried to pull himself along with the fingertips of his remaining hand. He didn't know how he could have moved so far away from where he'd fallen in. He felt his lungs spasm and fought to keep his mouth clamped shut to avoid sucking in more of the foul water.

Aben knew he had only a few more seconds, but between the blow to his head and the freezing water, his thoughts came slow. He tried to focus on the barking dog but it seemed further away now. Barely audible.

Where the hell am I?

Something brushed against his back. Even with little feeling remaining in his body he could tell it was something substantial. Not a fish. But he didn't dare risk looking away and further disorienting himself.

He clawed at the ice, kicked and pulled himself forward. And then his hand suddenly wasn't pressing against the ice, it was reaching through it.

Aben pushed himself into the hole and his upper body popped through, bobbing like a buoy. Prince yipped, an excited but worried noise, at the edge of the hole. When Aben saw him he never thought he could be so joyful and so pissed off at the same time.

"You damn dog. See if I follow you again."

He tried to grab onto the surface ice but his fingers were clumsy and of little use. He kicked and pushed himself far enough out of the hole that he could get his elbows onto the ice, then took a moment to catch his breath.

Aben got in four good mouthfuls of air before he felt something under the water grab hold of his belt. He had no time to react before the force of it pulled him off the ice and back into the water below.

When he looked down, he saw a zombie at his waist. Its skin was wrinkled and white, almost translucent. It looked to be around twelve years old and wore a Scout's uniform, the red kerchief still tied around its neck.

Aben was used to the cold now and that helped, a little. He reached down and grabbed the maul from his belt. He was unsure whether he'd be able to get enough force underwater to do much damage but he tried anyway. As he swung, the hammer end of the maul caught the boy in the jaw and it peeled off sideways in a way that reminded Aben of separating chicken wings. The zombie's jawbone floated away, spiraling into the murky water below until Aben lost sight of it.

Still, the zombie held fast to his belt. Aben went to swing again when another zombie grabbed his hair and ripped his head backwards. The sudden attack startled him and Aben dropped the maul which quickly plunged into the abyss. He remembered Bolivar telling him to get a haircut. He should have listened.

Aben was out of breath again and when he tried to propel himself upward the weight of the two zombies was too great to overcome. He could feel himself going down. Sinking.

Maybe this isn't so bad.

He'd seen men die much worse. He'd been party to a few of them himself. As far as ends went, this one seemed pretty easy. Probably better than he deserved.

Above Prince's frenzied barks grew further and further away. The sound of the dog was the only thing stopping him from accepting his coming fate. Damn it, he'd miss that dog.

Aben grabbed onto the hand which clutched his belt. His fingers sunk into the zombie's hand, puncturing the flesh which quickly gave way and came free like a glove. It reminded him a bit of losing his own hand back in a rural Pennsylvania police station and that wasn't a memory he cared to relive. With the skin gone, the zombie's finger bones lost their grip on him and the monster floated away.

That was easier than he thought and Aben began to think he might get out of this yet. He knew it had to be soon though because his lungs were seizing and he battled his body's attempts to breathe.

He reached over his head, feeling behind himself until he maneuvered his arm around the zombie's neck, then he pulled it closer to him. He felt its teeth smash against his skull. Felt its jaws working, chomping down on his hair and realized his unruly mane had some benefits after all.

Using all the strength he had remaining, Aben thrust his upper body forward, vaulting the zombie over his shoulder. That was the plan anyway. Instead its waterlogged body gave way and the monster's head popped free of its torso. The skull tumbled end for end through the water and Aben would be damned if its face didn't look surprised. He was too and it took him a good second and a half to realize he was still on the verge of drowning. After kicking his way back to the surface, his upper body poked through the hole in the ice and he gulped down mouthful after mouthful of air. He wasn't going to dawdle this time. He kicked, dragged and pulled until his upper body was firmly on the ice surface.

Prince kept barking, a sound so sweet Aben started to laugh, even if it was the damned dog that got him into this mess in the first place.

"How about you give me a hand, boy."

Prince plodded toward him, laid down on the ice and licked his face. That was enough.

CHAPTER THIRTY-SEVEN

Saw spotted the man first. He was so white Mitch thought he might be albino and he sat on the bumper of a big rig eating heaping spoonfuls of beans straight from the can. To Mitch, he looked old, to Mitch, everyone over twenty was old. He had an oblong face and mud brown hair that was pulled back in a ponytail. They'd seen his truck moving a few hours earlier then stayed a mile or so back to remain out of view until he stopped.

Mitch and Saw traded binoculars back and forth as they spied on him.

"What do you say, Mitchy? Time to give him our sales pitch?"

Mitch nodded. "Sounds good to me."

They left the death machine parked on the side of the road and approached. Mitch had a loaded and cocked pistol in hand and another in a holster on his belt. Saw was unarmed.

"Wotcha!" Saw called out when they were within shouting distance.

The man jumped to his feet, sending the empty container careening to the roadway as he rushed toward the driver's side door

"Easy now, easy now. We're as harmless as a couple mice and hope you can say the same."

The man didn't flee, but when he stepped away from the cab Mitch saw he was carrying a broken baseball bat, the fat end partially sheared off into a jagged point.

"Who are you?"

"Name's Solomon. But you can call me Saw. And this is my little buddy Mitch."

"Hiya," Mitch added.

The man didn't respond and didn't lower the bat. Mitch tightened his grip on the pistol.

"Polite thing to do now is tell us your name," Saw said.

"Everyone calls me Casper. And if you're harmless, why does he got that gun out like he's ready to use it?"

Mitch returned it to its holster. With a pistol on each hip he felt a little like an old west outlaw. He liked that.

"He's a little jumpy. Had some bad experiences with the zombies."

"Ain't we all?" Casper said and he lowered his bat.

"That's the truth."

They were within a few yards of the man now. Saw picked up the can and motioned to Casper to get ready. The man narrowed his eyes at first, but when Saw took a pitcher's stance, he caught on. Saw lobbed the can toward him. Casper swung and connected, sending the now dented can skidding along the highway.

"I'd reckon that's an easy double."

Casper smiled and Mitch was shocked at how easily Saw had brought down his guard.

"Are you all by your lonesome out here?"

"I am. You're the first people - living people - I've seen in almost two weeks."

"Shame what's happened, ain't it? Almost everyone dead or turned. Rest of us left to fend for ourselves. It's a hard life."

"Sure is."

Saw took a seat on the bumper, mimicking Casper's positioning when they approached. Then Casper resumed his seat beside him. Mitch watched.

"Where are you from anyway? You got a funny accent."

"Birmingham."

"Alabama?" Casper raised his eyebrows.

"England."

"That makes more sense."

"And you?"

"Cherry Hill, New Jersey. Little suburb of Philadelphia."

"You like it?"

"Not really. Too many spooks."

Mitch noticed Saw squint, confused. He mouthed "Black people" to him and Saw nodded understandingly.

"Ah, I get that mate. We don't got any spooks in our group."

"There's more of you?"

"Right on. Two more. Three if you count the mutt."

"Mixed race?" Casper asked with a sneer.

Saw grinned, showing his tiny, rotting teeth. "No, a real mutt. A dog."

Casper's sneer faded. Mitch moved a little closer to get a better look at the harsh, black ink - prison tattoos - that stood out against his lily-white skin. Among them was an "88" scrawled in the hollow at the base of his throat and a pair of swastikas on the back of his hands. Swell guy, Mitch thought.

"Why don't you come with? Spend a couple days with us, see if you like the fit," Saw said.

Casper didn't answer at first. Mitch half-hoped he'd say no. He liked their little group just fine and didn't see the need to add anyone else, especially some asshole Nazi wannabe.

"World's a dangerous place, mate. We could use a man like you."

Casper sighed, nodded. "Yeah, that sounds fine. You boys need a ride?" He cocked his thumb toward the semi.

"No, we've got our own. But bring that with. I have a feeling it might be useful."

Casper got into his rig and followed them back to Saw's dump truck. Mitch saw the man's eyes grow wide when he caught sight of it.

"Ain't that something?"

Saw patted the cab lovingly. "It sure is."

Mitch was amazed at how Saw had transformed the man from a potential foe to an ally, all within a few minutes. He's smoother than a politician. He thought his father could have learned a few things from Solomon Baldwin. Senator Son of a Bitch had tried to control people through empty threats and making them feel small. Saw fed into their needs and helped them be whatever they wanted to be. Saw was the type of father he should have had, not some self-important asshole in a fancy suit. Saw was the kind of man who could teach him about the world.

CHAPTER THIRTY-EIGHT

Saw's plan was coming together better than he'd hoped. No matter how many ways he looked at it, he couldn't find a flaw. After weeks of keeping it all to himself, he was ready to tell the others what he'd come up with.

He went to Jimmy's cabin first. Not because he liked him the best, he actually thought the old man was a right bellend, but because his quarters were the closest. Saw pushed the door open without knocking, an act he'd regret as soon as his eyes witnessed what was happening inside.

Jimmy was on all fours on the bed, naked as the day he was born. His face was contorted into a grimace that Saw couldn't decipher as pleasure or pain. Behind him, Lonnie hammered away. Sweat soaked his body and he seemed to struggle to keep pace with the frantic tempo he'd set. They were so caught up in the act that it took a moment for Jimmy to realize Saw was standing in the now open doorway.

"Oh, oh shit!"

Lonnie looked up, saw what was happening, and dropped backward on the bed, his hard dick flailing aimless in front of him. He grabbed the bedsheets to cover himself, but Jimmy had the other end, and the two played tug of war with it.

This is the lot I'm depending on? Maybe his plan wasn't so perfect after all.

Lonnie gave up on the sheet and reached for his pants which were discarded on the floor.

"Hells bells, men. Bugger each other till your arseholes fall out for all I care. Just get yourselves together and meet me in the lodge."

He turned away, smirked to himself, then glanced back. "Go ahead and finish what you were doing. I don't want you strolling in there with blue balls and a stiffy."

* * *

SAW WENT OVER THE PLAN IN HIS HEAD ONE MORE TIME WHILE THEY waited for Mitch to arrive. Aben absentmindedly scratched his stump with his remaining hand. Jimmy slouched in a chair at the end of the table and chewed on his mustache, not looking at anyone. Lonnie had been pacing back and forth, tiny, hurried steps. When Saw made the mistake of looking up, Lonnie grabbed his elbow and ushered him to the side.

The man was still sweating, his skin pallid. Saw thought he looked a half second away from puking up whatever food lay inside his stomach.

"What you saw there— I don't want you to— I'm not queer, I just—
"

Saw fought back a grin. "I meant what I said. It don't matter none to me. Now Casper, he'd probably be of a different mind so you might want to try locking the door lest he catch you two in the throes of passion sometime."

Lonnie looked toward Casper who sat at the table, interacting with no one except the cigarette he sucked on nonstop. Saw thought Lonnie shivered.

"If he'd seen what I did, I wouldn't be surprised if he'd cut your cocks off and shove 'em down your throats."

Lonnie nodded and took the seat furthest from Casper.

The door banged open and Mitch stepped into the lodge. His long hair was pushed in a dozen different directions and he rubbed at his eyes, trying to chase away sleep.

"Okay mates. Now that everyone is here, we can get on with it."

He told them about the island. About the people. And his plans for them.

* * *

ABEN WATCHED AS SAW UNFOLDED A MAP AND POINTED TO A SMALL land mass in the middle of a lake.

"This is the place. They've got themselves set up right good. But they aren't expecting us."

Aben looked from the map to Saw. The man's beady eyes were downright gleeful.

"And that's going to make it easier for us to take."

"Why?" Aben asked.

The question seemed to puzzle Saw and he didn't answer right away. "Because I want it."

That wasn't the answer Aben wanted to hear and Saw seemed to sense that. His expression softened. "Look, Aben, those people, they've got themselves their own safe haven out there. They should be flying a fucking welcome flag. But instead they're hoarding it all for themselves. What kind of people do that?"

Smart ones, Aben thought.

"That still doesn't give us the right to storm in there, guns blazing," Aben said.

"Wake up man. Did the Europeans have the right to take this country from the Indians? And did the Indians have the right to take it from whoever they stole it from? Did you have the right to march into Baghdad or wherever the fuck you were in the war?"

"I didn't want to go there either."

"But you did it. Because you're a soldier and what do soldiers do? What they're told."

As Saw laid out his plan, Aben had to admit, it seemed as close to a sure thing as possible if all the pieces came together. He hoped that never happened.

* * *

THE WEEKS AFTER CONSISTED OF WHAT SAW CALLED 'HARVESTING.' IN A police station, Casper had found a few of those long poles with a wire loop on the end, the kind dog catchers used to corral vicious animals. It proved the perfect tool to catch zombies too.

Saw led the way in his dump truck. The other men followed behind in the semi. When they'd get close to a town, they'd lay on the horns all the way there, making as much noise and commotion as possible. That usually resulted in a dozen or more zombies flocking toward the road by the time they arrived.

That's when Saw slowed down. He didn't want to run them down or tear them to pieces, he wanted to impale them on the metal poles or ensnare them in the razor wire he'd affixed to the death machine. He'd be going three or four miles an hour when he hit them, weaving back and forth and gathering as many as possible.

If a few managed to avoid the truck, it was up to the other three men to catch them. They were all slow zombies, by this point, which made it easy and not too dangerous for Mitch and Aben to draw them toward the rear of the rig's trailer. That's where the pole came in. Casper snagged them around the neck and then the group of them lifted and pushed the zombies into the trailer.

Before they went on these missions, Saw placed a pile of rotten meat at the front of the trailer. That seemed to draw the creatures further inside where they lost interest in the men who'd captured them.

So far, they'd filled four trailers with, Aben estimated, sixty or so zombies each.

* * *

Aben found Mitch playing poker with the other men. He was relieved to find Saw was not among them. He must have been off doing whatever the hell it was that Saw did when he was alone and those were details Aben didn't care to know.

"Hey Mitch?"

Mitch looked up from his cards.

"Can I have a minute?"

"Yeah, let me finish this hand. Got a good feeling about this one."

Aben glanced at the kid's cards. A pair of sixes.

Casper raised with a box of powdered donuts. Jimmy followed by adding a bag of licorice to the pot. Lonnie went out and Aben thought Mitch should do the same. Instead, Mitch tossed in three candy bars. Good ones too.

"Okay what do ya got?" Casper asked.

Jimmy threw down three aces. Casper a straight flush.

"Fuck!" Mitch threw his cards down while Casper cackled.

"Lose again, Mitchy. When are you gonna realize you're out of your league here?"

Hopefully soon, Aben thought.

"Come on." Aben strolled away.

Mitch followed, but not before kicking the pile of junk food, scattering it across the floor.

Aben continued until they were two rooms over. He felt that far enough from curious ears, but just to be extra careful he grabbed a tennis ball and began tossing it against the wall. He sat on the edge of the bunk and motioned for Mitch to join him.

Mitch flopped onto the bed beside Prince, scratching the dog's belly.

"I think that asshole cheats."

"He probably does. But you're still a shitty card player. Don't know why you bother."

Mitch sighed. "Helps pass the time. It's so fucking boring here."

"I won't disagree with that."

"What did you want me for anyway?"

Aben threw the ball harder.

Thwock! Thwock!

"I've been thinking about leaving."

"Oh yeah? Where does Saw want to go now? Hopefully somewhere warmer. This cold and snow shit's for the birds."

"Not just leaving this place, Mitch. Leaving Saw."

The boy sat bolt upright in bed. "Bullshit you are."

"I am. I'm tired of it all. Aren't you?"

Mitch broke eye contact with him and Aben thought maybe the kid shared more of his opinions on things than he cared to admit. "But where would we go? Back to crazy pastor Grady and his lone disciple?"

As much as he wanted to get away, even Aben wasn't up for that. "No. Somewhere else. We could take the dog and head south. Get away from the cold. Away from all this nonsense."

"I don't know."

"Just think about it. Think about how you want to spend the next year, or hell five years for that matter. Do you want to be a lackey for this bunch of weirdos?"

Aben threw the ball again. This time, Mitch caught it on the return bounce. He rolled it around between his palms.

"Okay, I'll think about it. But you won't leave without telling me first, will you?"

"Nah. I won't do that, kid."

Mitch nodded, passed the ball to Prince, and left the room.

The kid was brash, full of piss and teenage hormones, but Aben liked him despite that. Maybe, in part, because of that. And if Mitch decided to stay, he'd miss him but his mind was made up. He had to get away from this place, these people, before it was too late.

CHAPTER THIRTY-NINE

Aben woke with a pain shooting through his right side.

Bit, I'm being bit.

His eyes shot open and he found Casper and Lonnie standing over him. Lonnie held a gun on him. Casper some sort of baton. Aben wasn't sure what it was.

"Rise and shine, soldier." Casper poked him again and Aben realized he had the cattle prod. Aben's body tensed, raising off the bed as electricity coursed through him. After a few seconds, Casper pulled the prod away and Aben collapsed back into the bed.

Prince, who had been sleeping beside him, barked and snarled at them.

Aben struggled to catch his breath. "What the hell?"

Each man grabbed an arm and ripped Aben from his bed, dragging him out of the room.

"Let me go you bastards!"

Even though the men were smaller it was two against one and Aben had no chance of breaking free. They pulled him out of the bunkhouse and into the dim light of predawn.

His bare feet hit the snow and he felt the chill race up his legs and settle into his groin. So damned cold. He was wearing nothing but his briefs and was experiencing major shrinkage. He had a feeling that was the least of his problems though.

"If you assholes don't tell me what's going on real quick, I'm gonna hold a grudge."

He had a feeling he knew though. He hoped to God, if there was a God, that he was wrong, but he knew they'd never act on their own. Whatever was happening was happening because it's what Saw wanted.

They half dragged, half carried Aben up the access road that served as the entrance to the camp. Aben let his feet hang, determined to make it as hard on them as possible. Prince trotted along at their heels.

When they reached the main road, Saw waited for them. He stood in front of one of the tractor trailers.

"There's the man of the hour." He gave a sarcastic clap.

"What do you think you're doing, Saw?"

Saw took a step closer. "What did I do to turn you away from me?"

"I don't know what you're talking about."

"We've been together for what, four months now? Tell me what I've done to you that's so terrible."

"Nothing. But right now, you've got me standing in the snow freezing my pecker off and my patience is running thin."

"All I've ever asked from you, from any of you, is honesty. I must have done something to offend you for you to go behind my back and try to turn the others against me."

Aw, fuck. Mitch. "I talked about leaving, that's all."

"This is no prison. I'm not holding you hostage." Saw turned toward the truck. "Come on out, Mitch. Aben wants to say goodbye."

The door swung open and Mitch dropped from the cab. He came toward them but wouldn't look at Aben, not at first. He took his place at Saw's right side.

"Morning, Mitch," Aben said.

Mitch looked up, reluctant. He nodded. "Yeah."

"I guess this means you aren't joining me."

"Nope. It was never really an option either. Surprised you didn't realize that."

"Can't blame a guy for hoping."

Saw chortled. "Oh, but you can. A traitor is still a traitor even if his plan fails. I'm sure you Americans have heard of Benedict Arnold, after all. You know what happened to him?"

"I believe he ran back to England and lived out his days there."

"Really?" Saw asked. "They didn't hang him for treason?"

"I don't believe they did."

"Huh. You Yankees really are a sorry lot."

"Is that what you have planned for me? Hanging me? Why didn't you just shoot me in bed? Then these fellows could have slept in."

Saw grabbed a water pitcher from the bumper of the trailer. Aben could see something dark inside, through the nearly opaque plastic. "Naw, I'm not going to kill you. No sport in that, is there?"

He moved closer to Aben and Aben could smell something rancid inside the pitcher.

"You told Mitch you wanted to go, so I'm sending you on your way."

"Like this? No clothes or anything?"

"Oh, I've got a little something for you."

Saw tossed the contents of the pitcher onto him. It was cold and wet and heavy. Part liquid, part solid. As it dripped down him, he realized it was rotten meat and blood. He wiped some of the chunks out of his beard and chest hair and tossed them into the snow. Even Prince avoided the gore.

"I could think of better parting gifts."

"Who said I was done?"

Saw motioned to Casper and Lonnie. The men moved to the trailer doors. They banged on the metal walls with their hands, whooping and hollering.

Aben could hear the zombies inside going crazy. He knew where this was going. He didn't like it, but he wasn't going to lower himself to beg. Especially when he knew it was pointless.

"Now get the hell out of here," Saw said and turned his back on him.

Only Mitch still looked in his direction. Aben resented the kid for ratting him out, but for the most part he blamed himself and his own big mouth for getting him into this predicament.

"Mitch," Aben said. "You take good care of Prince, alright?"

Mitch nodded. He took hold of the dog's collar and scratched it behind the ear. "I promise."

"Thank you."

Aben walked away from them, up the snow-covered access road and away from the camp that had been his home for the last few months. Away from his dog.

He'd made it ten yards when he heard Prince bark and Mitch yelp. He risked a glance back and saw Mitch holding his hand to his mouth and the dog dashing toward him.

"Stay with him, Prince," Aben said but the dog, as usual, didn't listen. In seconds, it was on his heels. "Damn dumb dog."

When they were half a football field away, Aben heard the metallic screech of the trailer doors opening. He didn't bother looking back. He knew what was coming.

* * *

BEING ALMOST NAKED, ABEN ALSO LACKED A WATCH BUT HE GUESSED he'd been walking for six or so hours as the sun had passed overhead and began its slow descent. He'd started with a fifty-yard head start on the zombies. That was down to forty-five or so now. They were too far away to get a headcount but he estimated their number to be in the mid-thirties. He was surprised Saw wasted that many on him.

His feet felt like two numb cement blocks attached to the bottom of his legs and he had to shuffle to keep from falling. He knew his odds of surviving through the night were slim and he hoped he'd stumble upon a house or even a vehicle. Anywhere he could barricade himself for a while in the hopes that the zombies lost interest.

Prince plodded along beside, panting happily as if they were going on the longest, coldest pleasure walk in the history of mankind. Aben wish the dog was smarter, Lassie-type smart so he could say, 'Prince, fetch me a machete' and the mutt would actually go and find one. But the dog was just a dog and Aben told himself it wasn't fair to expect him to be anything extraordinary when he himself was about as ordinary as a living creature could be.

He wondered how many life choices had led him to this. How many times he could have done something as simple as turn left instead of right, that might have taken him down a different path. He thought this line of thinking to be of the pointless variety but as he walked, it seemed thinking was all he could do.

A few more hours passed and the sun dipped below the trees, casting long shadows behind him. He took a look back on the chance the zombies had taken an accidental detour, but they were still there and he judged them to be within thirty yards now.

He thought it felt colder, but it was hard to tell, most of him was numb. His remaining fingers had turned a blue-ish white and he kept flexing that hand to keep circulation flowing. On the slim chance he got out of this, he didn't want to be minus both mitts.

Darkness came quick after that, like someone turning a dimmer switch too fast. He couldn't see the road ahead of him nor the zombies behind him, but the low rumble of their growls and groans assured him they were still there. Prince was there too. His tongue hung so far out of his mouth it dragged on the snow in spots where it had drifted deeper.

Aben was tired. Physically, of course, but mentally too. A day of reliving his rotten life over and over again had taken a great toll. He realized it was pointless to keep walking. He knew that soon he would trip and be unable to get back up, or fall into a ravine he couldn't climb out of, or just get so damned exhausted that his heart blew up mid-step. But still, he walked.

* * *

IT TOOK ABEN A FEW MINUTES TO REALIZE THE REASON THE LAND AHEAD of him was getting brighter was because the sun was coming up. He'd stopped thinking sometime through the night but his body went on putting one foot in front of the other like someone had wound the key on a toy and it kept going and going and going.

Behind him, the zombies were less than ten yards away. Ahead of him laid endless road with no houses, no shelter.

Saw knew this. He knew there was nothing on this road for dozens of miles. *Bastard knew I didn't have a chance.*

The sun brought with it slightly warmer temperatures and some of the ice that had formed in his beard began to melt. His mouth felt like a desert and he pushed some of the hard, scraggly hair between his lips and sucked the moisture off it. It was only after the hair was in his mouth that he realized it was also tainted with frozen snot, along with whatever mélange of gore Saw had doused him in before sending him out to die.

Oh well, it's all wet so what's it really matter?

He wondered if he should have gone along with Saw's plan to attack the island. Maybe he was right and that the people there were selfish sons of bitches and they deserved to lose their haven. Hell, even if they were decent people, was it worth him having to endure this ordeal? But then he realized he brought some, maybe all of this on himself by leaving Juli and Grady. Listening to that little dude prattle on about God and punishments and redemption certainly wasn't as bad as this.

After a few hours of daylight, he stepped on a particularly slick spot of icy snow and went down on his ass. It didn't hurt. He was too numb to hurt. But he struggled to get back up. The first time he tried he fell on his face. The second he made it to his knees and got stuck there. Eventually Prince got close enough that Aben could rest his hand on the dog's back and push himself up.

Right away he started walking again, but a backward glance revealed the zombies were within twenty feet.

Only a matter of time, now.

He looked down at Prince who, despite being a dog with seemingly endless energy, panted hard and seemed to be almost as poor off as Aben. Large snowballs of ice had formed on his legs and belly and the whites of his eyes were blood red, like all the vessels in them had burst from the constant exertion. That pissed Aben off because even if he'd brought this on himself, the dog hadn't done anything to deserve it. He was just a dog, one whose only fault was being too loyal. Aben had accepted that the zombies were going to eat him, but he wanted to spare Prince.

"Hey Prince." The dog looked up at him. Despite its exhaustion it looked happy to hear his name and its ears perked up.

"How about you run ahead and fetch us a rabbit?"

Prince cocked his head to the side and Aben had to remind himself that the dog was just a dog.

"Get going now. Get!'

Aben gave him a pat on the rear end then pointed down the road. Prince remained at his side.

"How about a run then. Can you still run? Let's go."

Aben sucked in a big mouthful of frigid air and somehow managed to jog ten paces. Prince ran with him, excited and yipping. Dog speak for 'This is fun!'

When Aben ran out of steam the dog continued ahead a few yards, then looked back to him.

"Keep going, boy. I'll catch up."

Instead, Prince returned to his side.

Damn dog.

Aben was running out of ideas quick and the more he thought about the zombies eating his dog, the more angry and fearful he became. Damn it, this wasn't right and he wasn't going to let it happen. The only thing he knew to do was let out that rage.

"Get out of here!" He screamed at the dog. Prince cowered, his floppy ears slicked against his head. Seeing him like that made Aben's chest tighten and he fought hard to get a breath, "I said go! Damn dog, get away from me!"

He kicked snow at the dog but it only hunkered down, tail tucked.

"I said go!" He roared. Then he kicked Prince as hard as he could, aiming for the hindquarter that had been injured when he found it that past summer. His foot connected and the dog skidded five feet away, rolling over twice before landing in a puff of snow.

Prince stared back at him, its big brown eyes questioning, 'What did I do? I'm sorry.'

Aben never imagined anything could hurt like this. That damn dog was the only thing he'd ever loved but now just looking at it made him hate himself. In a life filled with terrible moments, this was the worst.

"Go! Get!" Aben grabbed a chunk of ice and hurled it at Prince. It hit the dog in the side and Prince gave a high-pitched yelp that might have been the most horrible noise Aben had ever heard.

And then Prince darted into the forest. Between the cover of the trees and the tears that blurred his vision, Aben quickly lost sight of him.

His bare chest rose and fell in hitching wheezes. He didn't know how much ground the zombies had gained on him and he didn't care. He collapsed to his knees, sobs racking his near frozen, exhausted body, and welcomed the end.

CHAPTER FORTY

After sending Aben on his merry way, Saw loaded Mitch into a Subaru Forester that he kept around for longer trips. It lacked the panache of his dump truck, but it got much better gas mileage. Besides, this trip didn't involve collecting things. This time, they were making a delivery.

They drove south out of the Pennsylvania mountains, crossing first into Maryland, then West Virginia. As they drove, the snow accumulation became less and less before disappearing entirely. Saw never ceased to be amazed that the US could feel like entirely different worlds within a few hundred miles.

Saw had given Mitch a few beers and the teen had a good buzz. They were halfway through West Virginia and Mitch was sufficiently slurring his words, so Saw thought it was time.

"Alright, Mitchy. Now listen careful because you have the most important job of everyone."

Mitch's glassy eyes grew wide. Saw could tell how much he reveled feeling important. "I'm up for it. I promise. I'll do anything you need me to do."

"That's a good lad. Very good."

When they made it to the overlook, Saw took out the same telescope he'd used months earlier to show Mitch the island. The teen got so excited he almost knocked it over.

"It's like an entire fucking town! There's houses and RVs and people. People everywhere."

"Exactly, Mitch. Looks like a place we could call home, does it not?"

"Shit yeah!"

Saw then showed Mitch the map. "There's only a couple roads that dead end in the lake. And this one," he pointed to a line he'd highlighted in yellow, "Seems like the one they'd be most apt to use."

They drove down the highway, away from the overlook and toward the flat ground of the valley. Saw had to stop twice along the way so Mitch could get out and piss and he worried a bit that he might have got the boy a bit too drunk, but he suspected everything would be fine.

Mitch asked him again about his role in the attack and Saw felt it was finally time to reveal the teenager's mission.

"You saw the gate through the telescope, right?"

Mitch nodded.

"Well, Mitch, your job is to open it."

Even though he was drunk, Mitch had enough of his faculties remaining to know that didn't make sense. "How am I supposed to open it, Saw? Wouldn't it open from the inside?"

"I'm sure it does. And that's where you're going to be."

"How?"

"We saw a boat, a right big one, at the dock by the gate. And that road I showed you, there was a pickup truck parked at the end of it. Only reason they'd need a boat and a truck is because they're making trips to the mainland for supplies."

He looked to Mitch and saw he still hadn't put the pieces together. "So, Mitch, what you're going to do is find them when they're out on a run and get them to bring you back to the island. I want you to find out as much as you can while you're in there. Who's in charge. What type of weaponry they have. Anything that might be important. Then, when we show up on January 15, you open the doors for us and we take over."

"I can do that once I'm inside, but I'm still not sure about getting in. How do we know they'll take me back with them? Or do you want me to do it by force, like hold a gun to the ship driver's head?"

This was going to be the tricky part. Saw hoped Mitch was loyal enough, and drunk enough, to go along with it.

"No, you can't come off as dangerous. No one will trust you if you shove a gun in their face. You got to be sympathetic. Completely unthreatening."

"I think I can do that."

"I know you can, Mitch, because you're going to be injured. Unless they're a bunch of total savages, they wouldn't let some kid who's hurt out there to fend himself. Of course, they'll take you in."

Saw watched Mitch as he furrowed his brow and considered this.

"Okay. That makes sense."

"Good. Now get out of the car."

Mitch did and Saw followed. They stood in the middle of the road. "Just remember, we'll be coming January 15 at dawn. So, have that gate open."

"That's almost two months away. You won't forget about me, will you?"

Saw grinned. Even though his rotten chiclet teeth weren't reassuring, he followed it up by putting his arm around Mitch's shoulder and that did the trick. "Absolutely not, Mitchy. You're like my son. I'd never abandon you."

Mitch surprised him by leaning in to Saw and embracing him. Saw hugged him back and, with his free hand, pulled a straight razor from his pocket.

"Are you ready now?"

Mitch let go and nodded.

"You might want to close your eyes. This is apt to hurt."

Mitch obeyed. Saw placed the blade first against his left cheek, an inch or so below his eye, then swept it down in an arc that connected with the teen's mouth. He was so quick and fluid with his movement that it was finished before the blood began to flow, but that followed within a second.

Mitch gasped, too shocked to scream, and raised his hand to his face. Saw quickly repeated the action on his right cheek but before he could finish, Mitch collapsed to his knees. Now he screamed. Shrieked. A sound so loud it made a woodpecker flee from a nearby tree and flutter away. Blood poured from the wounds and formed a puddle underneath him.

Saw rested his hand on the back of Mitch's head, running his fingers through his hair. "It's alright, Mitchy. You'll be alright. Just remember now, January 15."

The boy was sobbing as Saw returned to the Subaru, but Saw ignored him.

Don't worry, Mitchy. I'll make a man out of you yet.

Saw did a U-turn in the middle of the road, and drove away. He was almost certain you couldn't bleed to death from cuts on your face. Ninety percent, at least. And if he was wrong, so be it. He'd come prepared to smash down that gate if it was necessary.

He returned to the overlook and waited. Hours turned into days which became a week. Finally, on the tenth day, he saw the boat speeding away from the island. He watched in the telescope as it docked and three men moved from the boat to the truck. A few hours later the truck returned and Saw watched as a big man carried a much smaller man from it. They boarded the boat and sped toward the island. He didn't know what happened to the other two men who left the island and didn't much care because he knew his plan had worked.

"That's my boy, Mitch. I knew you could do it."

He packed away the telescope, casting one more glance toward the island before leaving. "You don't know it yet, but hell is coming."

PART FIVE

CHAPTER FORTY-ONE

The keys felt frigid in Emory's palm, like a handful of ice cubes, and he quickly dropped them into his coat pocket.

"Thank you for these."

Delphine nodded as a gust of wind caught her white hair and blew it across her face. "Least I can do. Especially if what you think is true."

Emory had heard rumors about Delphine's keys, and had noticed how she always seemed to come and go where and when she pleased. After he told her what he'd witnessed, she was quick to offer her assistance.

"Now go to Wim. Tell him to wait outside of the clinic and if I'm not out by 1:30 to come in and get me."

"You sure you ain't better off taking him with?"

Emory shook his head. Yes, *he* probably - no, certainly - would be safer with Wim at his side, but it was too risky. It wasn't long ago that Wim had been sentenced to almost certain death for defying Doc's orders. If he got caught breaking into the lab... Emory didn't have to guess what the punishment would be. He wouldn't take that chance. He loved Wim too much to risk his life on what might be the delusions of an old fool.

"No. This was my grand scheme and I bear the responsibility to carry it out and accept any consequences that might occur."

"If you say so."

Delphine left him then, and Emory's grand plan went into action. Oftentimes, as the years became decades, he'd thought that being old was the next best thing to being invisible. People ignored you, maybe because you were a walking embodiment of their own fears of aging. The upside to this was coming and going without anyone paying too close attention, and in the dim moonlight, it was even easier than expected to make his way to the medical clinic unnoticed. Once there, Delphine's keys opened all the locks, including those to steel double doors that were located at the far end of the clinic. It took considerable effort for Emory to swing them open and, when he did, he revealed a long, downward sloping corridor. The grade was so steep that he needed to slow his gait to half its usual lackadaisical pace.

A bright light illuminated the end of the corridor. The vision brought Emory back to the afternoon when he had to flee the tunnel after crashing his Mercedes. That had been one of the worst days of his long life and wasn't a memory he cared to relive. As he neared the light, the room came into view and helped him push those thoughts aside.

When he stepped into Doc's lab, his first observations were of the sheet covered steel gurneys which stood out in stark contrast against the gleaming white walls and floors. He knew immediately that the sheets covered bodies and, after making sure there was no one in the room, he went to them. Along the way, he saw marker boards covered with notes, dates, and diagrams. Sketches of human-esque figures, people with four arms, no legs, two heads, it was like a demented child's sketchbook and it made Emory feel ill.

"What perverse mind came up with this..." But he knew all too well who was responsible.

Emory approached the first gurney where the sheet was sunken down in the middle, like a valley in between the rolling hills of the human form. He peeled back the sheet, first revealing the dead, gray face of a zombie. Its eyes snapped open and it attempted to lunge toward him, but straps held it to the table. Emory pulled the rest of the sheet away, discovering that the creature was unclothed. Its midsection had been splayed open, all the organs and intestines gone, leaving behind just a black, putrid hole through which he could see the zombie's spine.

The sight horrified and disgusted him. He was ready to flee. This was proof enough of Doc's madness, but Emory had always possessed a healthy sense of curiosity and, with six more tables, he found it impossible to resist. He remembered Grant watching *Let's Make a Deal* on many afternoons. Are you going home with the zombie you already have or do you want to see what's under sheet number two? Let's try sheet number two. I'm feeling lucky.

There, he found a zombie whose head had belonged to a white man but its body was that of a black woman. The head had been sewn on so crudely that the stitches gaped apart and black fluid oozed out as it strained toward Emory.

The third reveal was a zombie with its rib cage split open and its heart missing. The fourth uncovered a man with every bit of flesh stripped off his body, all the muscles and tendons exposed. It stared at Emory through lidless eyes, its mouth opening in a pained growl.

Leave now, he thought. Go to Wim and tell him what's happening.

But there were still two gurneys to go.

Emory grabbed the fifth sheet, but before he could sweep it away he heard a voice behind him.

"They are some of my earlier work."

Emory spun around and saw Doc watching him. The man stepped toward him.

"I'm not terribly proud of them, but even DaVinci had to start somewhere."

"How could you?"

"Oh, it was quite simple really." Doc motioned to the zombie that had been disemboweled. "He was the first. One day, the question came to mind, do zombies shit?"

Doc was beside him and Emory took an instinctive step away. He didn't want to be close to this deviant.

"After all, they're voracious eaters. That's pretty much all they do. Eat. So, when they eat, where does all that meat go? I decided to find out. I had Phillip bring me a zombie and fed it can after can of chicken. Apparently, it was close enough in flavor to human flesh to suffice. Maybe we don't taste like chicken. Maybe chicken tastes like us. There's a question for you." Doc cackled at his own joke.

"After feeding it, I waited and waited. And waited some more. As it turns out, the digestive system of a zombie is quite slow. Nearly twenty-six hours passed but sure enough, zombies do shit. Perhaps that's why they walk so awkwardly, their pants must be full of it."

Another cackle. Emory thought the man seemed to be in love with the sound of his own voice.

"Once I knew that their bowels worked, I wanted to see what happened with the stomach and intestines removed. Would it die? Or cease eating?"

Doc took a bag of what looked like pale colored jerky and held it toward the zombie's mouth. Its head darted toward it and Doc pulled back with a gleeful grin. "Now, now, wait until its properly tendered." He eased the meat forward, then deposited it into the zombie's open, waiting mouth. "As you can see, they still eat."

Doc moved to the zombie with its chest open. "You take out their heart, they carry on. Lungs are equally expendable, if you were wondering." He headed toward the black and white zombie. "I cut this fellow's head off with a common handyman's saw. I thought for sure it would destroy it but that head remained alert. Hungry. We had her body lying around so I decided to play Dr. Frankenstein. I didn't even need a bolt of lightning. Just slap them together and on they go. It's like the easiest jigsaw puzzle ever made."

Doc discussed all of this with the nonchalance of a mechanic talking about swapping out engines. Emory supposed, to this madman, that's all he was doing. To Doc, these weren't human beings, they were toys and this lab was his playroom.

"Why though? What would possess you to do this?"

"Boredom mostly. Little boys pull the wings off flies or burn ant hills for the same reason."

"But the people here respect you. They practically worship you. Isn't that enough?"

Doc scoffed. "The people here are imbeciles. How could I ever be satisfied leading this group of dolts around by their noses. They're only alive because I saved them. And do you know how I found most of them? Advertisements in the tabloids."

"'The end of the world is nigh! Do you want a safe haven? A place where you can start anew? Apply now!'"

"Fools. All of them. I probably could have done a better job of choosing people to save, but this bunch is easy enough to manipulate. They haven't even realized that I was the one to unleash the virus in the first place."

Emory had suspected this ever since Wim told him about the red circle he'd seen on Doc's calendar, but knowing it was true wasn't the relief he'd expected. It only brought more horror. He wondered how much time had gone by. Shouldn't Wim be coming now?

"So, all of this is because of you?"

"Impressive, isn't it?"

"My God." Emory didn't know what else to say. The jubilance Doc displayed over being able to brag over these horrible accomplishments was unlike anything he could have ever imagined.

"God? He's a lightweight. It took him 14 billion years to make this world and I brought it to its knees in less than three." Doc clapped his hands together. "But wait, there's more."

He moved to one of the covered zombies, grabbed the white sheet and pulled it off with the flair of a magician. "I'm calling this one, 'mother', for obvious reasons."

The pregnant woman looked toward Emory and he realized she was alive - really alive. Her distended midsection looked almost big enough to burst and when Emory examined her closer, he could spy movement, tiny hands and feet pressing against the skin of her belly from the inside.

"The sperm was harvested from that fellow over there." Doc motioned to the skinless zombie. "He didn't mind. In fact, I think he rather enjoyed it. Anyway, a little back alley invitro and eight months later, here we are."

Doc patted the bulbous belly. Emory thought he saw one of the hands inside reach toward him but told himself that was impossible. Then again, looking at this abomination, was anything truly impossible? He was no longer sure.

"I'm quite excited to see what she births. Boy, girl. Human, zombie. Some sort of hybrid. The options are practically endless."

Tears leaked from the woman's eyes and Emory had to turn away. He couldn't handle any more.

When he turned, he saw Phillip standing in the background. His heartbeat quickened and pain shot through his chest. It's time, Wim. Don't wait. Get in here.

"You're a monster," Emory said to Doc. "And sooner or later they'll all know. Ramey will see what you really are."

"Yes, Ramey. She's been a massive disappointment. Once, I thought perhaps she'd be able to follow in my footsteps but she lacks the vision. A sad case, that one. But that's fine. My legacy will carry on in other ways. Regardless, I'm tired of this Scooby Do villain speech and no one's going to ride to your rescue at the last minute. Let's get on with it."

Phillip grabbed Emory around the neck, his forearm digging into his windpipe and making him cough.

"Don't suffocate the old fool, Phillip. That wouldn't be any fun."

Phillip's grip loosened enough to let him breathe.

Doc pulled a cotton swab from his lab coat and dipped it into the open mouth of the gutless zombie. He swabbed it around and, when he extracted it, the swab was dripping slimy yellow saliva.

"I still haven't solved the mystery of why people who were immune to the airborne version are susceptible to bites. I think the concentration of the virus is higher in the saliva. Their mouths are basically Petri dishes. Perhaps that's the reason, but no one seems immune to this."

Please, Wim. Please come. We're running out of time.

Doc moved to him, holding the swab at chest level. "It doesn't take an actual bite, of course. Just transference of the saliva." He was in front of Emory now. The swab was inches from his face. "Now say ah for the doctor."

Emory clenched his jaws so hard it made his brittle teeth hurt. Phillip grabbed his chin and tried to pull his mouth open, but Emory surprised even himself by managing to resist.

"Have it your way then."

Doc shoved the swab up Emory's nostril so forceful and fast the old man thought it might poke into his eye socket. Phillip released him and he fell painfully to the floor in a heap.

"Careful, old timer. Don't want to break a hip," Phillip taunted.

Emory pulled the swab from his nose and threw it aside. When he looked up, both men were on their way out of the room.

"What's that hotel say? We'll keep the lights on for you?"

And they were gone.

Emory held his finger over the opposite nostril and blew as hard as possible. Snot and the zombie's yellow, pus-filled saliva shot out his nose and onto the floor and he prayed it wasn't too late.

CHAPTER FORTY-TWO

Wim checked his watch. It was 1:27. He didn't want to wait for the half hour but tried to make himself.

"Getting close now?" Delphine's voice said behind him.

He didn't know how she'd managed to sneak up on him and didn't like it.

She'd come to him earlier that evening, just after he'd finished topping off the troughs with pig feed. She told him that Emory was sneaking in Doc's lab and that he didn't want Wim to know until he was already inside, lest he try to talk him out of it. Wim thought the plan brave but foolhardy and Emory was right, if he'd have known about it ahead of time he'd have not only tried to talk him out of it, he'd have stopped him by force if necessary.

If anyone was venturing into Doc's lab, it should be him, not an eighty-plus year-old man whose arthritis was so bad that he oftentimes couldn't walk more than a few paces in a minute. But it was done and now all he could do was follow his wishes and wait until 1:30. If he wasn't out by then, Wim was going in.

Wim turned to Delphine and noticed how the moonlight made her white hair almost glow. "Three minutes. Perhaps two now."

Delphine nodded then took a puff on a hand rolled cigarette. "Do you expect he'll find anything in there to make a difference?"

"I hope."

"I wouldn't, if I was you. You think the people here will care about what he did? Or what he's doing?"

"Wouldn't you? If it turns out he had a hand in the plague, then you'd be living with the man who killed billions of people. Wouldn't that matter?"

"Depends on your perspective, I suppose. One hand, you could say he's a murderer. Other hand, you could say he's a savior."

"A savior?" Has she lost her marbles?

"He saved them's what I'm saying. To some people, maybe lots a people, that might be more important than the killing."

"I'd hope not." Wim cast another glance at his watch. 1:29.

"People's selfish, Wim, is what I'm telling you. Long as they get something they want, they can overlook a lot of bad."

"Are you selfish?"

"I am. You are too."

"You think so?"

Delphine nodded. "The other day, when you saved all those people from the zombies, twas just one you really cared about. You wanted to prove yourself to Ramey."

"I don't know why you think that."

"Because I know men and they's all the same. You wanted to be a hero for her."

He didn't appreciate this line of questioning and didn't respond.

"Answer me honest. If there was a group of zombies chasing me and another group of zombies chasing her, which of us is you gonna save? You can only pick one."

He looked at her long enough to meet her gaze and immediately wished he hadn't. "Well, I believe Ramey'd have a good chance of taking care of herself."

"I might could too."

"I reckon that might be true. But I'd still watch out for you."

Delphine shook her head. "There's men that are built for lying.

Maybe most of em even. But you ain't one of em Wim, so you best stop trying."

Time was up, thankfully, and he moved toward the clinic. "Nice talking to you, Delphine."

"What I say about lyin?" She smiled a little when she said it.

Wim did too, then he went to see what Emory was up too.

CHAPTER FORTY-THREE

After regaining his footing, Emory managed to stumble out of Doc's lab and into the clinic. The further he walked the clumsier his feet became. Twice he fell and each time getting back up proved more of a challenge than the last. He thought his legs might give out so he took a seat at a desk to recuperate and catch his breath, which seemed to come in shallow, gasping wheezes.

Oftentimes since the epidemic swept the land, he found himself wondering what it was like to fall victim to the virus. What they felt. Whether they knew what was happening to them. Now his questions were getting answered.

There wasn't much pain, which both surprised and relieved him. The arthritis he dealt with daily was much worse. There was a headache, a dull throbbing that felt a bit like a hangover, leaving his head foggy and thoughts slow to come. The thinking was the worst. His memories raced away from him like road signs passed on an interstate. He struggled to remember what happened to him. Where he was. And as minutes passed, who he was.

It came back in flashes. He remembered marrying Wim and Ramey and how happy it made him. Then he remembered Christopher dead after the wreck, crawling soldier style along the pavement with his broken, twisted back. He could see Grant sitting on a dock in Menemsha, eating hot buttered lobster rolls as the setting sun lit him up like an angel. Emory thought he could still taste that lobster, caught fresh from the ocean that very morning, and his mouth flooded with saliva.

So hungry.

He wondered when he'd last eaten. It must have been days because he felt as if he were starving. And the hunger grew and grew, a deep, unrelenting, insatiable need.

Emory could feel his humanity slipping away. There was less of him with each passing moment. All that remained was the hunger. He wanted - needed - to eat. It was all encompassing, all consuming. He had no more thoughts of himself. Of his friends. Of the disease. Every thought he had was the same. Eating.

He rose from the chair on limbs no longer hobbled by pain. Without arthritis to slow him down, he ran.

* * *

WIM TROTTED TOWARD THE CLINIC. CAMP WAS EMPTY AT THIS TIME OF night and that was a relief because he didn't have time to be covert. Even if the Ark had been teeming with people, he doubted he'd care because Emory should have been out by now. He cursed himself for letting Emory go in alone, for taking all the risk upon himself.

The clinic was in view and Wim quickened his pace. He was thirty yards away when the door opened and a bit of light streamed out, silhouetting the tall man exiting the building. He thought it was Phillip. The long, rangy body had the cop's quick, leaning forward gait. Like he was always in a hurry to get somewhere and be a prick.

Wim sidled up beside a construction trailer and watched the man approach.

"If you hurt Emory, so help me God, I'll kill you." He'd killed hundreds of zombies but never a person. And up until now he thought himself incapable. But the very notion of his best friend being hurt by that arrogant son of a bitch flipped a switch inside Wim and he was angrier than he'd ever been before.

He wished he'd have kept one of Delphine's guns as he knew Phillip would be armed. He noticed a toolbox sitting beside the trailer and popped the lid. Inside were an assortment of wrenches, pliers, and hand tools. Wim settled on a screwdriver.

When he peeked around the corner of the trailer he saw Phillip was less than ten yards away. He wanted him gone so that he could continue forward and find his friend, but Phillip kept coming toward the trailer, toward him. Wim gripped the handle of the screwdriver tight in his right hand, in case he had to use it, then waited.

Pass on by, Phillip. Please, pass on by.

But he made a line straight at him. Like he knew he was there. Like he could smell him.

Wim backed away, around the corner, retreating until he neared the backside of the trailer. He could no longer see Phillip but that changed soon enough when the man appeared around the spot where Wim had been watching seconds earlier.

Only it wasn't Phillip. In the moonlight, Wim could see the ebony skin and realized it was Emory. His nerves settled and he broke out in a wide grin.

"My gosh, you had me scared. I— "

Emory kept closing in. Quick. Quicker than Wim had ever seen him move before.

"Emory?"

His old friend was ten feet away. Five.

When he came within arm's reach, Wim got a better look and he felt so sick he thought he might pass out. Emory's eyes were clouded over and gray. His mouth hung open and his tongue sagged out like an overheated dog on a summer day.

This wasn't fair. Emory was one of the best men Wim had ever known and he didn't deserve this. No one did, but especially not him. He wanted to cry but there was no time for that.

Emory was on top of him. Wim held him back, one hand on the

man's shoulder, the other in the middle of his chest. His head bobbed at him, trying to get a bite, but Wim held him out of range.

"Who did this to you?"

At the sound of Wim's voice, Emory cocked his head. His frantic attempts to attack slowed.

"Do you know me?" Wim asked.

Emory's cloudy eyes stared at his face.

Does he remember? Somehow?

"Emory, it's me. Wim."

Whatever recognition Emory may or may not have had disappeared as his upper lip snarled and he bared his teeth. A low, menacing growl rumbled out of his throat and he pushed forward, straining to get him.

"Don't do this. Please."

Wim let himself be pushed back a step, then two. Emory kept fighting, if anything with renewed vigor. Wim had seen so much horror in the last half a year, but this was worse than all of it put together. And he knew he couldn't take much more.

The next time Emory lunged for him, Wim took a step to the side and allowed the man to fall forward. Emory landed face down in the snow and when he crawled back to his knees the front of him was coated in white powder. It stood out in stark contrast to his ink-colored skin.

"I'm so sorry." Wim raised the screwdriver and swung it downward. The tool connected with Emory's skull just above his left ear. With a hard crack, the metal shaft sunk deep into his head. Wim jerked the handle back and forth twice and Emory went limp.

Wim pulled the screwdriver free and threw it into the snow. He grabbed his friend under the arms and raised him up. The now limp body sagged against Wim's chest and Emory's head lolled back and forth before settling down on his shoulder. Wim carried him like that, their faces inches apart, into the night.

CHAPTER FORTY-FOUR

After leaving the old, black man to die, Doc returned to his cabin and attempted to sleep, an act which had proven to be a great chore in recent weeks. His mind never stopped churning. Between ideas for new experiments, and fear of what was happening outside the Ark, he felt like he was awake thirty hours a day. Resting was impossible, but a few barbiturates kept him dead to the world long enough to keep his body functioning.

Even with the pills, he woke early, well before dawn. He was anxious to see what had become of the man and check on his other creations. When he reentered the lab, the first thing he noticed was the sheet on the floor. It was more red than white and had soaked up so much blood that some had drained from it, onto the floor like an over saturated sponge. He looked up from the sheet to the bed and patient it should have been covering.

What he found both excited and disappointed him. His pregnant, human patient was no longer pregnant, nor human. Her belly, which earlier looked almost ready to burst, had done just that. Tendrils of pale flesh rained down over her torso, and as he followed them upward, he saw the gaping hole where her midsection had been. Now it was just a blackened chasm, void of her own organs, as well as the child she'd been carrying.

As Doc moved closer, the woman's hand tried to claw at him but the straps held her at a safe distance. She groaned and growled, her teeth clicking together as she bit the air. He leaned in to examine her and realized the flesh hadn't burst after all. It had been ripped apart. From the inside out.

"Congratulations, ma'am. You're a mother. And it looks like you've given birth to a real fighter."

But, where is it?

Doc crouched down beside the bed, looking under and around it. Nope, no baby here.

How far could it have gotten? It couldn't be more than a few hours old, after all.

He followed the path of blood leading away from the mother. It was like tracking a slug that left a slimy trail in its wake, but after a few yards the blood, and the path, dried up.

Behind him, something metal fell and clattered against the floor. Doc jumped, then spun around and saw an instrument tray, which had been setting on a wheeled cart, had fallen. He rushed to the spot and dropped to his knees and saw nothing.

To his right came a gasp. He turned just in time to see the baby coming at him. It was light gray, the color of dirty dishwater, with black veins crisscrossing under its skin like a roadmap. It looked about a foot and a half in length and its belly was fat.

Not fat. Distended. Full of its mother's flesh. It reminded Doc of a Thanksgiving turkey, ready to carve.

It moved more quickly than Doc could have ever imagined and was only inches away when he swooped out and grabbed it by the nape of its neck. Its eyes narrowed and its tiny palm lashed out. It uttered a squawking hiss, some strange amalgamation of a baby's cry and a zombie's growl.

"There, there, little one," Doc said. "Nothing to be afraid of from me. I'd never dare hurt you."

The creature again hissed and cried, its tiny arms flailing, its legs kicking.

Doc saw its lips were covered in blood with bits of dried intestines stuck to its cheeks like a macabre Papier-mâché mask. He couldn't understand how it had done so much damage, especially in such a short amount of time.

He carried the infant to an examination table and laid it on its back. Then he took a speculum, inserted it into the infant's mouth and pried it open. He gasped at the sight.

"My, oh my. You're a special one indeed, aren't you?"

What Doc saw in the infant's mouth was a full set of tiny, sharp baby teeth. There were even scraps of tissue caught between them.

He held his finger in front of the newborn's mouth. Its head darted up, its tiny jaws clicking together as it tried to catch his digit but ended up with nothing but air. He set the undead infant on an examination table and grabbed an assortment of instruments. This was going to be so much fun.

Doc was prouder of this little mutant than he'd been the day his own daughter had been born. And with any luck, in another eight and a half months, it would have a sibling because, as his latest tests had confirmed, the zombie that Phillip had inseminated was indeed pregnant.

For a man who'd spent most of his working life toiling away, unappreciated, for the pharmaceutical companies, this was even more proof that he was every bit the genius he believed himself to be. He half wished he could bring everyone who'd doubted him back from the dead so they could see his creations. On second thought, he'd rather they stay dead. Those who remained would know his greatness soon enough.

CHAPTER FORTY-FIVE

Mitch – Wayne to those on the Ark – hated the cold, which meant he hated almost everything on the island. What kind of assholes build an end of the world compound in somewhere that has winters like this? Even wearing two pairs of sweatpants and a white parka so thick he looked like a Yeti, he felt like he was going to shiver to death. Could you die from shivering? He thought it certainly might be possible and he didn't want to be the test case.

He picked up the pace as he plodded through the knee-deep snow, which dragged and grasped at his legs as he worked his way to the gate. He wished he'd have taken a snowmobile. Who gave a fuck whether he woke everyone up with the noise. Soon enough Saw'd be here and most of these dickholes would either be dead or bowing at his feet.

It was almost a mile to the gate and that gave him time to think. Maybe too much time. As excited as he was for Saw and the others to arrive, he was still pissed at what the Brit had done to his face. Why didn't he carve up Lonnie or Denny like Christmas hams and send them here to get poked and prodded? Casper, he could understand, that bastard couldn't make a friend if his life depended on it, but the other two would have been fine guinea pigs. So why did Saw put *him* through this ordeal?

He wondered if it was some sort of test. Maybe Saw was trying to find out if he could be trusted. But Mitch thought he'd proved that by ratting out Aben. He didn't like to think about Aben and especially Prince. He missed the both of them. But Mitch was a good soldier and he knew that meant making hard decisions. And that should have proved his loyalty. So maybe this was all about trying to see if Mitch was tough enough. He knew the other men considered him a kid. Maybe Saw did too and this was the gauntlet he had to run to get his man card. After everything he'd been through, they better tell him he passed with flying fucking colors.

He was close enough to the gate to see it. And he saw Nestor's truck idling beside it, the tailpipe spewing white steam.

Way to waste gas, dickface.

When Mitch was within twenty feet, Nestor rolled down the truck window and waved. He had a big smile plastered to his wide, dopey face.

"Heya Wayne. What are you doing all the way out here?"

Mitch crossed the last few feet and leaned against the door. He could feel the heat radiating out and tried to lean in to be closer to it.

"Doc told me to exercise. Said it would be good for my recovery. Stronger my body is, the better it is for my immune system." He thought some of that might make sense, especially to this borderline retard.

"Well, if Doc said that, I'm sure he's right."

God, how stupid could these people be? "Think I can join you for a sec? My toes feel like ice cubes."

"Sure thing. Climb on up."

Mitch circled around the front of the truck and joined Nestor. The man tilted a thermos in his direction. "Coffee?"

"Thanks," Mitch took a sip. It was so hot he thought it might blister his tongue but it chased away some of the cold. He held the thermos tight to his body, trying to absorb the heat from it.

"Face is looking pretty good, buddy."

Mitch checked his reflection in the mirror on the visor. Nestor was lying. Even with the stitches gone, he looked like a patchwork quilt. Dark purple scars curved upward, starting at the corners of his mouth and ending just below his eyes. The one on the right side went askew and veered off toward his ear at the end. Saw couldn't even make his mauling symmetrical.

"It's getting there."

"I'm real glad you pulled through, Wayne. You're one of the good guys."

Nestor fished through a paper sack at his feet and pulled out a plastic bowl. "Hardboiled egg? I got two."

"Nah, that's okay, Nestor. I'm still working up an appetite."

"Okay then."

Nestor cracked one of the eggs on the dashboard and peeled off the shell, meticulous as he tried to get every last piece off.

Mitch was glad he was distracted because that allowed him to pull the fork from his pocket unnoticed. Mitch had filched it from the mess hall earlier that week. He bent the two inner tines back and forth until they snapped off. Then, he scraped the outer tines against a brick for a few days until they were so sharp he could prick his finger just by tapping it against the tips.

Nestor had finished peeling the egg and he popped the whole thing into his mouth. As he chewed, he held the other out to Mitch.

"Sure, you don't want it?" Tiny bits of partially masticated yellow and white egg spilled from his lips as he spoke through the mouthful of food.

"I'm good. Maybe Wim wants it though."

Mitch pointed out the driver's side window, feigning a wave. Nestor turned to look and, when he did, Mitch plunged the fork into the man's throat.

Hot blood spurted from the wound, spraying the dash, the windshield, Mitch's hand.

Nestor turned back to him, his eyes wide and confused. He opened his mouth.

"Way— "

Egg and blood tumbled out, preventing him from saying the name. Mitch watched the man as he choked and bled out. He didn't struggle as much as Mitch had expected. In under a minute, it was over.

Mitch exited the truck, walked to the gate, and lifted the lever which held it closed. He tried to push it open, but the snow was too deep, too heavy. He thought he made a mistake in killing Nestor so soon. He should have made the dumbass open the gate first.

Mitch returned to the truck but went to the driver's side this time. He opened the door and grabbed Nestor's coat, pulling him out of the truck where he tumbled into the snow. Then Mitch took his place behind the steering wheel.

He put the truck in gear and turned it so it was facing the gate. Then he eased forward until the grill pressed against the wood. Slowly he crept forward, pushing the fifteen-foot-wide gate until it was the whole way open.

Mitch looked ahead, toward the vast, featureless sea of ice that lay ahead.

"I did my part, Saw. Now it's your turn."

Mitch turned the Chevy toward the Ark. He knew driving the truck back to camp might arouse some suspicion but didn't feel like trudging through the snow again. Besides he'd just started to warm up and didn't feel like getting cold all over again. And if they suspected anything, so what? Soon they'd all be dead anyway.

CHAPTER FORTY-SIX

The hollow, metallic crack of the trailer door slamming against the outside wall woke Ramey. She sat up in bed, reached across the mattress and realized she was alone. The bed was cool under her touch.

Where'd you go, Wim?

The door banged again. Closed, this time.

Ramey reached for the light switch but she still wasn't used to sleeping in this room and couldn't find it in the dark.

"Wim?" She pushed the covers off herself, the cold air hitting her legs and making them break out in goosebumps. She was already tired of winter and it had barely begun.

Wim hadn't answered and that bothered her. She slid off the bed, pulling her nightshirt down as far as it would stretch, not that it did much to keep away the cold.

She was half way to the bedroom door when she heard the floor creak under heavy footsteps. She smiled, relieved.

"Come back to bed alre— "

A shadow filled the door frame but she immediately knew it was too slender to be Wim.

"I've been waiting to hear that for a long time."

Phillip stepped into the room. Ramey could see his big, wolfish teeth gleaming in the moonlight.

"Get out of here," she snapped. "Get out of our house."

"Oh, Ramey, it's not a house, it's a trailer. I know you're white trash but even you should understand the difference."

She couldn't believe her ears. Was he drunk? That was the only reason she could imagine him being so brazen.

"Get out right now. If you're here when Wim gets back, he'll beat the shit out of you and I won't even think about stopping him."

Instead of fleeing he moved closer to her. His breath hit her face. It smelled of tuna fish - his usual - but no alcohol. Somehow that made the situation more unnerving. Ramey realized her goosebumps now weren't caused by the cold. They were caused by fear.

She glanced around the room, looking for something she could use as a weapon if it came to that. Pillows, sheets, a paperback novel. Even the lamp was only a few inches tall and weighed mere ounces. She hated that she'd grown so comfortable and complacent.

Ramey took a few steps back until she hit the bed and ran out of room.

"Trying to run off on me, Ramey? That's no way to treat a guest. Pretty rude, don't you think?"

Phillip was less than an arm's length away. She was out of room. Out of time.

Time.

Ramey stole a glance toward the end table and spotted the wind up, metal alarm clock. Wim used it to wake up at some ungodly early hour so he could care for the animals.

"How about you lay down and spread 'em so I can show you how a real man fucks?" Phillip leaned in closer, pursing his lips.

"Fuck you!"

"Is that a promise?"

"Sure."

Ramey reached back, grabbed the alarm clock and immediately spun and swung. It connected with Phillip's eyebrow, opening a three-inch gash. The blood spilled from the cut into his eye, turning it red.

She didn't stick around to see the aftermath, jumping onto the bed, taking two steps then leaping off the other side. She made it to the door when she heard the distinctive sound of a round being chambered into a pistol.

"Bad idea, girly."

She took another step. One foot in the hallway.

"I'll blow your pretty head off."

Ramey half turned back to him. "Then you'd have to answer to my father. What do you think he'd say about that?"

"Probably 'job well done.'"

She saw something in his eyes, even through the blood, that made her think he was right. Or that he believed he was right. Either way, she decided running was a bad decision as long as the pistol was aimed at her.

"Okay. Then what happens now?"

"First you put on some shoes. Then you come with me."

Ramey knew this was bad news. She wanted no part of whatever Phillip had planned but for the time being, she had to placate him.

* * *

EMORY HAD OFTEN TOLD WIM ABOUT THE FIELD OF BLACK-EYED Susan's toward the east side of the Ark but Wim had never seen it in person. The way he described it, it was one of the most beautiful sights around. But the flowers were gone now, just barely tan, lifeless husks. Yellow tufts of fountain grass poked up from the snow and their feathery ends caught the wind, swaying back and forth peacefully. Wim wasn't a hundred percent sure he had the right spot, but he believed he was in the right neighborhood.

He eased Emory's body into the snow. Carrying it all the way out here, even through the deeper drifts, hadn't been as much of a physical challenge as he'd expected as the old man barely weighed anything. The emotions, however, were harder to handle. As Wim had carried his friend, he was unable to wipe away his tears and they'd frozen against his cheek in salty rivulets. Now he sat down beside Emory's body and picked the ice away with his fingernails.

"Why'd you have to go in there by yourself? Why didn't you tell me what you were planning to do?"

Wim knew Emory could offer no answers to his questions. And he knew crying about the situation wasn't going to change anything. He wished he could get Ramey and Mina. They deserved a chance to say their own goodbyes, and he could also use their support, but he didn't want to risk one of Doc's people seeing this scene and Doc claiming the body.

Wim took Emory's glasses off his face and carefully placed them in his pocket. Before he'd left camp, he'd taken a can of lighter fluid. Now he popped the top and aimed the can at Emory, spraying it over his body.

"I'm sorry about this. I wish I could give you the Christian burial you deserve, but I don't think anything short of a backhoe is getting through the ground right now."

Wim wished he could think of something profound to say. Some heartfelt words that could honor Emory and give him a proper send off. He hated himself for not being smart enough to come up with anything. Emory was a man who deserved to be honored. Wim could only hope the man knew how much he loved him when he was alive.

He then took out a book of matches and tore one off. He used his hands to shield it from the wind as he struck it, then used the lone match to set the whole pack ablaze. When he was confident it wouldn't go out, Wim held it against Emory's jacket which caught fire. The flames spread out in every direction and within seconds Emory's entire body was engulfed.

Wim backed away, then sprayed more lighter fluid into the fiery inferno. The orange flames reached up, like fingers grasping at the air. Wim tossed the can into the blaze and turned his back on it. He wiped fresh tears from his face and heard a pop as the can blew. The heat of the fire was so intense he felt sweat break out on his back.

CHAPTER FORTY-SEVEN

Phillip had secured Ramey's hands behind her back with zip ties. He'd allowed her to slip on a pair of boots but no coat and the near half mile walk to the clinic left her almost. By the time he pushed her into the building, she thought she might need medical treatment.

She hadn't seen anyone during the trek and that worried her. Where was Wim? She wondered if, somehow, Phillip had gotten to him. That couldn't be true though. She wouldn't allow herself to go there.

It took her eyes a few moments to adjust to the florescent lights. Why were they on anyway? She was sure they were always shut off at night.

Phillip closed the door behind them and locked it. He moved to a bin filled with medical supplies and grabbed a long bandage.

"Put it on," he said.

She considered protesting, but decided that would be unwise.

The cut on his brow had stopped bleeding. It appeared almost frozen. As she removed it from the paper packaging, she realized he was staring at her chest - at her cold nipples which poked against the thin fabric of her shirt.

Ramey slapped on the bandage and gave it an extra hard push to stick it down, hoping to cause him as much discomfort as possible. Much to her dismay, Phillip barely flinched.

What was up with him? Why was he so calm? The last few weeks he'd been nervous almost to the point of twitchy. It was like the real Phillip was tucked away in a pod somewhere and this man before her was an impostor.

"Will you at least tell me why you brought me here? If you wanted to rape me you could've done that at the trailer."

Phillip opened his mouth to answer, but then his eyes drifted past her.

"Rape?" It was her father's voice and it came from the edge of the room. Ramey turned to see him standing at the opening to a long corridor.

"No need to disparage the young man's character. He was simply doing as told."

Phillip backed away from her as Doc neared them.

Doc noticed the wound and raised an eyebrow. "Fist?"

"Alarm clock," Ramey said with pride.

Doc nodded. "Ah." He pointed to a metal cabinet with a red cross on it. "Get some ibuprofen and give us some time alone."

Phillip did as told, locking the door as he left. Ramey wasn't as relieved to see him go as she'd expected. After almost dying multiple times trying to find her father, she suddenly had no desire to be alone with him. And deep down, even though she was reluctant to admit it to herself, she was afraid of him.

Doc stared at her for a long while. It only added to her discomfort and Ramey found herself again tugging at the shirt. Doc noticed and finally spoke up.

"Oh Heavens, Ramey. I was there when you were born. I changed your diapers. Don't be so bashful."

That sounded a little more like her father and some of the apprehension she'd built up faded. "I asked Phillip and he wouldn't answer. So, will you tell me why I'm here?"

Doc's face turned sober. "I'm afraid I have some bad news to share. There's been another death."

He sat down on a metal stool with casters on the bottom and used his toes to sway back and forth.

Oh God. Not Wim. Not after everything we've been through.

She didn't want to say it aloud though. That would be giving into her father who was enjoying this self-created suspense all too much. She bit the inside of her lip and refused to allow herself to say anything,

Doc looked disappointed that she wouldn't take his bait. "Your friend. The Afro-American fellow."

"Emory?" Ramey could barely get the word out. Her mind was a roller coaster of emotion. She was thanking God repeatedly that it wasn't Wim but poor Emory. So gentle and caring and sweet. If her own father had a tenth of Emory's compassion the Ark would be an entirely different place.

"Yes, that's him. Apparently, the old fellow's ticker finally gave out. Sad."

Ramey felt her eyes sting like they'd just been doused in gasoline and tears quickly followed. She looked down at the floor, not wanting her father to see her pain.

Doc pulled himself to her, still not rising from his seat. He set his hand on her knee. "It's okay to cry. I know you were fond of him. That you admired him. So much so that you chose him to marry you and William."

Ramey's head snapped up. Doc looked like a hazy mirage through her tears. Was he smiling?

"Yes, I know all about that. I'm hurt that I wasn't invited. I'd have brought a nice gift, I assure you"

"How?"

Doc pushed himself away. The stool carried him a few yards from her and he held his arms out to the side like he was flying. "Please, now. Do you think so little of me to believe that anything happens here without my knowledge? For Christ's sake, Ramey, I created this world!" Anger colored his voice. "I am all-knowing and all seeing."

He stood up so quick the stool skittered away, rolling until it clattered to a stop against a wall.

"So, what, you think you're God now?"

"If the title fits. Although I think that's a bit of an understatement myself. God, at least for the last two thousand years, has been a supervisor. He lets his underlings drive the action. I prefer to be more hands on." He grinned, nostrils flaring.

Doc strolled toward the corridor. "Come. I have such sights to show you."

* * *

IT WAS BARELY DUSK WHEN SAW STOPPED HIS DUMP TRUCK AT THE EDGE of the ice. It looked solid enough, but he wanted to be certain so he grabbed a sledgehammer from the empty passenger seat and brought it with as he jumped down from the cab. The frigid wind caressed his cheeks and he realized he couldn't stop smiling.

Three tractor trailers approached from behind him. He held up his hand for them to wait. Casper was in the first rig and he nodded, the brakes screeching as he came to a full stop.

Saw stepped onto the ice which had taken on the pinkish red cast thrown by the morning sunrise. The whole sky was lit up with it. Saw thought it was beautifully fitting for the blood which was to come. He raised the sledge over his head and brought it down with all the strength he possessed. It slammed into the ice, the force of the blow pulsing up his arms. But the hammer had made little more than a divot in the thick ice. Saw grinned and licked his blackened teeth.

He returned to land and motioned for the men to roll down their windows. They did.

"Ice is hard, mates. Plenty strong enough for us here but further out, who knows. Once you start driving, I expect you not to stop until we hit the island. You push those pedals to the floor and don't even think about slowing down. Because today's the day we're taking what's theirs and making it ours."

That bought a cheer from Denny and Lonnie. Caspar only watched with blank, emotionless eyes.

"Are you ready?"

Lonnie hit his air horn as an answer. The others followed.

Saw returned to his dump truck, shifted it into gear and drove onto the ice. It held.

In his rear-view mirror, he saw the others follow. Casper first, then Lonnie, with Denny bringing up the rear. They fanned out so the four vehicles were in a mostly straight row.

Saw shifted again, picking up speed. He could feel the wheels slipping under him but that only made him drive faster.

The other trucks followed suit, barreling across the ice and rapidly closing in on the island. White clouds of displaced snow rose around them like a fog that chased them as they drove, obscuring the bottom halves of the trucks and making the rigs look as if they were floating across the frozen lake.

Saw could feel his pulse pounding, could hear it in his ears. He'd been wanting this fight for months. Ever since he saw the island for the first time. Whether they had twenty cans of soup or enough food and supplies to last a decade didn't matter to him. His men might want their provisions, but all Saw cared about was battling men who could fight back. He'd grown bored with the zombies who were too stupid to even care when you killed them. He wanted - needed - to cause pain. It had been too long.

* * *

ABOUT THREE FOURTHS OF THE WAY TO THE ISLAND, SAW CAUGHT Lonnie's rig swaying to his left. That quickly escalated as the truck jackknifed and the trailer spun around. When he took a closer look, he realized what was happening. The ice under Lonnie's truck was giving way. The tires shrieked against the ice, spewing wet clouds as it ripped through the surface.

"It's breaking, Saw! I'm gonna fall through!" Lonnie's voice squawked through the CB radio.

Jimmy's voice, full of panic, crackled through the speaker. "Saw, we've got to help him!"

Saw looked sideways and saw Jimmy's rig slowing down and

veering toward Lonnie. He grabbed his CB and pulled it to his mouth, his lips pressed against the cold plastic. It tasted like stale cigarettes.

"Don't slow down, no matter what happens!" He pushed his own gas pedal until it wouldn't go any further, the diesel engine roaring and the pipes belching jet black smoke into the air.

The cab of Lonnie's 18-wheeler dropped and, even over the screaming of his own truck and Lonnie on the radio, Saw could hear the ice break. The next second, Lonnie's rig was gone and a puddle of dirty water erupted from the ragged hole like a wet belch.

Lonnie's squalling continued over the radio and Saw heard Jimmy's voice consoling him and crying as Lonnie went down. He shut off the radio, not interested in the conversation.

To his right, Casper sped along beside him undeterred.

Within minutes the island was in sight and the gate was wide open.

Good boy, Mitchy. I knew I could count on you.

"I'll lead the way, boys," Saw said into the CB. The remaining two trucks fell back and Saw drove through the gate. He spotted a lump of a human form sprawled in the snow and grinned. *Yep, very good boy.*

The tractor trailers entered behind him. The snow was two feet deep but the convoy plowed through it, speeding straight ahead until it reached the center of camp. The spectacle of their arrival had drawn the attention of a dozen or so men and women. Two of them ran but the others stared ahead, shocked and curious and too stupid to move.

Saw jumped out of the dump truck, landing in a puff of snow. He looked at them. "Ladies. Gentlemen. My name is Solomon Baldwin but all me friends call me Saw. It's a pleasure to meet you."

Another person, a middle-aged man, ran, dashing toward one of the several buildings which were laid out to form something like loose concentric circles.

Saw looked behind him and saw Casper and Denny waiting. "He must of heard of me."

Denny laughed. Casper stared blankly ahead.

"Aw right, boys. Let's get this party started."

Saw pulled out his pistol and shot the running man in the back. He fell into a snow drift, then tried to crawl away on his hands and knees.

Caspar and Denny threw open the doors at the rear of their trailers. Then they slammed their hands into the outer walls, banging the aluminum like they were playing the bongos. Saw could hear movement inside. The more his men beat the walls, the louder and more agitated the creatures inside grew.

The first zombie that dropped free was a woman with spiked, red hair. She got up from the snow and looked around like a tourist in some exotic land. Then she saw one of the islanders and headed toward him.

More zombies followed. They poured out of the trucks in a way that reminded Saw of how cartoons depicted lemmings going over cliffs. There were around eighty in all and they hadn't eaten for weeks, Saw had made sure of that. He wanted them good and hungry.

"Now while my zombie friends 'ere get their feet under them, let me explain how this works. You folks can either stay here and do whatever I can tell you to do, or you can run, in which case then you'll get eaten. The choice is yours."

A woman sprinted away. Two others followed. The best part, Saw thought, was that there was nowhere to go. They thought they were safe on this island. Only now did they realize they were trapped.

Casper poked a few zombies in the back with a makeshift spear and sent them in the direction of the runners.

The other islanders stayed.

Saw smiled at them. "Wise decision." He turned to Denny and motioned to a wood sided building. "Put them in there."

Denny shuffled them toward it.

Saw turned to Casper. "Break down the door to every other building on the island. We want our horde to have free reign."

Casper kicked open the door to an Airstream camper. A man inside screamed as two zombies charged through the opening.

Overhead, a siren started to wail. Saw grinned. "They put some music on for us, mates. How considerate."

The man who'd been in the Airstream fell out the open doorway.

His right arm was spurting blood from several large bite wounds. The zombies followed him back into the snow and descended upon them. Saw took in the chaos surrounding him, proud as could be of what he'd started.

* * *

WHEN SHE STEPPED INTO THE LABORATORY, RAMEY COULDN'T understand what she was seeing. The men and women who roamed through the white room were zombies, but unlike any she'd seen before. They were mutated and mangled, their bodies cut apart and sewn together like someone had snipped photos from a magazine, torn them to pieces, then taped them back together haphazardly.

She gasped when she saw them, but when she noticed her father's behavior, the situation turned even worse and more bizarre. He looked at them, not with fear or disgust, but with pride. He was beaming with it.

"What the hell have you been doing down here?"

Doc turned to her, a lunatic's smile on his face. "Creating, of course. Aren't they grand?"

He's gone mad.

Ramey wondered when it happened. He couldn't have always been this crazy. Surely, she would have noticed. She couldn't have been that blind, could she?

Doc moved away from her toward the corner of the lab where a plastic tote sat on metal shelving unit.

A zombie with two heads came toward Ramey. She stumbled backward.

"Don't be afraid of them. I've removed all their teeth. They're harmless as kittens."

She looked closer and saw their lips curved inward over empty gums. "I can't believe this is what you've been doing all these months. You're sick."

"What would you have suggested I do, Ramey?"

"Why not try to find a cure?"

Doc turned to face her. "Oh please. Do you really think it was just some happy coincidence that I built the Ark mere years before the zombie apocalypse? You're smarter than that Ramey." He stepped toward her, clutching the towels. Ramey stepped back.

"I don't want to cure the disease. I made it."

Ramey's mind was reeling. He did this? Everyone who had died? It was all because of her own father. She couldn't comprehend it. She realized she was crying.

"Why would you do this? To prove you're smarter than everyone? To be infamous? Or did you hate everyone that much?"

"What's the point in limiting myself to just one?"

Doc sat back against the counter. "Really, Ramey, tell me why what I did was so wrong? Mankind before the plague was already lost. You had religions blowing up people because their messiah promised them sex with virgins. You had maniacs running countries, starving their own citizens. People like your mother were so pathetic that they'd sell their own bodies to get whatever they needed to feed their addictions. They spent more time looking at memes on their phones than talking to people they supposedly loved. People didn't value each other. Humanity desperately needed a wakeup call and I gave it to them.

Ramey couldn't handle the sound of his voice. The noise made her want to puke. The sight of him was even worse, because in his face she could see herself. "I hate you."

"I'll add you to the list."

Ramey turned to the door. She'd had enough, heard enough. Her fingertips hit the lock and started to turn it.

"Ramey, one more moment, please. That's all I ask of you."

Go. Run. Don't listen to him.

But she turned around.

Doc held up a bundle of towels and she realized the towels were swaddling a baby. Doc had raised a red bottle to its lips and it drank.

"This is my greatest achievement thus far. She was born just a few hours ago."

"Oh my God. Are you feeding it blood?"

Doc bobbed his head. "She can eat meat in small amounts, but I believe this provides more nourishment."

Ramey got closer. She could see the baby now. The black veins standing out against its pale skin, the wispy bits of hair that sprouted from its head, its cheeks as they sunk it and puffed out with each sucking mouthful and swallow.

She grabbed Doc's hand, the one that held the bottle and tried to pull it away. "Stop it! You can't do this!"

The baby opened its eyes. They were gray and lifeless, yet somehow, still hungry.

Ramey's breath caught in her throat when she saw them.

Doc looked down on the baby, smiling. "She has her father's eyes."

Ramey looked at the zombies that wandered about the room and found the one with its stomach shredded. She realized it had given birth, if you could call it that, to this monstrosity. She couldn't imagine how that was even possible.

Doc motioned to a gurney where another zombie was strapped to a table. There was a barely noticeable incline in its profile at the midsection. "That one is Phillip's breeder. She's two months along now! I'm hoping it's a boy. They can be the Adam and Eve of the new world."

Ramey had seen enough. She turned to run, but as she did a red light flipped on, bathing the white room in its crimson luminescence. A moment later, the siren wailed.

CHAPTER FORTY-EIGHT

The sirens woke Mina from a sound sleep and she bolted upright in bed.

"The zombies are back, Birdie. This time they's gone eat you," her father's voice said.

She realized he might be right. The last time the siren went off, it was because of zombies. Then, Wim and Delphine saved the day but could that possibly happen again? Sooner or later their luck was bound to run out. In many - most - ways, her luck had run out a long time ago.

She wrapped the sheet around herself as she moved from her bedroom, across the narrow hall to Emory's room. The door was closed and she lightly rapped her knuckles against it.

No response came.

She knocked again. "Emory? Don't you hear that?

No answer.

Emory wasn't normally a sound sleeper. He was an early riser too which made the fact that he was still in bed unusual. Mina turned the knob, eased the door open, and saw the room was empty.

His bed either hadn't been slept in or he'd already made it. She hoped the latter as she moved up the hall and into the kitchen.

There was no coffee brewing. No dirty cups in the sink.

This is bad.

"Damn right its bad. Zombie's got him just like the got your last boyfriend."

"Shut up!" She screamed out loud.

In her head, her daddy laughed and laughed.

Mina grabbed a jar of pickles from the countertop and hurled it against the wall. Juice and glass and bits of exploded gherkins flew through the air, covering everything from the floor to the ceiling in the tiny kitchenette. Mina knew she'd have to clean up the mess and that just made her angrier.

She reached for a plate. Why stop now? But noise outside the trailer drew her attention. She realized Emory must be outside, listening to her throw a tantrum like a crazy person. She didn't bother with the plate and instead moved to the door.

As Mina opened it, she expected to see Emory's wrinkled, kind face but instead she saw zombies. Half a dozen of them. Their faces unfamiliar except for the fact that they were dead. Mina stumbled backward, slamming the door closed.

"Told ya, Birdie! But you never did listen to your daddy."

Mina closed her eyes. She was imagining this. It wasn't real. Maybe it was a dream and she'd wake up again in her bed only this time everything would be quiet and the smell of brewing coffee would fill her nostrils. That's right, only a dream. Nothing to be scared about.

Hands banged against the thin metal door of the mobile home. More joined it. Soon it was like a band of undead drummers hammering away.

Mina realized it wasn't a dream but she still kept her eyes closed.

* * *

WIM WAS A HUNDRED YARDS FROM THE CENTER OF CAMP, CRESTING A small bluff when he saw the tractor trailers. He realized the siren had nothing to do with his Viking-esque send off for his friend. The Ark was under attack.

In the distance, he could see people running. But there were too many. There were no more than forty people left on the Ark. He saw two times that many figures. Maybe three. He squinted, trying to make out details but the distance was too great for his aging eyes to find any. But he knew whatever was happening was bad.

He made his way to Delphine's cabin. The door hung ajar and he crept toward it with caution. For once, he was happy to have snow because it muffled the sound of his approach. He listened carefully but could hear nothing aside from the siren. Wim took a deep breath and stepped into the cabin.

He realized he was alone. The cabin looked ransacked and her cache of firearms was strewn across the floor. Wim wasn't sure how many she'd had before this, but all the pistols and revolvers were gone. All that remained were three rifles and a shotgun. He took a bolt action Remington 770, loaded it, and shoved as many .30-06 cartridges into his pockets as would fit. He wasn't as comfortable with that particular firearm as he'd been his Marlin, but if the scope was sighted in, he thought it more than capable.

Wim left the cabin and went back to the overlook. He leveled the rifle toward camp and peered through the scope. He gasped as he realized the new additions to camp weren't people, but were instead zombies. He then looked to the tractor trailers. Even though he wasn't a scholar like Emory, it only took him a moment to realize what happened.

Who would bring zombies here and set them loose like attack dogs? His next thought was to wonder where Ramey was. As soon as that came to mind, he recalled Delphine telling him he was selfish. Maybe he was, but he knew everyone on the Ark was in danger right now and he had to trust that Ramey could handle herself, at least for a little while.

He lined the crosshatch of the scope over the face of a zombie and shot. It fell. He pulled back the bolt handle to eject the spent cartridge, fed in a new round, then locked the bolt back in place. He aimed, shot, and killed another zombie. Then the whole process started over again.

* * *

CASPER HERDED A GROUP OF MEN AND WOMEN TOWARD SAW. THERE were eight altogether, five men and three women. One of them caught his eye. She looked to be around 40 and was thin as a twig but had a look in her eyes that was different from the others. It wasn't the blank defeat he'd already grown familiar with. There was life there, and maybe rage. Saw always liked his women feisty and as she passed by, he grabbed her forearm.

"Aren't you a pretty bird?"

Her head snapped toward him eyes blazing. Oh yes, he liked this one. "What's your name, love?"

She tried to pull away but had no chance of breaking Saw's grip. Saw dragged her closer, their faces inches apart. "I asked you a question."

"My name's Wilhelmina."

"Ah. So, are you a Wilma or a Billie?"

"I'm a Mina."

"Very pretty. Please to meet you, Mina. My name's Solomon but you can call me Saw."

He released her expecting her to run. But she didn't. She stared at him. Saw motioned to Casper. "Put them inside."

Casper pushed them toward a cabin which had become a makeshift holding area but, before he made it all the way there, a zombie ten yards from them collapsed. It took Saw seeing the blood around its head to realize it had been shot. He hadn't even heard the gunshot over the air raid siren.

Fookin' thing's giving me a headache. He'd need to shut that off soon but now he was curious who'd just killed one of his zombies. Before he could even begin to formulate a plan, another fell. Saw spun around, looking in every direction but couldn't see anyone with a gun.

A third zombie hit the ground. Saw could feel his pulse quicken.

His face felt hot and his palms tingled. Now this was the excitement he'd been craving. He clapped his hands together.

"Heads up, mates. We've got ourselves a war!"

Casper closed the cabin door, locking Mina and the others inside. He took out a pistol of his own and Saw thought he saw emotion on the pale man's face for the first time. Panic.

Another zombie dropped. Saw raised his gun overhead and fired off a few rounds. "Hello, out there! How many bullets you got"

"Not as many as we do."

The voice was familiar but it took Saw a second to place it. He spun around and saw Mitch and Jimmy approaching from the rear. Mitch carried a duffel bag and struggled under the weight of it. Denny had an arm around the throat of an old woman as he shoved her forward.

"Mitchy!" Saw said. Mitch dropped the bag just as Saw threw his arm around his shoulders in a half-hug. "You done good, lad. Real good."

He was shocked at the teen's appearance. He looked a bit like a Halloween decoration, the kind they sell in the back of the stores out of view of the kiddies. He didn't think he'd cut him quite that bad. But the ends justified the means.

"Thanks, Saw. But I'm not done."

Mitch unzipped the bag and threw back the canvas flap, revealing twenty or more pistols, a couple shotguns, and hundreds of rounds of ammunition. Saw tousled the boy's hair. They made a good team, they did.

Saw took another pistol. He now had one in each hand and he held them sideways in front of him, just like he'd seen them do in the action movies he watched voraciously.

"Almost no one here has guns," Mitch said. "This old bitch stock-piled most of them. And there are four or five guys who are wannabe cops. That must be who's shooting."

Almost on cue another zombie's head blew up and it collapsed into the snow.

"Anything else I should know, Mitchy?"

"Yeah, lots. Like the guy who runs this place is a fucking lunatic. But I can fill you in on that later. Right now, I'd rather not get shot."

Saw nodded. The teen was wiser than his years. "Aw right, Mitchy. Let's find ourselves the shooter."

Jimmy almost had the old woman to the cabin when she called out. "I can tell you that."

Saw turned to her. She looked halfway to ancient. Add a couple bandages and she could pass for a mummy with dirty white hair that fell almost down to her scrawny ass. "You can, huh, granny?"

She nodded. Saw glanced at Mitch who shrugged his shoulders in a "maybe" gesture.

"Well, then, spit it out."

Delphine tried to move toward him but Jimmy held her back. He tightened his grip around her throat and she barked out a cough.

"Let her go," Saw said and Jimmy did.

Delphine took a couple steps toward him, not even flinching when a zombie was shot and fell a few yards away.

"I know you're old and all, but as you can see," Saw motioned to the dead zombies, "Time, as they say, is of the essence."

Delphine looked at him from head to toe and Saw thought he was being studied. "I want a promise first."

He appreciated the audacity that she thought she was in a position to make demands. "And what's that?"

"When you're done with the killing here, you give me back my island."

"Your island?"

Delphine nodded. "Been in my family for generations. Biggest mistake I made was giving it up."

"Okay, love, let's say I'll do that. How can you help me first?"

Delphine turned away from him, staring out into the distance. "The man shooting your zombies is named Wim Wagner. And he's about a hundred yards that way." She pointed a crooked, bony finger toward the bluff just as Wim took out another zombie.

Saw followed her finger. He couldn't see anything but he believed her. He turned to Jimmy.

"Kill him."

Jimmy reached into the bag and traded his own gun for the biggest pistol he could find. Then he jumped on a snowmobile, fired the engine, and disappeared into the white.

* * *

WIM WAS RELOADING THE RIFLE WHEN HE HEARD THE WHINE OF THE snowmobile engine approaching. Under the circumstances, he expected the rider to be of the unfriendly variety and decided to head toward a less conspicuous location.

A quick dash through the path brought him to the box. The lock had never been replaced after Delphine shot it to pieces and its door hung slightly ajar. Wim never imagined he'd go back inside by choice, but the snowmobile was very close now and it was the only structure in the area.

"Damn," he muttered to himself as he stepped inside and pulled the door closed. He couldn't hold back a shiver.

The snowmobile sped past the box. Wim waited. "Keep on going." The sound of the engine faded. He started to get his hopes up. Then it stopped. Wim knew it hadn't gone far enough beyond him to be safe and he wondered if he'd been spotted. Then, he realized his footsteps in the snow provided a perfect map to his hiding spot.

The steel walls of the box were most likely bullet proof but all it would take was pulling open the door and Wim would be the epitome of a sitting duck. He decided to not wait until that happened and eased the door outward. All appeared clear. But he took his time and looked both ways before moving into the open.

He made it two steps before he heard the voice. "Put down your gun and turn around real slow."

Wim set the rifle against the side of the box.

"Halfway there," Jimmy said.

Wim did a slow 180 until he came face to face with the man who had one of the larger pistols Wim had ever seen aimed at his chest.

"Hands up," Jimmy said.

Wim obeyed but he thought he saw the top of the pistol trembling in the man's tight grip. "I don't know what you're here for, but no one has to die. I was only shooting the zombies. Not any of you. Although I could have should I wanted to."

Wim saw the man swallow hard. He realized he was no cold-blooded killer. He was probably easily swayed and had fallen in with a rough lot.

"Trust me, I have no intention of defending this place. If you want it, take it. All I ask is that no one get hurt. That includes your people. I'm Wim, by the way."

Jimmy lowered the pistol a few inches but still held it ready to fire if the need arose. "Jimmy."

Wim thought the older man's eyes looked red and swollen, as if he'd been crying. That solidified his belief that this man wasn't a murderer. "Well, Jimmy, let's go back to the others and try to talk this out. I'll leave my rifle here to show you there's nothing you need to worry about, all right?"

He saw Jimmy look past him, toward camp, considering the offer. Then he nodded. "Okay. Let's do th— "

The side of Jimmy's face blew out in a tidal wave of blood, bone, and brains. He didn't even have time to look shocked before he fell, but Wim certainly was. He looked toward the direction of the shot and saw Phillip and Buck jogging toward him. Buck held his .44 Magnum in his hand and smoke seeped from the barrel.

"You're wwww- welcome," Buck said as they reached Wim.

"You didn't have to kill him. He was reasonable."

Phillip sneered, waved his arm toward camp. "Reasonable? You stupid hayseed fuck. Have you seen what they've done?"

Wim grabbed the rifle. "I wasn't talking about the lot of them. Only him." He glanced down at Jimmy's body where liters of blood gushed from his skull, melting the snow underneath all the way to the ground.

"You can believe that if you want, but we're under attack. How about you stop talking and start shooting?"

The two men rushed past him, toward camp. Wim turned in that direction but didn't follow right away. If they wanted to deal out death, he was content letting them do it on their own. He wanted to find Ramey.

* * *

RAMEY EMERGED FROM THE CLINIC, BURSTING INTO THE CHAOS THAT had consumed camp. She couldn't believe her eyes. There were zombies everywhere she looked. Some ate. Some stalked new prey. She saw Darry, one of Phillips cohorts on the security force, shoot a male zombie in a Pittsburgh Penguins jersey only to be overwhelmed by five more of the creatures.

His gun kept firing as they forced him to the ground . She saw random sprays of blood, but the zombies continued their attack. She couldn't tone out his screams as they ate him.

Santino, another of the Ark's cop wannabes, came on that scene too late. He unloaded his pistol into the zombies. Three of them fell and remained motionless. This opened the view and Ramey saw the remaining zombies chomping on Darry's face and neck. His nose was gone as was one of his ears. Blood bubbled from his mouth. Santino rushed toward them. He cracked the zombie that was eating Darry's cheek over the head with the butt of his gun and it went down.

The other zombie looked up, a chunk of flesh dangling from its lips. Santino kicked it in the face and sent it sprawling into the snow. He stomped its head with his boot over and over again. As he smashed its skull in, Santino missed seeing Darry sit up, but Ramey saw it all.

Darry's face was mostly gone but he had one good eye and that eye found Santino. He flopped onto his knees, then staggered to his feet. He fell against Santino's back, his hands catching in the tall man's belt and pulling his pants down enough to expose his ass crack. Santino tried to turn around to see what or who had hold of him, but Darry's weight made movement difficult. Darry's teeth chomped into that exposed section of flesh between his back and butt. Santino groaned and managed to pull himself free of the zombie's grasp, but it was too late.

As Santino was being eaten, Ramey remembered his cold eyes as he dragged Wim to the box. Men like Santino were almost as big of parts of the rotten core of the Ark as her own father. She was so caught up in watching the situation unfold that she didn't see the zombies coming at her from the side until they were close enough to smell. She spun around and saw two of the monsters were less than five feet away. One was short and round, a fireplug of a man. The other was a gray-haired woman in a bright pink jogging suit. Fortunately, neither were fast of foot as Ramey had no weapons. Rather than fight with her bare hands, she ran.

* * *

WIM SHOVED OPEN THE DOOR TO DOC'S CABIN. THEIR TRAILER HAD been empty and this was his next guess as to where Ramey could be, but as he scanned the quarters it looked like he'd struck out again.

He hadn't been inside the cabin since the day he arrived - or was brought to - the Ark. The man's desk was cluttered with papers and notebooks but the main room was empty. Wim moved on to check what laid behind the three closed doors.

The first opened to an empty bedroom. The second to a cramped bath. The last door revealed an oversized closet but instead of clothing, it was filled with books and journals. He almost left, but a photo of Ramey caught his attention and he moved to it.

He realized it was attached to a file and he opened the folder. There were basic statistics, height, weight, date of birth. Then what looked like a medical history. Much of it may as well have been in a foreign language for as much as Wim understood it, but one column made a sort of sense. It was headed with 'Vaccines' and contained dates for diseases such as chickenpox, the mumps, measles, etc. The last line was curious though. It was dated three years earlier and labeled only 'Test'.

Wim sorted through the files underneath. They all had photos of men and women he knew only from the Ark. All had vaccine records and all had more recent entries in the 'Test' column. A gunshot outside the cabin stole his attention but before he left, he folded Ramey's file in half and shoved it inside his coat.

Outside Doc's cabin Wim saw Butch shoot a bearded zombie in a blaze orange hunting jacket. The bullet ripped through the creature's forehead and exploded out the back of its head.

Butch spun toward him, pistol raised, until he realized it was Wim and not another zombie. "Wwww - what were you dddd-doing in DDDD - Doc's cabin?"

Wim shook his head and moved toward him. "There's no one inside. You don't think they got Doc, do you?"

If Buck had been smarter, he'd have realized Wim didn't give a fig about Doc's well-being, but the man wasn't a bright bulb. "He's in the llll-lab. He's safe there."

More gunshots came from closer camp. Buck looked in that direction, then back to Wim. "YYYY - You gonna help or not?"

"I've been helping."

Buck headed toward the sound of gunfire. Wim followed only because it took him closer the clinic which was his last hope for finding Ramey safe. If she wasn't there, he knew she was either out here in the chaos, or that the attackers already had her.

* * *

OF ALL THE PEOPLE RAMEY COULD HAVE RUN INTO, THE LAST ONE SHE wanted to see was Phillip, but that was who she literally crashed into as she made the corner around the mess hall.

He looked panicked and afraid, his pale freckled skin flushed. He tried to mask his fear with anger. "Why aren't you still with Doc?

"How long have you known he was crazy?"

Neither had an answer for the other and, as a group of nine zombies approached, there was no time for follow ups. Phillip shot and sent a round flying through the afro of a black zombie. It kept coming.

"Give me a gun," Ramey said.

Phillip glanced her way before shooting again. That bullet hit the zombie above its left eye and it collapsed. "This is the only one I got."

"Bullshit."

She knew he usually kept a gun in an ankle holster and she also knew he'd never head out into a situation like this with only one firearm. "Come on, Phillip. Let me help. I can shoot."

Ramey hadn't fired a gun since before coming to the Ark and even then, she was far from a crack shot, but she knew she'd feel more comfortable with a gun in hand rather than nothing at all.

A zombie which Ramey recognized as a man who dished out food in the Ark's mess hall headed the group coming at them. She saw he was missing most of its fingers and several large chunks of skin on one arm. Phillip shot and killed him, then squatted down and grabbed the small gun off his ankle. He pushed it at Ramey.

"It's loaded but only holds six."

Ramey accepted it and chambered a round. She shot at a zombie who was missing so much flesh on its cheek that Ramey could see her teeth. The shot missed.

Well, my accuracy sure as hell hasn't improved.

Phillip looked at her and opened his mouth, likely to insult her, but before he could get out the words, a gaunt, Asian-looking zombie grabbed Phillip's coat. Shocked, Phillip squeezed the trigger of his pistol and sent a bullet into the snow. He tried to squirm free but another zombie, a fat man in a tattered three-piece suit, got ahold of his arm.

The rest of the zombies were at them now. Ramey fired the pistol and hit a zombie that didn't look much younger than herself, in the mouth. She saw its teeth shatter and its arms flail as it fell into the snow. She steadied herself and aimed at a zombie wearing a blue scarf with white snowflakes embroidered on it. The bullet hit the woman just under the center part of her hair and she fell.

There was a garbled mixture of a grunt and a squeal behind her and Ramey turned to see the other zombies had forced Phillip to the ground. They had his jacket open and were ripping at his shirt. Ramey shot one of them in the back of its head and it fell on top of Phillip's legs.

The zombies had torn Phillip's shirt and were working on his stomach. Ramey saw their long, ragged fingernails puncture his almond white flesh. Dark red blood bubbled from the wounds. Then their fingers went deeper. She could see their digits writhing under his skin, like his belly was full of worms.

Phillip screamed as their hands jerked and yanked and pulled at his flesh and the tissue underneath. She heard the wet tearing sound as it gave way and his intestines were revealed. The monsters moved on to them and ripped them free, eating them like sausage links.

Ramey couldn't bear to see any more. She looked away from the carnage and her eyes found Phillip's face. It was a mask of agony. Tear streamed from his eyes. Snot from his nose. Blood and saliva from his mouth.

"Shoot me!" He cried. "Please, kill me!"

Ramey knew it was the humane thing to do. Phillip's time on Earth was down to seconds. There wasn't any coming back from this.

She raised the little pistol and closed one eye as she aimed the peep sights at his face. As she started to put pressure on the trigger, she remembered what she'd seen in her father's lab. The things her father had said. Phillip knew everything he'd been up to down there. Not only knew of them, but took part in them.

With that in mind, Ramey decided he deserved everything that was happening to him right now. One of the zombies had progressed past his intestines and pulled free a kidney, or maybe it was his liver. She hadn't done well in anatomy. The organ came free with a thick sucking sound and Phillip shrieked again.

Ramey turned her back on him and listened to the sounds of his death as she walked away.

* * *

DOC'S LAB WAS ON THE OPPOSITE SIDE OF THE CENTER OF CAMP AND between it and Wim were the tractor trailers, the zombies, and the men who had attacked camp.

Buck sidled up next to him as they surveyed the scene. "You thththth - think we can take them?"

Wim thought the odds were against it and all he really cared about was getting to the clinic. He pondered their situation for a moment and came up with something resembling a plan.

"Not head on we can't. We need to stay hidden. I'll go left, you right, but stay out of sight and don't waste any ammunition."

"What about the aaaa - assholes who brought them here?"

"Do what you want."

"What about you?"

"I'll work on the zombies."

Wim didn't wait for Buck's opinion. He dashed away, taking refuge at the corner of a small building that served as one of the Ark's outhouses. He poked the rifle barrel around the corner, aimed, and began to shoot.

* * *

SAW HUNKERED DOWN BEHIND ONE OF THE OVERSIZED WHEELS OF THE dump truck. Mitch was on his heels. The zombies - his zombies - kept dropping. Another fourteen since he'd sent Jimmy to find the shooter. Now Jimmy hadn't returned and the shooting had recommenced and Saw didn't need to be a MENSA candidate to figure out what happened.

"Where the fuck is he?" Mitch asked.

"Probably dead." Another zombie fell. For the first time, doubt had crept into his mind. Saw thought he might lose this battle and that didn't sit well with him. He motioned to Casper who had been guarding the door where the hostages were being kept. "Grab one of them and bring them out here."

"Who?" Casper called.

"I don't fucking care. A woman."

Casper disappeared into the building and emerged a moment later with the old hag who'd ratted out the shooter. Casper held her by her long hair with one hand and had a pistol pressed against the soft flesh under her chin with the other.

"You wait here," Saw told Mitch as he stepped into the open. He went to Casper and the woman. The shooting had stopped, for the moment. "Give her to me," he told Casper and the man shoved her toward him.

Delphine stumbled in the snow and went down on her hands and knees. She began to push herself up but Saw stepped on her hand. He felt a few subtle pops as her fingers broke.

"Whoever's out there shooting." He glanced in the direction of the shots. "For every one of my zombies you kill from here on out, I'm killing one of your people. And if my math's right, your numbers'll run out long before mine do."

Saw stood over her, his pistol pointed down at the back of her head. "So, how's about you come out and we settle this man to man?"

He waited. Nothing. But no shooting either so that was a plus. "Come on now, mate. This old girl's getting cold laying in the snow like she is."

Saw stared ahead trying to see the shooter, anything that would give him up, but found nothing. Then he caught movement to his right. A man emerged from behind a shed. He held a pistol and it was aimed at Saw.

"Thanks for joining us. Now toss me that gun of yours."

The man shook his head. "I dddd - don't think I will."

Christ, what a bunch of misfits, Saw thought. It was hardly the best of the best that had survived the apocalypse. "If you're wise you will, mate. There's three of us." He looked to Mitch, then Casper, then back to the man. "And one of you. Be smart now, won't you?"

Buck looked at them, his head swiveling around, taking it all in, but he didn't lower the gun.

"If you want me to kill this old girl to prove I mean business, I will. Then her blood's on you. Is that what you want?"

Buck took another step closer. "YYYY - You shoot her, I shoot you."

"I'd like to see you try that, nigger," Casper said, his voice dripping with hate.

Saw saw Buck's eyes change. Where there was something that could pass for courage before, now there was fury. "Aw, fook."

In a quick motion Buck spun away from Saw and dropped to his knees. Casper shot but he was aiming for where the man had been standing, not at the new, low profile. Before he could readjust, Buck fired.

The bullet hit Casper in the hollow between his collar bones. At first it was a black spec against his white skin but then blood gushed out like water from a hole in a dam. Casper tried to plug it with his finger but the blood kept coming.

Saw realized everyone was looking at Casper dying on his feet. He lifted his gun away from Delphine's head and pointed it at the stuttering shooter, and pulled the trigger. Buck never saw the bullet coming before it punctured the side of his head and sent him to the ground.

* * *

WIM WINCED AS BUCK WENT DOWN. HE ADMIRED THE MAN FOR HAVING the courage to walk into that scenario, but then again it hadn't worked out too well for him.

Earlier, when he looked through the scope he'd seen Wayne at the older man's side and realized it had all been a set up. And, with a sickening feeling in his gut, he understood that this was all his fault. He'd brought the boy into camp against all of Doc's rules and against common sense. At the time, it seemed like the right thing to do. Only now it had led to even more death in a world where the living were already in short supply.

He couldn't dwell on it now though. There'd be plenty of time to beat himself up later if he survived. Now, he needed to fix the mess he'd created.

There were eight zombies roaming through the area. A ninth rose before Wim's eyes as Casper's eyes went blank and he took a shuffling step forward. Wim thought he seemed like as good a choice as any. He watched through the scope as he shot the newly undead man in the head and put him down for good.

Wim reloaded and shot, reloaded and shot, as fast as he could maneuver the bolt action rifle. Nine zombies became three in less than a minute.

* * *

MINA STOOD IN THE NOW OPEN DOORWAY AND FLINCHED AS ANOTHER zombie was killed. She watched as Saw peered around the camp, trying to find the source of the bullets but having little luck.

"I've had about enough of this," he said. "I don't think this hunk of rock's really worth fighting for anyway." He motioned to Mitch.

"What do you say, Mitchy? Anything here worth taking?"

Mitch shook his head. "It's too damned cold here. We've got most of the guns. All that leaves are canned goods and farm animals."

"I don't think we got time or the manpower to lift a couple piggies into the trucks anyway."

Mitch nodded in agreement.

"Then let's get the hell outta 'ere."

"What about her?" Mitch pointed to Delphine who still knelt in the snow, clutching her crushed hand.

"Her?" Saw stared down at her. "You asked me earlier, when I was done killing, that I'd give you this island back."

Delphine peered up at him and nodded.

"Aw right then. But there's one problem."

"What's that?"

"I'm not done killing."

Saw shot her in the face, the bullet blasting through her eye. Her weathered, wrinkled skin contorted into a grimace and she fell into the snow.

Mina turned away from the sight of it and looked at the dozen or so cowering men and women in the room. The faces of strangers. She doubted she'd said a hundred words combined to all of them put together. Could she really stay here with them? On this island overrun with zombies? Even if they somehow managed to kill the monsters, it was only a matter of time before someone else showed up to take or destroy what they had. And it was obvious fighting wasn't this lot's strong suit.

"I think you managed to find ya'self a group of people even more worthless than you, Birdie. And that's saying' somethin'," her daddy's voice said.

Saw jumped onto the truck's running board and leaned into the cab.

"Gonna be just you and a bunch of chickens. A flock of birdies waiting to get picked off by a cat."

"I'm no chicken, Daddy," Mina said.

A woman to her right looked at her, her face a mask of fear and confusion. "What did you say?"

Mina ignored her. She stood up, head high. She was tired of cowering. She ran out of the building just as Saw emerged from the truck. In his hand, he held a white propane tank, the kind people used on their grills. Taped to the side of it was a road flare. He struck the flare and the light of the fire turned his face red. He looked every bit the Devil.

Mina watched the man throw the heavy tank with one arm. It soared past her and she could see it clear as day. There was even a blue label that read 'Bernzomatic'. The tank hit the ground and skidded across the snow before coming to a stop in front of the building where she'd been hiding moments ago. She realized she had a choice, but only seconds to come to a decision. She could run to the tank and try to move it away, or she could run from it and let the man who attacked their camp finish what he'd started.

She heard men and women inside the building shouting, but they were too scared to push past the fire and escape. Instead, they stayed where they were.

They aren't worth risking my life over. Mina ran from the fiery blaze, watching as Saw aimed his gun at the tank and shot. It exploded with a roar and made her stumble, almost falling. The yelling inside the building transformed into panicked, agonized shrieks as the wood building was set ablaze.

Saw climbed into the truck and sat down behind the wheel.

Don't go. Not yet. "Better hurry, Birdie."

Mina knew her daddy was right for once. She ran to the truck as Saw began to back it away from the camp. She picked up the pace and caught it before he could make the turn. Mina slammed her hand against the driver's side door.

Saw peered down from above her. He rolled the window down. "Mina, was it?"

She nodded. "Are you going somewhere safe?"

Saw glanced over at Mitch. He flashed a leering grin that showed his black, broken teeth as he turned back to Mina. "Everywhere's safe when I'm around, love. Ain't that right, Mitchy?"

"Sure is."

Mina stared up at him. The man was a revolting sack of muscle and rage. He was the type of person she'd have crossed the street to avoid before the plague, but the world had changed now and she had a strong feeling inside that this new world was made for men like Saw.

Mina took one more glance back at the men and women who called the Ark home. Most died in the fire. Zombies tore through the ones who managed to escape the blaze and the humans were too weak or too dumb to even fight back.

She looked up at Saw. He still smiled. "Will you take me with you?"

The door opened. Saw extended his hand. "All you had to do was ask."

Mina grabbed his palm and he hoisted her up with one arm, with the ease of lifting a pillow. She got her footing on the door frame and Saw spun her around so she fell into his lap. She could feel his hot breath on her neck. It was sickeningly sweet, like rotten meat. But when she felt his strong hands on her thin waist as he lifted her over him and sat her in the seat, she felt protected. She realized she wasn't afraid any more. And that's all she wanted out of life.

Take that, daddy.

* * *

WIM THOUGHT HE MIGHT HAVE LOST HIS MIND. HE'D JUST WATCHED
Mina voluntarily join the man who'd attacked them. Who'd set loose
zombies. Who'd killed Delphine right in front of them. He didn't see
how it could be real, but as the truck backed away, then did a U-turn
in the snowy landscape before heading toward the gate, he was left
with no other choice but to believe it.

He didn't care about killing more zombies. He only needed to find
Ramey and be gone from this awful place. Away from this land that
made people do crazy, terrible things. He thought again, as he had so
often in the past, that he'd been right all those years to stay on his
farm, away from society. If this was how people treated each other, he
wanted no part of it.

Wim jogged toward camp, closing the remaining distance in less
than a minute. A man from the Ark grabbed his arm as he passed by.

"Did you see what happened, Wim?"

Wim jerked his arm free and didn't answer. He kept going,
ignoring the people and the zombies. Let them fight each other. He
wanted no part of it any more.

* * *

RAMEY SAW WIM STORM INTO THE CLINIC. SHE WAS TWO BUILDINGS
away and ran after him.

"Wim!" She called out. But the door had closed.

She wanted to get to him before he found her father. She didn't
want him to see what Doc had done. The things he had created. The
shame she felt over being his daughter burned a hole inside her and
she couldn't imagine Wim knowing that the man who had created
her, was also responsible for so much evil and madness.

Ramey passed the first building. Halfway there. As she moved
beyond the second, four zombies staggered into her path. One of
them was on fire, the flames licking at his clothing. The smell of

burning hair assaulted Ramey's nose. The other zombies were uninjured, aside from being dead.

She knew she had no weapons to fight them, and that running was her best choice, but her pulse was thrumming in her ears and she couldn't remember the last time she'd been this angry. She wanted to kill them.

A zombie in athletic shorts, a tank top, and sweatband lunged for her. Ramey hopped to the side and avoided its grasp. She shoved it in the back as it stumbled past her and it did a face plant into the snow.

The other three came toward her. You're being stupid. Run away. But still she didn't run.

The lone female zombie in the quartet was a sixty-something year old who was shaped like a bowling pin and whose gray hair was wound up in a tight perm. She snarled at Ramey and swatted with French manicured nails. Ramey jumped back, out of her reach. She scanned the area around her, looking for anything she could use to battle the creatures. There was nothing. She backed away, retreating around the corner of the building. Searching.

Someone had been installing a brick facade on the building when the snow started to fly. A few bags of mortar mix leaned against the door, along with a two-foot-tall stack of bricks. It wasn't much but it was something. Ramey grabbed a brick.

The bowling pin zombie shuffled around the corner and Ramey was ready for her. She slammed the brick into the woman's face, connecting with her brow. There was a crack that reminded Ramey of peeling a hardboiled egg and the dead woman's skin split open revealing white skull underneath.

The zombie blinked. Then she began to lean backward, slowly at first but speeding up as the momentum built until she crashed against the building and slithered down the side. When she hit the ground, she remained motionless.

The burning zombie was at Ramey's shoulder. She could feel the heat coming off it. And the smell. God, it was sickening, like a crematorium crossed with roadkill on a hot, August afternoon.

Ramey swung the brick and hit it in the jaw. It groaned and a few broken teeth spilled from its mouth, along with a slimy trail of black drool. She hit it again, this time catching it above the ear. Her fingers were singed by the flames and the zombie went down so quick that she fell on top of it.

She felt the fire against her body and rolled off. Her jackets smoldered and she dropped the brick so she could beat at it with her hands.

In her distraction, she didn't realize there was a zombie behind her until it grabbed hold of her chestnut colored hair. The zombie dragged Ramey backward and she skidded along the snow. She was away from the bricks now. Helpless.

In front of her, the fitness zombie approached. But something was different. Now, in his hand, he held a small trowel. As he stepped toward Ramey he kept raising it up and stabbing it down repeatedly.

Ramey didn't know if it was trying to use the tool as a weapon or if it was some sort of bizarre muscle memory. Maybe he'd been a brick-layer in between running marathons. But either way, he was getting closer.

She tried to yank herself free from the zombie that held her hair but its fingers were entwined in her long locks. Ramey changed course and did a 180 so that she was no longer on her ass, but on her knees.

Ramey could see the zombie that held her was wearing flannel pajamas with tiny footballs printed all over them. Her head was at groin level and that gave her an idea. Ramey didn't know if crotch shots worked on zombies, but it was worth a try.

She punched as hard as she could manage. Her fist sunk deep into the creature's groin. The sensation reminded Ramey of pounding out bread dough.

And somewhat to her surprise, it worked. The zombie released her hair as it stumbled backward. Ramey turned away from it, ready to retrieve the brick. But she turned right in time for the zombie with the trowel to swipe the blade down, into her face.

The metal sliced into her cheek, cutting a deep gash. She felt a hard jolt as the trowel hit her cheekbone. As the pain rushed through her, she jerked her head which sent the tool skidding to the side. An L-shaped chunk of flesh hung from her face and she thought it felt extra cold as the air hit the wound.

The zombie fell into her, knocking her back, crashing into the building. The back of her head hit the wall and everything blazed bright white, whiter than the snow. She lost herself for a moment but came to when she landed on the ground, and the zombie landed on top of her.

It belched a mouthful of putrid, rotting air into her face and she thought she might puke from the smell of it. It lunged toward her, but Ramey reached up and caught its headband with her thumb. The material stretched, stretched so far, she thought it might have enough leeway to still bite her, but finally it stopped. Its head bounced forward and back, forward and back. Every time it came close its vile breath sent new waves of nausea rushing through her.

In the fall, the fitness zombie had dropped the trowel and now Ramey strained to reach it with her free hand. The exertion, coupled with the blow to her head, kept making her vision go fuzzy. Her thoughts came slow, like she was half-asleep and part of her just wanted to close her eyes and make it all stop.

But she knew doing that meant death and she wasn't about to die yet. She tried one more time to grab the trowel, her fingertips glancing across the frigid metal. Just a little further. She stretched as far as possible with the zombie pinning her down. She touched the trowel again, could pinch the metal between her index finger and thumb. Now she was able to pull it closer. She flipped it around and grabbed the wooden handle.

The next time the zombie's head bounced toward her, Ramey was waiting. She rammed the trowel into its mouth and didn't stop pushing until it hit bone. The corners of its mouth were sliced open and the blade jutted out from between its teeth like it was chewing on a cigar.

The creature flailed with its arms, now less interested in the hot meal beneath it than the tool stuck in its mouth. Ramey took advantage of the distraction and pushed it off her.

She rolled away from it, then bounced to her feet. That strange feeling like she was floating in a pool returned and she held her arms out at her sides to steady herself. Get it together, Ramey. If you go down now its game over. She held as still as possible until the feeling faded. Good. Now forget about the zombies and find Wim.

She ignored the fitness zombie which thrashed on the ground, and the pajama-wearing zombie which was again stumbling toward her, its injured nuts forgotten. There was no time for them. There was only time for Wim.

*   *   *

WIM FOUND THE CLINIC EMPTY WHICH WAS PRETTY MUCH WHAT HE expected. He headed toward the open doors which led to Doc's lab. Its downward corridor was cloaked in red light and he felt like there was a fair chance he was walking straight into Hell, but he continued.

Halfway into his descent, the first moving thing he saw was a zombie with two heads. He blinked hard, thinking he must be seeing things, but when he opened them, the creature was still there. It staggered toward him, traveling up the tunnel. Its heads lolling aimlessly atop a bloated, purple neck.

It reminded Wim of the two-headed calf that had been born on the farm all those years before. His pa had called it an abomination. What would the old man think if he were here to see this horrible creature?

Pa had done the merciful thing and put the calf down. Now it was Wim's turn to do the same. He shot the head on the right. It flopped backward as a spray of brains exploded out the back of its skull. But the creature kept coming. Wim ejected the cartridge, loaded a new one and closed the bolt. He shot again, hitting the second head. The bullet caught it just above its eye and the force whipped its head sideways and he saw a fissure open where the head was attached to the oversized neck. He thought it might come loose, but before that could happen the monster collapsed in a heap. Wim continued.

The remainder of his journey was uneventful and the opening to

Doc's underground lair was unimpeded. He kept the stock of the rifle against his shoulder, ready to shoot, as he stepped inside.

It really is Hell in here.

The room was filled with Frankenstein-type zombies which staggered about, bumping into each other, into gurneys, into the walls. The creatures seemed even more clumsy or maybe stupid, than their normal counterparts, if zombies could even be smart or dumb, let alone normal.

Wim saw a female zombie with its stomach torn open and all her insides missing coming toward him. He aimed the rifle.

"William! Don't!"

Wim turned to see Doc in the back corner. He held what looked like a fat, blood covered baby in his arms, but that couldn't be possible.

"Don't shoot her. She has no teeth. She's harmless. All my creations are. Look closer if you don't trust me."

Wim did not trust the man and had no desire to take a closer look, but he squinted into the scope and peered at the female zombie's mouth. He realized Doc was right. Her mouth was a scarred mass of hollow gums and nothing more. He checked a second zombie, this one looked as if it had been skinned from head to toe. Its mouth hung open giving Wim a good look. Again, it was toothless.

He knew Doc was a liar, but he didn't see any point in checking the others. He lowered the rifle.

"You're worse than them, you know?" Wim said.

Doc shrugged his shoulders as he rocked back and forth. "Worse isn't the word I would use, but I know your vocabulary and intellect is limited so I won't take that personally. Tell me, William, have you even so much as glanced at a dictionary or thesaurus? And s, you don't embarrass yourself, the latter is not a kind of dinosaur."

Wim was tempted to shoot him right then but did not. He wanted answers, not more death.

Doc rose from the stool on which he was sitting and took a few steps in Wim's direction.

"Did you kill Emory?"

"Of course, I did."

Wim had no doubts of this, but the blunt matter-of-factness of Doc's answer sent his temper soaring.

"The old coot was too smart for his own good. He thought he was being quite sneaky, breaking into my lab, but he never thought to ask the most rudimentary question: Why would Delphine of all people, have keys to this place?

Wim processed this, all the while feeling dumb that he wasn't putting the pieces together quick enough. "You mean Delphine— "

"Told me everything."

Wim processed the fact that Delphine had betrayed them. That she'd got Emory killed. He suddenly felt a whole lot less bad about seeing her get shot.

"Congratulations, by the way," Doc said.

Wim tried to get out of his head and back to the matter at hand. "For what?"

"Marrying my daughter, of course. It wounded me to not receive an invitation. Never mind the fact that you didn't have the courtesy to ask me for her hand."

Wim shook his head, trying to clear it of Doc's ramblings. He looked closer at the object Doc was carrying. It was a baby. Where the heck did he get that? It didn't matter. He pulled the folder out of his jacket and held it up to Doc.

"What's this mean?"

"You've been snooping in my house. Naughty boy, William. Very naughty. Santa won't be bringing you any gifts this year."

Wim stepped toward him. They were only a few feet apart now. He shoved the file at Doc's face. "Tell me!" His voice was so full of rage that he surprised himself.

Even Doc flinched. He pulled the newborn closer to his chest. "Easy now, you'll scare the baby."

"Why does it say 'test' under vaccines? What did you do to her?"

Doc's momentary fear dissipated and his crazy jackal grin returned. "What did I do to her? I saved her you buffoon."

Wim felt like he was being spoken to in riddles and he couldn't decipher whether Doc was intentionally being confusing or if he really was too dumb to understand. He felt some of the anger leave him, replaced by self-doubt. He'd already been responsible for the attack on the Ark. He'd trusted Delphine, who in turn, betrayed them all. Maybe he was in the process of fowling something else up. When he spoke, his voice was on the verge of wavering. "What do you mean?"

Doc's smile grew so wide Wim thought the man's face might split in half. He was loving this. "Come now, William, you're not even living up to my, admittedly very low expectations, of you. What does the chart say?"

Doc reached out and snatched the file from his hand. He held it up, displaying it for Wim to see. Shoving it in Wim's face now. "Vaccines. Administration dates. Batch numbers." He threw the file at Wim. The pages bounced off Wim's face and fluttered to the floor. "Connect the dots. Tell me what it means!"

Wim's confidence was gone. He thought about what he was being told, tried to understand it. "You gave Ramey a vaccine. I get that. But for what?"

Doc waved his free arm around the room, then toward the corridor. "For this! For the plague. Are you figuring it out now?"

Wim was. He didn't want to say it but he knew Doc wasn't going to do it for him. So, he spit out the words. "Ramey isn't really immune."

"Winner, winner, chicken dinner! Of course, at the time I told her it was the flu shot. Which in retrospect, wasn't entirely a lie, now was it? If I hadn't given her the vaccine before I came here, she'd be just like every other zombie wandering around eating people to survive. I saved her, just like I saved all of my followers here on the Ark."

"That's why you knew she'd come here."

"Of course. Where else would she go? I told you before, William, *all* of this is because of me."

Wim took a step backward. He was ready to go but he had one more question. And he knew he might not want to hear the answer. "But Hal— "

Doc nodded. "A most unfortunate, but not unexpected, development. Hal didn't get sick because you brought the boy, and the virus here. The virus is everywhere. Hal got sick because his vaccine wore off."

"When was he vaccinated compared to Ramey?"

Doc thought about for a second. "About fourteen months afterward."

Wim felt his chest tighten and his mouth go dry. He struggled to get out words. "How long..."

"Does she have? I'd say your guess is as good as mine, but that would be untrue. I'd anticipated that we'd all need boosters every five years. Hal's time ran out in less than three."

The idea that there was still hope buoyed Wim's spirits and he recovered, at least somewhat. His grip tightened on the rifle. "Then I'm going to bring her here and you're going to give her the booster shot right now."

Doc's eyes blazed. "I will not."

Wim clenched the rifle in his hands. "You will."

"Let me rephrase that for you. I cannot. Because there is no booster. Not yet. I've been dabbling with one but..." He looked around the room, his face full of pride as he took in the monsters he made. "I've been rather distracted."

Doc turned back to him. "So, Ramey's life is in your hands, Wim. Proceed with your plan to leave the Ark, to run away and live as man and wife until one day, you wake up and your dearly beloved has become yet another flesh-eating ghoul... Or stay here with me. Keep the Ark safe and I'll refocus on developing the booster. It's your choice."

"No, it's not."

Both men looked toward the corridor where Ramey stumbled down the tunnel, toward them.

Wim was too shocked at first to move. He saw the ragged wound on her face and wondered what had happened.

Doc saw it too, and to him the torn away section of flesh on her face looked oddly boot-shaped. His hand went to his own birthmark.

"Ramey, I love the new addition. You're becoming more and more like me with each passing hour."

"I'm nothing like you, you sadistic asshole. I hope to God my mother was cheating on you and I'm not really your daughter."

"Well, she was a bit of a whore."

Ramey ignored him. "I hate you. I hate you and I'd rather die out there than ever have to see your face again."

Wim could see her trembling. He'd never seen her so angry and it worried him.

"That's why we're getting the fuck out—"

Before she could finish, her body went limp. Wim caught her and stopped her from falling to the floor. He took a closer look at the wound, saw it was not a bite wound, and was able to breathe again. He lifted her limp body cradling her in his arms and held her tight against him.

He glared at Doc. "I want you to know, if she ever turns I'm coming back here and I will kill you."

Doc held his hands up and faked trembling, mocking. "Ohhhh, I'm very scared. Why not just do it now, because her fate is predetermined. It would save you the return trip."

One of Doc's zombies, this one comprised of two different ethnicities, stumbled between them. Wim was glad he didn't have to look at Doc's face any more. He turned away and carried Ramey up the corridor.

Doc called after him. "Ta ta, William. Until next time…"

Wim didn't look back.

CHAPTER FORTY-NINE

Wim set Ramey on a snowmobile and climbed on behind her. She was slowly regaining consciousness but he held onto her tight with one arm while he steered with the other.

They sped through camp. It seemed like everyone was dead and that the zombies had taken over. He avoided all of them as he left camp. They passed the buildings that had been their poor excuse for a home for months, passed the box. Wim stopped when he reached the house trailer.

"Stay here," he said to Ramey.

She was still groggy, but she understood and nodded. "Don't keep me waiting long."

"I won't."

Wim climbed off the snowmobile and up the steps into the trailer where the door had been left ajar. He scanned the tight quarters where he'd lived since June. It was a dump as far as homes went, but he had fond memories of his friends. Now they were both gone, albeit in different ways.

He moved to his bedroom and crossed to the nightstand. There he took the handkerchief Emory had given him the day he married them. Wim held it to his nose and could still smell the man's aroma on it. He felt his eyes start to burn and hurriedly shoved it into his pocket. There wasn't any time for that. Then he took a Polaroid photo Delphine had snapped of the four of them together. Even though she'd cut off the tops of his and Emory's heads, and despite the events of the day, seeing it made him smile. He carefully tucked it into his shirt pocket.

He passed by the bathroom, stopping to grab a small first aid kit, then exited the trailer.

Ramey appeared more alert and smiled up at him. "Thought maybe you went in there to take a few of those plaid shirts. I know how attached you are to them."

Wim grinned despite himself. "I thought you liked 'em."

"Not quite as much as you, big boy."

He went to her and took her face in his hand. He examined the wound. The bleeding had stopped and it looked clean but he wasn't taking any chances. She winced as he poured peroxide over it, but she was a tough girl and he loved that about her. In the wind, it dried fast and he covered the L-shaped cut with a 4x4 bandage.

He paused before he resumed his seat on the snowmobile.

"Is there anything you want to take with?"

Ramey grabbed his collar and pulled him into her. "Only you, Wim. You're all I need."

She kissed him. It was long and deep and made him forget about the day's pain. She had a way of making everything better.

* * *

RAMEY NOW SAT BEHIND HIM, HOLDING HIS WAIST, AS THEY DROVE OUT of camp and to the gate which still hung ajar. The snowmobile skidded down the little hill that led to the dock, but they avoided it and went straight onto the ice.

Chunks of snow bounced up as they rode and the cold wind prickled their faces but neither seemed to mind. They passed the gaping hole in the ice where Lonnie's rig had disappeared and continued to shore. The road that dead-ended in the lake was empty.

Saw and his truck were nowhere to be seen. All that remained were tire tracks in the snow.

Wim slowed to a stop when he reached the road. He dialed back the throttle so he could hear something other than the whine of the engine.

"Where should we go?" He asked her.

Ramey squeezed his chest through his coat. "To that little cabin you told me about the night you married me. The one in the mountains."

"Well, it wasn't a particular one."

"I know. Any will do as long as there's a porch with a view. Because you promised me sunsets and stars, remember?"

"Of course, I do."

He gunned the engine and they drove on.

* * *

THE END

If you enjoyed The Ark (and I sure hope you did), please take a moment to join my mailing list to receive news about the upcoming books in the series as well as my other books and stories. You'll also receive first chance at discounts and specials. http://eepurl.com/P8lc9

As an indie author, every review helps keep me writing. If you'd consider writing a review, it would mean the world to me. You can find links to all of my books on Amazon. https://www.amazon.com/Tony-Urban/e/B00HZ77O1O/

AUTHOR'S NOTE

Thank you! Thank you! Thank you!

I'm amazed at the success of the "Life of the Dead" series and I hope you've enjoyed the first 3 books. I can never thank my readers enough for taking a chance on a new author and for investing your time into reading about the characters and world I've created. It's a dream come true and I'll be forever grateful to you.

"The Ark" was a challenging book to write and took months longer than expected. At times, I wondered if it was ever going to come together. Even though I knew how it would end, getting there proved a challenge because the characters I love so much were put through such hardships. I wanted to make life easier on them, but I had to stay true to the story.

In the end, it was worth all the challenges. I'm so excited to share this book with fans of the series. And, I have some news.

Initially, I'd planned on 4 books for the series, but there's going to be a novella that bridges the gap between books 3 and 4. That book, "I Kill the Dead" will be crazy fun and epically gory. And, I promise, it will be less emotionally taxing – for all of us!

I continue to be blown away that the books I wrote in rural Pennsylvania are now being read all over the globe. Again, thank you for taking a few hours out of your life to take a chance on this book and on me!

I love hearing from readers, it absolutely makes my day, so if you'd like to reach out, please visit my website or send me a friend request on Facebook. The links are:

http://www.tonyurbanauthor.com

http://Facebook.com/tonyurban

Tell me about your favorite characters, your favorite scenes, and what you think will happen next!

And Happy Reading!

ABOUT THE AUTHOR

A professional photographer, writer and fan of general weirdness (both real and imagined), Tony has traveled tens of thousands of miles seeking out everything from haunted locations, UFO crash sites and monsters like Bigfoot and the Mothman. In a previous life, he worked in the independent movie industry but he finds his current career much more exciting.

Tony's first writing memory involves penning a short story about taking a road trip with his best friend and his dog (two different creatures) to watch KoKo B Ware in a professional wrestling event in Pittsburgh. He wrote that epic saga while in the 3rd grade and it was all downhill from there.

His first books were a series of offbeat travelogues but recently his zombie apocalypse series, "Life of the Dead" has been a bestseller online and grossed out readers all over the world.

His ultimate goal in life is to be killed by a monster thought by most to be imaginary. Sasquatch, werewolves, chupacabras, he's not picky.

If that fails, he'd enjoy making a living as a full time writer. Which of those two scenarios is more likely is up to the readers to decide.

For more information:
tonyurbanauthor.com
tony@tonyurbanauthor.com

Made in the USA
San Bernardino, CA
15 April 2019